BACK YONDER

Chronicles OF THE *Ozarks*

Brooks Blevins, General Editor

BACK YONDER

AN OZARK CHRONICLE

BY WAYMAN HOGUE

WOODCUTS BY HOWARD SIMON
EDITED BY BROOKS BLEVINS

The University of Arkansas Press
Fayetteville
2016

Manufactured in the United States of America

ISBN: 978-1-55728-698-7
e-ISBN: 978-1-61075-584-9

20 19 18 17 16 5 4 3 2 1

♾ The paper used in this publication meets the minimum requirements of the American National Standard for Permanence of Paper for Printed Library Materials Z39.48-1984.

Library of Congress Control Number: 2015955400

CONTENTS

SERIES EDITOR'S PREFACE

In the preface to *The Ozarks: An American Survival of Primitive Society*, the first nonfiction book on the people of the Ozark region, Vance Randolph confessed that he had no interest in townsfolk and prosperous farm families who had "been more or less modernized by recent contacts with civilization." Seeking to entertain general readers in the process of informing them about this little-known highland region in the middle of the nation, he dwelled instead on "diverting and picturesque" practices of "the 'hill-billy' or 'ridge-runner' of the more isolated sections." Randolph's Ozarks was a place divorced from the march of time, its inhabitants a people whose isolation and hidebound dedication to the ways of their ancestors rendered them exotic relics in an age of electricity, radios, and automobiles. Randolph knew he was presenting an incomplete picture of his adopted region, a place more complex and heterogeneous than even he could appreciate. Yet, his decision to "essentialize" Ozark people and their culture—to home in on the people of the backcountry "whose way of living ha[d] changed very little since their sturdy forbears wandered west from the southern Appalachians"—set a precedent that other chroniclers of the Ozarks would dutifully and willingly follow. Whether infused with a romantic fascination for ancient ballads, fox hunters, and weaving grannies or informed by a modernist critique of the intellect-stultifying poverty and backwardness of the benighted hill country, these chronicles of the Ozarks all agreed that "the average urban American" who visited the region would feel "himself among an alien people." The tens of thousands of readers of these books were almost certain to convert generalizations into regional stereotypes.

Randolph admitted that "the Ozark country and its people cannot be adequately described in any one book," and Depression-era publishers evidently agreed. *The Ozarks* proved but the opening salvo in a decade-long barrage of firsthand, "nonfiction" books explaining the mystery, the peculiarity, sometimes even the deep-rooted problems of the Ozarks. Before the United States entered World War II, at least half-a-dozen additional nonfiction Ozark books and a number of novels set in the Ozarks hit the market, all of them published far away from the region and all of them designed to entertain and inform general readers. Some of the nonfiction works—the anthropology-inspired, "documentary" books on the region—followed Randolph's blueprint, albeit usually in a more hyperromantic spirit. Like Randolph before them, armchair anthropologists and folklorists dwelled on colorful regional anachronisms such as moonshiners and superstitions, cultural survivors that, they hoped, would stave off the creeping specter of American homogenization in this age of nationwide radio broadcasts and expanding consumer culture. These Ozark opuses also included memoirs, a clinical observation of the socioeconomic challenges of life for the poor of the region, and even a book of unusual portraits and character sketches by an Ozark native. Such works existed side by side with the Depression-era's conscious fictional representations of Ozark life and Ozark people, from the radio comedy of *Lum and Abner* to the plays of Weldon Stone, from the big-screen comedy of the Weaver Brothers and Elviry to the novels of writers enamored with the region's romantic underbelly.

Though all the Ozark writers of the era differed in ways subtle and sometimes significant, they could agree on at least one point—there was something special about the people who lived in the Ozarks. Bridging the gap between the almost blind romanticism of the region's boosters and the middle-class, outsider condescension of a few detractors was the era's mantra that regionalism was exceptionalism. In the case of the Ozarks—and its highland southern relative Appalachia—this notion of regional uniqueness came wrapped in a set of assumptions about the inhabitants and lands of the highland South. These assumptions, which most writers of the era and their readers accepted, included the idea that mountaineers, with lifestyles more like America's pioneer generation than its post–World War I generation, were in effect our "contemporary ancestors"; that the pure "Anglo-Saxon" strain of their blood was reflected in their ancient British folk ballads and in a hillman's dialect sprinkled with peculiar "Elizabethan" words and phrases; and that generations of isolation from the currents of American culture and commerce had created in the mountains and hills a backward society in need of outside assistance and education. On the flip side of this bundle of assumptions was the belief that this backward society that had maintained ancient Anglo-Saxon cultural artifacts that elsewhere in America had been lost to the homogenizing forces of modernity or drowned by the waves of new immigrants that flooded the shores of the United States before anti-immigration legislation stemmed the tide in the 1920s. These highland characteristics, though largely dismissed by modern scholars as erroneous or at least exaggerated, infused the chronicles of the Ozarks with a spirit of wonder and discovery. Their authors often came across as sojourners writing back to mainstream society from the exotic recesses of the North American landscape.

All of these characteristics had become standard elements of the discourse on Appalachia and the Ozarks by the time of the great offering of Ozark books in the Depression decade. The era's cultural critique of the ills of unfettered capitalism and its temporary love affair with domestic exotics who seemed to survive and sometimes thrive in the face of almost insurmountable odds further leavened the fascination with the region. Not surprisingly then, the Depression decade engendered an intense interest in and appreciation for regionalism and the sturdy downtrodden who often composed regional populations in the national consciousness. So powerful were the portraits of the Ozarks that, in spite of the tremendous changes that took place in the region after (and before) 1941, the images of the static Ozarker, the unchanging and romanticized, exceptional Ozarks, remained the dominant currency in the public (and for years even the academic) marketplace of ideas of the region and its people.

The Ozark books of the Depression era played a crucial role in establishing the simplistic and reductionist stereotypes, both positive and negative, of Ozarkers and the Ozarks. It is for that reason that the University of Arkansas Press has launched the Chronicles of the Ozarks series, which will reprint some of the era's Ozark books with introductions and editorial notes that place each book and its author against the backdrop of the era and its popular assumptions and myths of life in the Ozarks. While it is important to understand the books' flaws and misconceptions in the interest of a fuller understanding of the development and persistence of regional stereotypes, it is also important to remember that these books were written to entertain an audience of general readers and that none of them was meant to be a scholarly scientific study. It is our hope that you will find them as entertaining as did readers in the 1930s and 1940s. It is also our hope that you will read them with an appreciation for the image shapers that they once were and for the cultural artifacts that they have become.

Brooks Blevins

INTRODUCTION

Two books, released in the spring of 1932. Both recounted the hardships and joys of post–Civil War "pioneer" life in rural America. The books were primers on ways in the old days—gardening, butchering, camp meetings, courting, sugar making, cow milking, butter churning, hunting, and trapping. Both unfolded in the dramatized, reminiscent narratives of obscure authors who were only then, in their sixties, publishing a first book. You have undoubtedly heard of one of the writers, and you've probably read that first book. *Little House in the Big Woods* introduced the world to Laura Ingalls Wilder. By the time the last of her eight *Little House* books hit the shelves eleven years later, Wilder had become one of America's most beloved authors of children's books. Her worldwide fame would blossom in succeeding decades, peaking in the 1970s and 1980s when millions of people tuned in each week to watch Laura, Pa, and the Ingalls family on the popular television drama *Little House on the Prairie*.

The other book? You are holding it right now. Chances are you had never heard of Wayman Hogue before coming across this reprint of *Back Yonder: An Ozark Chronicle*. Hogue had no sequels to offer, and it is doubtful that sales of his one book inspired his publisher to request a follow-up. Yet, one does not have to strain to find similarities between Wilder and Hogue. Born less than two years apart in the backwoods of a postwar nation—she in Wisconsin, he in Arkansas—both drew on a wealth of memories to re-create the lives of common folk in rural America, both the humdrum activities of everyday life and the occasional fears and pleasures that enlivened the backwoods family and chased away the drudgery of nineteenth century for at least a little while. Both wrote in a direct, unadorned style, and each had a knack for recognizing a good story and knowing how to craft it, even to the point of favoring a yarn well told over the absolute facts of the matter. And the Ozarks figured prominently in the lives of both writers. Wilder scribbled her stories inside her cozy farmhouse in the Missouri Ozarks, to which she had moved some forty years earlier, while Hogue's memories of a boyhood in the Ozarks came flooding back to him after being gone from the region for more than forty years.

Perhaps most intriguingly, Wilder and Hogue both reared daughters who became successful writers. Wilder's only child, Rose, was already a noted novelist and magazine contributor by the time her mother published *Little House in the Big Woods*. Rose Wilder Lane's impact on her mother's career as a writer was no doubt substantial, and the extent of that influence—as goad, unofficial editor, contact with the publishing world, and perhaps even rewriter—has been debated by scholars.[1] Hogue's own work was likely influenced by his daughter, Charlie May Simon. Though only beginning her career as a writer in the early 1930s, Simon would establish herself as one of the nation's leading mid-twentieth-century authors of juvenile fiction. Today, almost forty years after her death, Charlie May Simon remains a major figure in the literary heritage of Arkansas, the state she called home for most of her adult life.[2]

Back Yonder: An Ozark Chronicle obviously did not rival the popularity or cultural impact of the *Little House* books, but it does occupy a position of importance in the literature of the Ozarks. The first nationally published and widely distributed "memoir" of a life in the Ozarks, *Back Yonder* found an eager audience in an age when American readers were only beginning to become acquainted with this middle-American highland region. Though out of print and largely forgotten since World War II, the book did not lack for fanfare upon release, as the full-page review on the front page of the *New York Times Book Review* would indicate. Even *Little House in the Big Woods* did not receive such royal treatment; its review was relegated to a single paragraph on page nine two weeks later.[3] But, as both Wilder and Hogue could attest, where you start off doesn't matter so much as where you end up.

Where Hogue started off was a long way—more so figuratively than literally—from Memphis, the place he called home for about sixty years, the place where he wrote *Back Yonder*. Charles Wayman Hogue—he was known as Charles W. throughout his adult life but used his middle name when writing—was born December 22, 1868, in what is now Faulkner County, Arkansas, most likely in the rural community of Naylor, about eighteen miles northeast of Conway.[4] His father, Benjamin F. "B. F." Hogue, a veteran of the Confederate 10th Arkansas Infantry, was himself born and raised in the same area.[5] His mother, Mississippi-born Miranda Nicholas Rodgers Hogue, was seven-and-a-half years older than Charles's father. In fact, B. F. Hogue was her second husband, and census records indicate that Miranda (a war widow perhaps) was already the mother of three children, all daughters, at the time of her marriage to B. F. in late 1865. Census records further reveal that Miranda would give birth to perhaps as many as nine more children during her marriage to B. F. Hogue, though by 1900 only five of her dozen children were still living.[6] It was perhaps this complicated and apparently tragic family history that prompted Charles W. Hogue to simplify his family story in *Back Yonder*. The young Wayman of *Back Yonder* grew up in a tidier family with a mom, a pop, and only three siblings. The sisters' names in *Back Yonder*, Lelia and Nora, match none of the recorded names for the real-life daughters of Miranda Hogue. Charles W. Hogue did, however, use the actual name of his older brother, Jim (James E. Hogue). As we shall see, *Back Yonder*'s alteration of family names and family make-up was but one of many instances in which "creative" overtook "nonfiction" in this work of creative nonfiction.

Although Hogue notes in *Back Yonder* that his family moved into the remote Ozark Mountains (110 miles from Little Rock and 80 from the nearest railroad) when he was two years old, surviving records place the Hogue family in their native Faulkner County for at least the first twelve or thirteen years of Charles's life. B. F. Hogue's name appears in a number of Faulkner County records throughout the 1870s, and in 1880 a census taker found his family, now with eight children, residing in Faulkner's Newton Township.[7] Thus, during his formative years, Charles W. Hogue's family lived only forty miles from Little Rock and less than twenty miles from the nearest railroad.

B. F. Hogue paid his personal property taxes in Faulkner County in 1881, but it appears that the family left the county soon afterward. Where the Hogues went and what they did in the early 1880s is unclear. Perhaps the family did indeed sojourn in the remote recesses of the Ozarks during this period, and maybe the author simply bumped this move backward by a decade in the book so that the Wayman of *Back Yonder* could experience the exotic Ozarks as a wide-eyed little boy and not as a self-aware teenager raised within shouting distance of civilization. Regardless, B. F. Hogue's name resurfaces in public records in the mid 1880s, this time on the personal-property tax rolls of Casa Township in Perry County, in the Arkansas River Valley some fifty miles to the west of the family's longtime Faulkner County abode. If the *Back Yonder* account of Wayman's leaving home to attend college in Little Rock is at least a close approximation of reality, then it is quite possible that his stay in Perry County was a comparatively brief one.[8]

In spite of the rather romantic portrait the author paints of an independent, self-sufficient backcountry family with only the most tenuous connection to markets and modernity, county mortgage books and other records show that B. F. Hogue was already caught up in the postwar commercial cotton economy by the time Charles W. was big enough to scamper through the fields while his father plowed. There is even some indication that B. F. Hogue may have lost his 160-acre farm in the early 1870s and joined the growing ranks of landless tenants for a few years. By 1879, though, the agricultural census found him the owner of a 122-acre farm in eastern Faulkner County valued at seven hundred dollars, about the average for the time and place. Like most of his neighbors, B. F. derived the bulk of the family's cash income from the sale of cotton, to which he devoted eighteen acres.[9] Again, why Hogue would manipulate the facts of his family's backstory remains uncertain. As far as self-congratulatory, rags-to-riches stories go, his family's actual middling modesty would have made for a triumphant tale. But the hardscrabble, unrewarding labors of a cotton-belt family in danger more from crop liens than from panthers didn't exactly stroke a yearning for nostalgia in the same way that Ozark school days and courting ways did.[10]

Coming of school age amid the conservative retrenchment of the post-Reconstruction era in Arkansas, in a family with few material advantages, Charles W. Hogue likely received little more than the standard one-room-school education of the age. In many poor rural districts, sparse public funds, limited by state-mandated millage caps, resulted in brief and sporadic school terms. But Charles and his brother, both obviously possessed of no mean level of ambition, managed to exceed the educational attainments of the great lot of their peers. (Hogue recognized that the fulfillment of ambition owed much to gender. "Nora said that that was the advantage of being a boy," he writes. "We boys could get out and make a living for ourselves, while she, being a girl, was forced to stay at home and marry the first rag tag of a mountaineer that came along" [297].) James E. Hogue attended the small Methodist college in Quitman for a time and eventually made his way to Vanderbilt before returning to Arkansas to practice law.[11] Inspired by his older brother, the Wayman of *Back Yonder* attends an unnamed high school or academy in an Arkansas River Valley town before making his way to the capital city for an education at "Little Rock University." The location of any high school that Charles W. Hogue may have attended is unknown, and the "Little Rock University" of the book was almost certainly Little Rock Commercial College, a business training school that also offered a smattering of "classical" courses such as languages and higher mathematics.[12]

As is often the case in *Back Yonder*, the young adult Wayman of the book appears to be a creative composite of the historical Charles W. Hogue and the writer's imagination. By the early 1890s, Charles W. Hogue was living in

Drew County in the Delta. He may have been enticed to the southeastern part of the state by a teaching job, as was the Wayman of *Back Yonder*, but it is just as likely that he ventured so far away from his mother and father to stay with or be near his brother James, who took up the practice of law in Monticello in 1891. It is a near certainty that Charles W. did not marry a fellow high-school teacher, as does the Wayman in the book, for his bride, Mary Gill, the daughter of a Drew County cotton farmer, was barely seventeen years old when they married on Christmas Day, 1892. Charles W. and Mary may have never taught school at all. The 1900 census found their young family—including children Georgia, Charlie May, and Abner—living in a rented house, along with two adult boarders, in Greenville, Mississippi. Charles W. was employed as a traveling salesman.[13]

In 1902, Charles W. Hogue moved his family to Memphis, where Mary had their final child, a daughter named Zula, and where Charles appears to have pursued a career as an artist. In six of the first eight Memphis city directories in which his name appeared, Charles W. was identified as an artist or as a manager or associate of Morning Star Portrait Company.[14] In later years he appeared variously as a salesman or business owner. His two forays into entrepreneurship—once as head of his own manufacturers' agents firm and once as the owner of a jewelry store—were short lived, and after 1920 Charles W. appeared only as a salesman or traveling salesman until being identified as an author in the early 1930s.

Though little is known of their many years in Memphis, the Hogues appear to have been a comparatively solid, though not particularly prosperous, lower-middle-class family. Charlie May Hogue inherited her father's artistic ability and sensibilities, eventually studying art in Chicago and Paris and marrying fellow artist Howard Simon, whose Japanese-inspired woodcuts illustrate *Back Yonder*. There is no evidence suggesting that any of Charles W. and Mary's other three children ever pursued post-secondary education. Georgia and Zula found work as stenographers or in other female-dominated clerical and secretarial roles, while Abner, after a stint in the navy, worked variously as a carpenter, produce dealer, traveling salesman, and factory operative. Though there is also little evidence to indicate that Charles W. maintained anything more than casual contact with his Hogue relatives, he and Mary established close bonds with many members of the Gill family. This led to tragedy when a nephew they raised was killed in World War I. Charles W.'s latter years were scarred by tragedy and loss, beginning with the death of his grandson and namesake, US Navy ensign Charles Wayman Hogue, in the Pacific in December 1944. By the time Charles W. Hogue died at the age of ninety-six in 1965, he had outlived his wife and two of his four children.[15]

He had also survived what was meant to be an old-age exercise in creative reminiscence, *Back Yonder*, by more than three decades. Because Charles W. Hogue left behind no known papers for posterity and because Charlie May Simon's papers contain little material pertaining to her father's writing, there is no accurate record of Hogue's published writings. It would appear that his "national" publications consisted only of *Back Yonder* and a 1931 *Scribner's* story containing three vignettes that would appear almost verbatim in the book the following year. Any other published writings likely appeared in the Sunday magazine sections of newspapers or in regional folklore publications. After *Back Yonder*, it seems that Hogue left the writing to daughter Charlie May, who published her first notable article in *Scribner's* in 1933 and her first book, *Robin on the Mountain*, in 1934.[16] Unlike that of Laura Ingalls Wilder, the childhood story of Wayman Hogue was used up in one burst of storytelling, leaving no room for a sequel.

Nevertheless, Hogue's single book found an eager and approving audience in 1932. Reflecting the Depression-era backlash against ostentation and its appreciation for the sturdy commoner, the *Bookman*'s Elizabeth Stead Taber praised *Back Yonder* as "strong and durable, and in its strength and simplicity achieving a real beauty." "[I]t shows how life can be lived simply," she continued, "in its fundamentals, with a satisfying completeness." Likewise, the *New York Times Book Review*'s Percy Hutchison complimented Hogue for eschewing "artistic furbelows" and proclaimed *Back Yonder* "as engrossing as it is refreshing" and "as rich in its fundamentals as it is inarticulate of graces." So taken was Hutchison with Hogue's story of the courting of his sister Lelia—"one of the finest things of the kind in mountain literature"—that the reviewer devoted half of his extensive critique to its summary and analysis.[17] Above all, reviewers lauded *Back Yonder*'s "sincerity" and "genuineness." Hogue, after all, reminded readers that his chief aim was "to confine myself to facts." The reviewer for the *New Republic* appreciated the "singular integrity" of the author's "literal record."[18]

As we have already seen, *Back Yonder* is no "literal record." Just how sincere and genuine you deem it probably depends upon how comfortable you are when confronting fact laced with fiction. My first reading of *Back Yonder*, some twenty years ago, provoked an ambivalent reaction. Even then, before I had ever probed into Hogue's past, the specifics of his memoir—or perhaps more accurately, the *un*-specifics of his story—struck me as suspect. Yet, the author's overall presentation of late-nineteenth-century life and his matter-of-fact descriptions of folkways rang true. Sam and Lelia may not have existed in a technical sense, but the community's courting and marriage rituals that brought order and meaning to their relationship feel genuine. And in *Back Yonder* it is the folkways and rituals that are the primary characters anyway.

For historians and other scholars who have referenced Hogue's accounts of an Ozark boyhood, the geography of *Back Yonder* is often maddeningly unspecific. The author never once invokes the name of a county, he fails to identify the town in which he attends school as a teenager, and he uses a bevy of colorful yet difficult-to-locate locales (Bear Creek, Bull Mountain, Wild Cat Slough). Even the name of

Wayman's home community, Gravel Hill, is common enough that it appears in a number of different locations on a modern topographical atlas of Arkansas—none of them in Faulkner County. The reader could be forgiven for suspecting that Hogue's penchant for generic, backwoodsy-sounding, often fictionalized locations was just so much literary prevarication. It could be that his fuzzy geography was in response to an editorial mandate that all locations sport earthy names that would satisfy the expectations of readers who wouldn't know one Ozark town from another anyhow. Or perhaps Hogue really didn't want us to know just where "back yonder" was.

Maybe Hogue left the reader guessing because of the disturbing possibility that this chronicle of an Ozark boyhood did not actually take place in the Ozarks. After all, the physical backdrop of *Back Yonder*, in gently rolling but far from hilly eastern Faulkner County, does not match the mental image of the remote and rugged terrain conjured by Hogue. Physically, the area is not included on modern geographers' maps of the Ozarks.[19] Rather, Naylor and its Newton Township and environs lie atop a nondescript, upland extension of the Arkansas River Valley. It is not exactly bottomland or flat country, but neither is it the Ozarks. One could build a stronger case for inclusion in the cultural Ozarks, but geocultural boundaries depend in large measure on regional identity, and most folks in the area of Hogue's boyhood do not—and likely did not—consider themselves Ozarkers.[20]

Were it not for Hogue's intentional exaggeration of

his family's backwoodsiness and his native county's tenuous claim to an Ozark cultural identity, the modern reader could cut him some slack for simply observing the regional boundaries as they were defined in his day. Nineteenth-century maps generally applied the label "Ozark Mountains" or "Ozark Plateau" to a broad territory stretching from the outskirts of St. Louis to the Ouachita foothills of southeastern Oklahoma. Even Vance Randolph, in his 1931 book, *The Ozarks: An American Survival of Primitive Society*, the first "anthropological" study of the region, defined the Ozarks so broadly as to include the Arkansas River valley and the Ouachita Mountains. As the twentieth century progressed, however, geographers and other regional observers began to narrow the physical and cultural borders of the Ozarks, with the Arkansas River valley constituting a southern boundary.[21] Certainly, in the days of Hogue's boyhood there would have been little regional consciousness in the Ozarks, even in the remotest, most *Ozarky* areas. There was, however, a widespread recognition of the differences between the people of the flatlands and river bottoms and those of the upland, no matter how gently undulating the terrain, and an affiliation with the uplanders could have prompted Hogue to place his family retroactively in the Ozarks once that region's image came into clear focus in the twentieth century.

If it is possible that one of the seminal books on the Ozarks, the first reprinted classic in the Chronicles of the Ozarks series, was not actually set within the boundaries of the physical region—and certainly not in the remote backcountry that the author portrays—then what are we to make of Charles W. Hogue's decision to frame the stories of his childhood within the rugged hills and among the colorful folkways of a region he may never have called home? We will never know his true motivation, but a few observations may provide a window into Hogue's literary endeavors and murky geography, as well as insight into the burgeoning Depression-era fascination with all things Ozark.

Charles W. Hogue would likely be baffled by the notion that anyone would treat *Back Yonder* as memoir. Given his penchant for fictionalized names and places, the long passages of character dialogue, and the obvious liberties he took with geographical location, chronology, and family makeup, Hogue aimed above all else to entertain readers. This he did by combining his own boyhood memories with other neighborhood and family stories from his childhood and dramatizing them for effect—the very combination employed by Laura Ingalls Wilder. He had a storyteller's, not an autobiographer's, sensibility, one that he likely passed on to his daughter Charlie May whose own flare for the dramatic shone through in her autobiographical accounts.[22] He wrote what he knew but did not hesitate to "improve" memories and family stories and insert his own dramatizations of unrelated historical vignettes when it enlivened the narrative. The latter is evident in the chapters "The Gold Mine" and "The Hanging," both of which are almost certainly fictionalized.

In her introduction to Laura Ingalls Wilder's *Pioneer Girl*, the *Little House* author's original memoir that remained unpublished until the twenty-first century, Pamela Smith Hill observes that Wilder's daughter Rose Wilder Lane "built her professional career by fictionalizing what she published as nonfiction." This creative nonfiction style—"literary journalism" as it was called at the time—infused Wilder's *Little House* books as well. But, whereas Wilder ultimately abandoned the first-person, adult-voice approach of her initial manuscript in favor of a third-person, juvenile, novelized narration, Hogue's first-person account established the illusion of memoir.[23]

Hogue's dedication to literary journalism is perhaps most obvious in his decision to relocate the memories of boyhood in a timeless, almost mythical Ozark landscape. No manuscript versions of the book have survived, nor has any editorial correspondence, obscuring any window into the process of crafting the stories that would constitute *Back Yonder*. The timing of the book's publication is instructive, though. Before the 1920s, the Ozark region remained an amorphous, mostly undiscovered area in the minds of Americans, a place that seemed similar enough to Appalachia that most assumed it was simply a smaller, western version of its larger sibling to the east. Harold Bell Wright's wildly popular 1907 novel, *The Shepherd of the Hills* (and the copycats that followed), introduced readers to a romantic, fictionalized version of the Ozarks, but "nonfiction" accounts of the region remained extremely rare before the latter half of the 1920s, when Vance Randolph, Otto E. Rayburn, Charles J. Finger, Charles Morrow Wilson, and other writers began to crank out a steady stream of observational magazine articles on the peculiar ways and antiquated cultural relics of the region. By the early days of the Depression, the Ozarks had joined Appalachia in the minds of the reading public as a southern mountain region whose inhabitants continued to live quaint anachronistic lives free of both the material comforts and economic dependency of modern society. A picturesque time capsule of archaic folkways, the Ozarks intrigued post-crash mainstream Americans as the kind of place they could visit should they ever want to see how their ancestors lived. The Ozarks had been branded, in other words, and the mere mention of this odd regional name invoked a bundle of images and presuppositions. Inspired by Ozark writings perhaps, or at the very least aware of the powerful currency of the region's image, Hogue (and his editor, maybe Charlie May?) poured his stories into this ready-made mould. "An Ozark Chronicle" had a zest to it, a marketable geographical and cultural shorthand that would have been lacking in "An Arkansas River Valley Upland Chronicle" or even in "An Arkansas Chronicle."

Back Yonder's most insightful and erudite reviewer, Columbia University English professor and poet Mark Van Doren, recognized the mythical, romantic nature of Hogue's Ozarks. "For all Mr. Hogue appears to know, Arkansas was inhabited by white people exactly like his parents and his neighbors three thousand years ago," Van Doren, perhaps shorn of romantic fleece by his own boyhood on a Midwestern farm, wrote in the *Nation*. "[W]hen he describes his return to the hills after many years spent elsewhere, he cannot believe that the people down there will ever be any different from what they are now or from what they were when he was a boy in the eighties." But Van Doren's peek behind the curtain, his deconstruction of *Back Yonder*'s perpetuation of the image of a timeless Ozarks peopled by America's "contemporary ancestors," was not meant to expose Hogue, much less to demean. "[H]e manages to do what more artful authors merely try to do," observed the Columbia professor. "[H]e gives his world that simple, solid reality and permanence which it would seem we cannot give a thing when we are aware of wanting to do so."[24]

Hogue obviously did not strictly confine himself to facts, despite the claims of his foreword, and any student of history cites the book's details at her own peril. But his flourishes of creativity and dramatization need not detract from the "solid reality" at the heart of *Back Yonder*. By the 1930s the popular and domestically exotic Ozark region had become so identified with pioneer lifestyles and folkways that any Arkansas story awash in mountain ballads and moonshiners was drawn into the Ozark vortex. Yet, *Back Yonder* reminds us that the characteristics of an "Ozark" lifestyle were so widespread in the late nineteenth century that they were not confined to the narrow hollers and rugged hills of the Ozarks. Only in the twentieth century would the myth and romance of the Ozarks suggest otherwise. Hogue's first-person memories and stories of a rural childhood in the 1870s and 1880s—whether in Charles W.'s Faulkner County or in Wayman's mythical mountain recesses—possess the same kernels of permanence and reality as do the third-person narratives of Laura Ingalls Wilder's *Little House* books. Both authors captured the essence—albeit an admittedly sanitized essence—of a time and place long since forgotten. Both also described people not terribly unlike you and me. It is this essence—the essence of humanity—that keeps *Back Yonder: An Ozark Chronicle* relevant and entertaining after all these years. No matter where Charles W. and Wayman merge into one Charles Wayman Hogue—no matter where fact ends and fiction begins in *Back Yonder*—relevance and entertainment constitute a solid legacy for an ambitious Arkansas farm boy and a valuable contribution to the Chronicles of the Ozarks.

Brooks Blevins

NOTES

1. On the relationship between Laura Ingalls Wilder and Rose Wilder Lane, see John E. Miller, *Becoming Laura Ingalls Wilder: The Woman behind the Legend* (Columbia: University of Missouri Press, 1998); William Holtz, *The Ghost in the Little House: A Life of Rose Wilder Lane* (Columbia: University of Missouri Press, 1995); and Laura Ingalls Wilder, *Pioneer Girl: The Annotated Autobiography*, ed. Pamela Smith Hill (Pierre: South Dakota State Historical Society Press, 2014.)

2. Toran Isom, "Charlie May Simon," *Encyclopedia of Arkansas History and Culture*, http://www.encyclopediaofarkansas.net/encyclopedia/entry-detail.aspx?entryID=41, accessed April 3, 2015. As scholars have debated Rose Wilder Lane's impact on the *Little House* books, it is tempting to speculate on the level of influence that Charlie May Simon may have exercised on *Back Yonder* as story consultant, editor, or even ghost writer. The almost complete lack of any surviving manuscript items or book-related correspondence between father and daughter, however, obscure any working relationship that might have existed. A brief letter from father to daughter, likely written in the early 1950s, reveals that even into his eighties Charles W. continued to send Charlie May Ozarks-related stories. Papa to Charlie May, April 1, no year, Folder 15, Box 4, Charlie May Simon Papers, Preservation and Special Collections Department, University of Memphis Libraries.

3. Percy Hutchison, "The Hill Folk of the Ozarks," *New York Times Book Review*, April 10, 1932, 1, 11 and Anne T. Earton, "Little House in the Big Woods," *New York Times Book Review*, April 24, 1932, 9.

4. Charles W. Hogue Tombstone, Memphis Memory Gardens, Find A Grave, http://www.findagrave.com/cgi-bin/fg.cgi?page=gr&GRid=88459552, accessed March 27, 2015.

5. B. F. Hogue Tombstone, Little Rock National Cemetery, Find A Grave, http://www.findagrave.com/cgi-bin/fg.cgi?page=gr&GSln=Hogue&GSiman=1&GScty=65&GRid=3135808&, accessed March 27, 2015. Conflicting sources record B. F.'s middle name as Franklin and Frederick.

6. Manuscript Census, Tyler Township, Perry County, Ark., 1900, 333; Manuscript Census, Muddy Bayou Township, Conway County, Ark., 1870, 12 and Conway County, Ark., Marriage Book A, 1851–1875, A/061 26, A/308 14, Conway County Courthouse, Morrilton, Ark. Hogue's mother is listed in various records as Marinda, Maranda, Amanda, and Miranda, and her maiden

name is also alternately identified as Nichols. She was first married to Chesley Allen Thomas Rodgers in Conway County, Arkansas, in 1855. Faulkner County was carved from Conway County in 1873.

7. Manuscript Census, Newton Township, Faulkner County, Ark., 20. The 1880 agricultural manuscript census for Faulkner County includes B. F. Hogue in Cypress Township, just to the south of Newton Township.

8. Manuscript Census, Newton Township, Faulkner County, Ark., 20; 1881 Personal Property Tax Book, Faulkner County, Ark. and 1886 Personal Property Tax Book, Perry County, Ark. It is possible that the Hogues moved to Perry County even earlier. The 1884 Personal Property Tax Book for the county includes a listing for the household of what appears to be George and Fred Hoag. If B. F.'s middle name was Frederick, as one family historian believes, then it is possible that this could have been B. F. Hogue. Betsy Beacham, e-mail message to author, April 1, 2015. B. F. Hogue later homesteaded a tract of Perry County land in a valley of the Ouachita Mountains in 1899. Benjamin F. Hogue Homestead Patent, General Land Office Records, U.S. Department of the Interior Bureau of Land Management, http://www.glorecords.blm.gov/details/patent/default.aspx?accession=AR2770__.174&docClass=STA&sid=n4q5bbmg.3ju#patentDetailsTabIndex=1, accessed April 2, 2015.

9. Agricultural Manuscript Census, Cypress Township, Faulkner County, Ark., 1880. On page 18 of Faulkner County Deed and Mortgage Book A is the record for a mortgage on Hogue's yoke of oxen, ox wagon, and cotton crop, all of which would be forfeited if he failed to pay W. J. Sipes $100 by December 1, 1873. This would seem to be consistent with a renter's mortgage, as the crop mortgage for a landowner would typically list the farm itself as collateral. Faulkner County Probate Court Book One (Faulkner County Courthouse, Conway, Ark.) notes smaller cotton-crop mortgages for Hogue in 1878 and 1879, both of which list livestock and crops as collateral.

10. As with many elements of the Hogue family, there is a bit of confusion regarding the occupation(s) of B. F. Hogue. He appears to have farmed most of his life, but the 1900 census for Perry County's Tyler Township lists his occupation as "Practice Medicine." B. F. Hogue was also referred to as Dr. Benjamin F. Hogue in a biographical sketch of his son, James E. Manuscript Census, Tyler Township, Perry County, Ark., 1900; Fay Hempstead, *Historical Review of Arkansas: Its Commerce, Industry, and Modern Affairs*, Vol. II (Chicago: Lewis Publishing Co., 1911), 613.

11. Hempstead, *Historical Review of Arkansas*, 613. See also *Bench and Bar of Arkansas, 1935* (No place: B. F. Face Publishing Co., c. 1935), 59.

12. Goodspeed, Biographical and Historical Memoirs of Pulaski, Jefferson, Lonoke, Faulkner, Grant, Saline, Perry, Garland and Hot Spring Counties, Arkansas (Chicago: Goodspeed Publishing Co., 1889), 505–6, 513. Due to Hogue's laxity with the facts and the absence of historical records from Little Rock Commercial College, it is unclear whether or not he actually attended the college. If he did so, it is most likely, given his career as a salesman and business owner, that he completed a basic business course and not a traditional "liberal arts" course of study.

13. Hempstead, *Historical Review of Arkansas*, 613; Drew County, Ark., Marriage Records, 382 and Manuscript Census, Greenville, Washington County, Miss, 23. The Hogue family was involved in a census anomaly in 1900, appearing in the census of two different counties in two different states. On June 1, 1900, the enumerator for Prairie Township in Drew County, Arkansas, found the young family living in a rented house near the home of Mary Gill Hogue's parents. Charles W. was listed as a life insurance agent. Eighteen days later they were recorded in the Washington County, Mississippi, census. Given that their infant son Abner was identified as having been born in Mississippi in April 1900, it seems likely that Charles W. and Mary had temporarily relocated near the Gill family so that Mary would have assistance with the newborn baby and the other two small children while he continued to travel for work. Manuscript Census, Prairie Township, Drew County, Ark., 43.

14. R. L. Polk and Co., *1902 Memphis City Directory* (Memphis, Tenn.: R. L. Polk and Co., 1902.) All subsequent city directories, with corresponding reference data, were consulted through 1943. Directories available on-line through Shelby County, Tenn., Register of Deeds Office, http://register.shelby.tn.us/, accessed April 4, 2015; hereafter *Memphis City Directories.*

15. Jody Parsons, "Howard Jacob Simon," *Encylcopedia of Arkansas History and Culture*, http://www.encyclopediaofarkansas.net/encyclopedia/entry-detail.aspx?entryID=2335, accessed April 3, 2015; *Memphis City Directories*; Genealogy Materials, Series II, Box 3, File 3, Charlie May Simon Papers, University of Arkansas-Little Rock Special Collections; Mother to My Dear Children, no date, Series I, Box 1, File 19, Charlie May Simon Papers, University of Arkansas-Little Rock Special Collections; "King Pointers in World War II," http://kingspointww2.org/hogue-charles-w/, accessed March 28, 2015; and Memphis *Commercial Appeal*, March 2, 1965, 11.

16. Wayman Hogue, "Ozark People," *Scribner's*, May 1931, 509–20 and Charlie May Simon, "Retreat to the Land: An Experience in Poverty," *Scribner's*, May 1933, 309–12.

17. *Bookman*, April 1932, 88 and Hutchison, "The Hill-Folk of the Ozarks."

18. *Bookman*, April 1932, 88 and *New Republic*, April 27, 1932, 307.

19. For a widely accepted illustration of the physical boundaries of the Ozarks region, see Milton D. Rafferty, *The Ozarks, Land and Life*, 2nd ed. (Fayetteville: University of Arkansas Press, 2001.)

20. Identifying the boundaries of cultural regions is an inexact science at best. Though most of the handful of people with whom I discussed the issue of regional identity in the Enola and Mount Vernon areas of Faulkner County claimed that their communities were not in the Ozarks, the allure of the Ozark "brand" can cause people to stretch regional boundaries in order to affiliate with the Ozarks. For example, in its promotional literature Hendrix College claims that "Conway is at the foothills of the Ozark Mountains." See https://www.hendrix.edu/discoverhendrix/default.aspx?id=38286, accessed April 3, 2015.

21. Vance Randolph, *The Ozarks: An American Survival of Primitive Society* (New York: Vanguard Press, 1931), 3. Curtis F. Marbut's *Soil Reconnoissance of the Ozark Region of Missouri and Arkansas* began the process of narrowing the region's physical boundaries. This study, published in 1914, included no territory south of the Arkansas River and differentiated the territory north of the river but south of the Boston Mountains (including all of Faulkner County) as the "Ouachita Ridges and Lowlands," which he described as a "subdivision" of the Ozark highlands. Marbut, *Soil Reconnoissance of the Ozark Region of Missouri and Arkansas* (Washington, D.C.: U.S. Department of Agriculture, 1914), 8–9.

22. Simon, "Retreat to the Land," *Scribner's*, 309–12.

23. Wilder, *Pioneer Girl*, xxx, xxxiii.

24. Mark Van Doren, "In the Ozarks," *The Nation*, June 8, 1932, 656.

BACK YONDER

AN OZARK CHRONICLE

BY WAYMAN HOGUE

WOODCUTS BY
HOWARD SIMON

MINTON, BALCH & COMPANY
NEW YORK
1932

Printed in the United States of America by
THE KNICKERBOCKER PRESS, NEW ROCHELLE, N. Y.

TO MY WIFE

MARY GILL HOGUE

I LOVINGLY DEDICATE

THIS BOOK

FOREWORD

IN WRITING this book I have kept but one thing in view—that is, to confine myself to facts. I have made no attempt to hold the mountain people up to ridicule, neither have I made any effort toward defending them for any of their shortcomings.

I have described conditions, not as I imagined them to be, nor as I have read about them; but I have attempted to picture conditions as I actually saw and lived them. Wherever I have used dialogue I have quoted the conversation as spoken, to the very best of my memory.

In writing the dialect I have made no attempt to conform to any of the rules governing mountain vernacular, but I have quoted each word exactly as I heard it spoken and as I was taught to speak it.

W. H.

CONTENTS

BACK YONDER

BACK YONDER

CHAPTER I

OUR HOME

ABOUT the first recollection I have of my existence was one day when I was playing in the yard by myself. With a stick I was digging a hole in the ground, when suddenly it occurred to me that there might be danger of digging down to where the Bad Man lived. I had been taught that the Bad Man dwelt down under the ground and that the Good Man lived in the skies.

I jumped up, and looking at the hole I had dug, I thought of how mean the Bad Man had been described to me, and I made a face at the hole, defying him and daring him to come up. I then thought of how powerful the Good Man had been pictured and I made a face at the skies. Thinking over what I had done, I became a little afraid and compromised the matter by saying, "I'll lak ye both if you will let me alone an' not hurt me."

I do not remember the exact house in which I was born, for when I was about two years old my father moved and settled in another county. This was in the northern part of Arkansas, in the Ozark mountains. We were a hundred and ten miles from Little Rock, the state capital, and eighty miles from the nearest railroad.

I had two sisters and a brother, and as I write, a vivid picture of my family rises up in my memory. There is my mother, exacting, commanding, and of a strong determination of mind. My father, friendly, jovial, and always trying to put his best foot forward. Lelia, precise, studious, and refined. Nora, tom-boyish and nervous. Jim, self-assured and executive.

There is nothing I remember more vividly than our old home and its surroundings. I remember the "big house," one large room built of scalped logs, chinked and daubed, and floored with puncheons made of split logs with the flat side up and the surface hewn smooth. It was roofed with boards riven from choice oak and had overhead joists made of unbarked poles five or six inches in diameter.

There was no loft or ceiling, but some long boards were placed across the joists on which were stored baskets of apples, bags of peanuts and sacks of cotton. I also remember how, in the fall of the year, my mother would slice pumpkins in rings and string them on a stick to dry. These sticks containing rings of pumpkins extending from one joist to another were a familiar sight.

There were two doors in the big house, one on each side, called the front door and the back door. There were no windows, and all light and ventilation came from the open doors and the unceiled cracks in the walls between the logs.

Best of all I remember the huge fireplace at one end of the big house. This fireplace was made of stone quarried from a nearby hillside and cemented together with a mortar made of clay. The extending chimney was built of split sticks heavily daubed and lined with clay, which when dry was very substantial. Sometimes this lining would crack and fall off, leaving the wood parts exposed, and when the weather was cold and the fires large, my father would have to throw water up the chimney to extinguish the blaze.

The doorsteps were made of three sawed blocks which stood on end, one above the other.

I still remember the kitchen, a smaller house of one room that stood out in the yard, facing the back door of the big house, and connected with the big house by a hewn log that was used as a walk from one house to the other.

In the kitchen there was a small fireplace, on the sides of which were skillets and lids, a tea-kettle, a coffee pot, boiling pot, fire shovel, a pair of tongs, and a pair of pothooks, either resting against the walls or hanging suspended from nails or pegs driven into the walls. There was a stationary bench made against the wall on one side of the dining table. The other seats at the table were supplied with chairs brought from the big house at meal times.

The loom, when not in use, stood in the back part of the kitchen, and on it reposed two or three pairs of batting cards. The coffee mill was fastened to the wall, and the churn occupied space on the hearth near the fireplace.

Against the jambs, strings of red pepper, small bags of garden sage and hands of tobacco were sometimes suspended. Near the door there was a shelf attached to the wall on which rested—in addition to a can of home made lye soap, a jar of salt and a jar of lard—a cedar water bucket with a gourd dipper hanging on a nail just over it. Under the shelf was a barrel containing meal with a meal sack spread over it to keep out the dust.

Just outside the kitchen door and against the wall was a small bench on which there was another cedar water bucket, a tin wash pan, a sardine box filled with lye soap. Hanging over the basin was a towel made from a worn-out meal sack.

The entire family slept in the big house. There

were three large cord beds, two in the back part of the house—one in each corner—and the third in a corner next to the fireplace. In place of slats there were ropes running through and around the railings and woven tight. On this network of ropes rested the beds. First there was a straw mattress and on this a full heavy feather bed.

My father and mother slept on one of the beds in the back of the house and my sisters on the other, and Jim and I slept on the bed near the fireplace. We also had a trundle bed under one of the large beds, which could be drawn out and used for company. My mother could always take care of still more company by making down a feather bed in the middle of the floor.

The spinning wheel, when not in use, usually stood by the wall, and there was a large old trunk placed back between the beds, which was used for storing quilts and clothing.

A heavy board was built over the fireplace, which was used as a mantel. On this usually could be seen a large Seth Thomas clock, bottles containing castor oil, turpentine and camphor, and a cake of mutton suet.

Over each door were two forked sticks nailed to the wall with prongs extending outward, called gun racks. A rifle rested on one pair of these gun racks and a shotgun on the other. There was a shot pouch hanging suspended to each of the racks.

We had no rockers and all of our straight backed

chairs were bottomed with hickory bark, white oak splits, corn shucks or cowhide.

Our library consisted of a Bible, a small but very thick hymn book, a dream book, a letter writer and an almanac.

The usual way of lighting our house by night was with pine. The heart of the seasoned pine, when split into strips, made a splendid torch, and the knots of decayed pine were very rich in rosin. A pine knot thrown into the fire lighted the whole room. Sometimes, when out of pine knots, we used candles which we molded ourselves. I also remember seeing my mother put sycamore balls in a saucer of grease and light the end of the stem. This made a dim flickering light.

A small rail fence enclosed our yard. It was also well protected by two large and faithful dogs, "Watch" and "Savage." Off by itself in the yard was the smoke house, where meat was hung and smoke-cured.

A short distance from the yard-fence was the barn, usually called the "crib and stable." The lower part of the crib was used for storing corn, and the upper part, called the fodder loft, was used for storing unthreshed oats, fodder and hay. On one side of the crib was a stall in which we housed our horse and mule, and on the other side was a storage for wheat, tobacco, dry hides and baskets of wool.

The crib and stable were surrounded by a heavy rail fence staked and ridered, and we referred to this enclosure as "the lot." Adjoining the lot was the cow pen. We had no shelter for the cattle, sheep and hogs, and they were forced to take the weather as it came.

The outside walls of the crib and stable were often adorned with the skins of wild animals, such as deer, wild cat, and sometimes bear. The walls of the smoke house were ornamented with skins of fur bearing animals such as racoon, fox, mink and skunk, where my father had tacked them up to dry. The skins of an otter and a beaver, stretched over a board with the pelt side out, were a familiar sight.

Our vegetable garden was on the side of the house opposite the lot, and it was protected by a fence made of long sharp pointed pickets called palings. The palings were pointed at the top to prevent chickens from flying over into the garden, and they were set close together at the bottom to keep out rabbits and fowl.

Our house was built with respect to convenience to water. About a hundred yards from the house was a large spring with a swift outflow from which we obtained our household water. A few feet from the mouth of the spring was a small excavation through which cold water ran, and in it were placed buckets and jars of milk in order that they might keep cool. They were protected from hogs and cattle by a small rail pen. Near the spring was a large wash kettle and two tubs made by sawing a barrel in halves.

Our field of about thirty or forty acres of cleared land extended down to and included a small creek bottom. In going to the field we passed through the orchard. This was an enclosure of about ten acres independent of the rest of the field.

Our house was situated about a mile from the "big road." This was a rocky, rough, and seldom traveled highway, and was the only road leading out of the vicinity. A creek ran through our property, between our house and the big road, which would often become swollen too deep and swift to ford, and as there was no other way of getting from our house to the big road, we just had to wait until the water subsided.

In describing our old home, I have described the average home of the mountains. It was not much worse and not much better than any other in our neighborhood. It was such a home as my grandfather and my great-grandfather had lived in; we had the same conveniences, the same advantages and disadvantages, as did our ancestors of a hundred years back.

CHAPTER II

A CHUNK O' FAR

ABOUT the first work I ever did was to pick up chips. My father, in cutting up logs into firestick length, left a lot of chips, and my job was to pick up the chips and take them into the kitchen as my mother needed them. When a little larger, I was able to assist Jim in bringing in small wood.

Since our house was far from airtight during the severe cold of the winter we had to keep heavy fires going. In making a fire we raked the ashes from the back, and my father laid in a back stick, as heavy as he could carry. He then placed another smaller stick in front, each end resting on a rock about the size of a brick. We knew nothing about andirons then. In between the two sticks of wood, we piled smaller wood, and built on up.

We had no friction matches, and it was very important that we keep fires from going out. To do this we covered the fire with ashes before we went to bed, so that we would have live coals to start with the next morning. However, it was often the case that the fires went completely out anyway, and we then had to go to a neighbor's house and "borry" some fire. Many were the times when I had to get up in the cold and go to John Stewart's house a half mile distant, and "borry a chunk o' far," before we could build a fire in our house.

When we had to go off to borrow fire, we wanted it for immediate needs, and we therefore went in a hurry, got it in a hurry, and came back in a hurry. Even now, when a mountain man visits a neighbor and hints at going, the neighbor will say, "What's yer hurry? Did ye come arter a chunk o' far?"

We could solve our fire problem by creating the spark ourselves. On several occasions I have taken flint and held it just over some dry cotton lint and given the flint a downward stroke with my closed pocket knife. On doing this a spark would fly from the flint and strike the lint. I would blow this until it ignited and the fire was started.

I was ten years old before I ever heard of a cooking stove. We did all of our cooking on the kitchen fireplace. This necessitated fire in the kitchen every day

in the year. The chips which I so often had to unwillingly quit my play for and bring in were used in cooking. The chips quickly burnt into coals, which were necessary in baking. My mother would rake out some coals, and put over them a three legged skillet in which she placed biscuits. She then put a lid over the skillet and heaped coals on the lid. In this way she baked wonderful biscuits; I have never eaten any since as good.

All of our coffee came to us green, and my mother roasted it over the kitchen fire and ground it as she needed it. She made coffee by boiling the grounds and water together in the tea-kettle. When we were out of coffee, a good substitute could be made from parched corn meal and molasses.

Since we produced nearly everything that the family consumed, there was always plenty to do about the place. My father, Jim and I were kept busy tending the fields, caring for the stock, getting in the firewood, tanning hides, hunting, trapping and fishing. My mother and sisters had a great deal of work to do. Besides cooking, milking and churning, and attending to the house, they had to make all of our clothing, from the raw material to the finished product. As far back as I can remember, my mother and Lelia would sit up late at night and knit. They had to make all the hosiery, gloves, shawls and nubias and as the winter was approached they naturally had a great deal of knitting to do.

Every girl had to learn to cut out and make men's and women's clothing. Not only that, but she had to learn to manufacture the cloth from which the clothing was made. They carded the wool or cotton into rolls or bats, and with a spinning wheel spun it into thread, and with a loom wove it into cloth. My mother wove a heavy woolen cloth that she used in making clothing for my father, Jim and me. She wove a lighter wool cloth, called linsey, that she used in making dresses for herself and the girls. She also wove an all cotton cloth that could be used for making shirts and women's underwear.

We children went barefooted about eight months in the year. Should the weather get too severe before we had the money to buy the one pair of shoes each that we had a year, my father was able to make a kind of moccasin out of tanned cowhide that served as a temporary relief.

We used to get choice wheat straw and plait it into hats which served for the summer. We had warm coonskin caps in the winter. I was fortunate if I could get a fifty-cent wool hat once a year.

Corn was the predominant crop and we had to raise it plentifully, as we used it for bread and fed it to our stock and poultry the year round. In that country corn is not perishable and will keep for two or three years. Besides corn we grew wheat, oats, tobacco, sorghum, potatoes and a little cotton. We had no market for any of these products, and they were all for our own consumption.

We had good orchards and very often the yield of large red apples was excessive, but it was unprofitable to market them, as we had to haul them too far. Sometimes, however, my father did take a load of red apples to the river bottoms and peddle them out.

We raised our cattle and sheep with little trouble, as there was cane in the creek bottoms, which they could feed on in the winter, and the herbage on the hillsides afforded splendid grazing in the summer. I remember how I used to have to go after the cows. In the late afternoon when Lelia and my mother wanted to milk, and the cows were not back, they would send me after them. We had one cow belled so we could locate the herd. I would go out into the woods and listen for the bell, and when I heard it, I quickly located the cows and drove them home.

It was important that we raise plenty of sheep, as they supplied the wool out of which we made our winter clothing. We sheared them once a year and that was in the spring so that the wool would grow back in time to keep them warm in the winter. I always dreaded to see sheep shearing time come, for I had to hold the sheep while my father sheared them.

The fruit of the oak, the acorn, is very fattening for hogs, and when the acorns fell plentifully, we said the mast was good. When there was good mast, our hogs thrived without much feeding. They ran in the woods, but my father always called them up at night to feed them, so that they might sleep near the house. The hog call still rings in my ears as I picture my father outside the gate, uttering in a loud tone of voice the droll, howling call, "Peegoo-eee, pig, pig; pe-goo-eee."

A great day it was when hog killing time came around. My father usually had a man to help him, and my mother had a neighbor woman to help her. The scene is familiar. The large wash-kettle with a fire under it heating water; the sloping barrel filled with hot water; my father and his helper taking the hog by its feet and sousing it into the barrel, drawing it out and trying the hair to see if it would pull easily, then drawing it out on a bench, and with great activity pulling and scraping off the hair.

When the hog was butchered, the sides, or the middlings, hams and shoulders were hung up in the smoke house. Every day for a long time I had to make fires under the meat sufficient to create a good smoke. This was kept up until the meat was well cured. From this practice, of course, originated the term "smoke house."

It is surprising how little we felt the need of money. We had almost no use for it. I remember my father gave me a quarter once, and I carried it around in my pocket for several months because I had no way of spending it. Finally a pack peddler came by, and

I spent my money for a Jew's harp and a pocketbook. Corn, meat and lard were never sold outright. If a man was in need of these things, he simply borrowed from a neighbor until he could supply himself by his own production.

There were some things, however, that we could not produce, and it took cash to buy them. We had to have shoes, farm implements, dishes and cooking utensils, such staples as sugar, coffee, salt, soda and dye stuff, and household remedies, such as castor oil, turpentine and camphor gum.

My father was able to raise the necessary money for the family in various ways. He trapped for fur such animals as the otter, the beaver, the mink, the skunk and the raccoon. Then we raised a great deal of poultry and eggs which he occasionally took to market. Sometimes he went to the river bottoms and worked during the fall of the year. Cotton picking on the river plantations offered employment for men and women and children during the harvest. The mountain people take this work only as a last resort, because they enjoy their freedom too much to work willingly for some one else.

We rose early. When the chickens began crowing for day, we got out of bed. It was considered disgraceful for a man to be found in bed at sun-up. He was laughed at and called lazy. We knew nothing about an eight-hour day or a six-hour day. We worked when there was work to do and quit when it was through.

I will always remember when I learned to plow. We had two yearlings named Jolly and Brandy that my father was breaking in to work. Jim had been assisting him some, but I was considered too small to be of any help. However I made such a noise about it that my father let me hold the lines and drive Jolly and Brandy, while Jim held the plow. We were plowing new ground, and my father said he was breaking in the boys, the oxen and the land.

We had an implement called rope works, with which my father made ropes. These ropes were used for plow lines, halters, bridle reins, and for many other purposes. The rope was about the only kind of string we had, except rawhide or tanned leather. We did not have any cotton or hemp twine. Therefore we had to tan a great many skins to supply the need for cord. Tanned squirrel skin made a nice shoe lace, and well-tanned buckskin was used for hamstrings, mending harness and for tying bundles to our saddles. Nearly every boy and man at all times had a buckskin string in his pocket, as it was handy when a good strong cord was needed.

The long winter evenings were spent around the fireside. My mother and sisters were kept busy knitting. My father passed away the time in such duties as mending old shoes, cutting buckskin into strings or molding bullets for the next day's hunt. Jim usually assisted my father, and my duties mostly were to keep the fires mended and the room lighted. "Chunk up the far, Wayman! Throw in a pine knot, Wayman!" were oft-repeated commands that I obeyed until I got to nodding and became so sleepy that I had to go off to bed.

There was not much reading going on in our house. Lelia and Nora studied the "Letter Writer" and song book, my father read the almanac to learn what the weather forecast was, and Jim studied the dream book. My mother always read the Bible on Sunday afternoon, when we stayed at home. One day Jim traded his Barlow pocket-knife to Joe Burton for a badly worn copy of "Peck's Bad Boy." Joe could not read, and as he was through looking at the pictures, he had no further use for it. My father and Lelia read and re-read the book aloud, while the rest of us listened attentively. Not long after this my father brought home a yellow back, paper-bound book that he had borrowed from Squire George. The title of the book was "The Adventures of Dr. Rattlehead." This book was a side-splitter and well illustrated. We read it so much that we soon learned it by heart. One day my mother, in coming home from Aunt Lou's, brought home a book. I do not remember the title of it, but it was a history of Jim Copeland, a notorious free booter who plied his nefarious practices in the early days of the state.

With this supply of literature the family managed to get along fairly well until the advent of the history of the James boys.

Sometimes a book agent came amongst us, but it

was seldom that he did any business. Somehow, the people were not favorably impressed with book agents, as they were nearly all "furriners," and it was supposed that they were following that avocation for the sole purpose of trying to "beat work." However I remember one instance where my father subscribed.

One day about noon a man rode up to our house and inquired for my father. He was down in the field, and my mother sent Jim after him.

"Paw," said Jim, "they's a man at the house wot wants ter see you."

"Who is it?" asked my father.

"Dunno," replied Jim. "He looks lak a furriner."

My father came on up to the house.

"Good morning, Mr. Hogue," said the stranger. "O'Neal is my name. I am taking orders for the 'Royal Path of Life.' I have heard a *great* many say that you are a man well educated and well read and that all your family enjoy reading good books. With your permission I will just show you a few sample pages of this wonderful work."

The agent then produced his prospectus and began turning the pages in rapid succession, as he continued his sales talk. All of us except my mother stood by, looking at the book as the agent described it.

"Hit looks lak a good book," my father said after the agent was through with his talk. "What do youens thank uv it?" he asked, addressing Lelia and Nora.

Lelia thought that it was a handsome book and

would make a mighty good showing when laid on the mantle when company came. It would give to our house the appearance of the "rich folks' " dwellings.

Nora liked it, but she thought of a better use for it. On account of its size she had an idea that it would be nice to cut out the leaves and paste them on the walls when we got through reading it, as it would make the room more attractive.

Jim and I liked the book, especially the pictures, but we did not think they were as funny as those in the almanac.

My father did not know much about what was in the book, but he noticed that it had gold letters on the back and sides, and he concluded that it must be a valuable book.

So the consensus of opinion was that while the book would not measure up to the standards of "Peck's Bad Boy" and "Doctor Rattlehead," it was a fairly good book, and my father wrote his name under the others. Dinner was ready then, so he asked the agent to stay.

During all the proceedings my mother had said nothing, but stayed back in the kitchen and frowned unapprovingly. She didn't like furriners to begin with and was displeased at my father's buying the book, and she was downright angry with him for asking the agent to stay for dinner, because she had to dip into the little coffee and brown sugar that she was saving for Saturday night when the preacher and his wife, Brother and Sister Yates, were coming for supper.

"School is comin' on," my mother said to Lelia, "an' yore paw haint got narry a cent to buy books and slates and pencils with, an' yit youens want him to buy that ole book from that stuck-up furriner. An' youens kep on after him till he had to take two papers when one would have done."

When a weekly newspaper was established in our county it supplied a long felt want. In loading the shot gun we had to have a lot of wadding and this was hard to get. Last year's almanac was soon exhausted, and we had a hard time finding paper for gun wadding. Therefore we began taking the county weekly as soon as it came out.

One day a sheet writer came to our house, and among the papers he was soliciting for, was the Weekly Arkansas *Gazette*. Lelia and Nora liked the looks of the *Gazette* and wanted my father to stop the county weekly and subscribe for the *Gazette*. My father didn't want to do it and that brought on a long argument as to which was the better paper. My father liked the county paper because it was softer and sleazier and made better gun wadding and there was just enough of it for his purposes. The girls liked the *Gazette* much better. It was larger, was of a better grade of paper, and easier to cut and notch, and so much better to use for making mantle scarfs. Also, because there was so much of it, they could soon save up enough to paper the house.

My father could not see his way clear to give up

the county weekly, so he compromised matters by taking both papers.

School had often been spoken of, but though I was eight years old, I had never been. One day when we were all over in the back part of the field, Jim O'Quinn came along and said,

"Youens hurry up an' git yer crap laid by. The free school starts at Gravel Hill week come Monday. Youens git ready to go."

CHAPTER III

SCHOOL

ON the first Monday morning in July the four of us were off to school. Nora carried her books and a gallon-size new tin bucket with a tight fitting lid, in which was packed our lunch. Lelia wore shoes and carried her books in one hand and a red rose in the other. Jim, with his books in one hand, carried in his other, suspended to a string, a quart-size whiskey flask filled with buttermilk. I carried a red apple stuffed in each of my pants pockets and was equipped with a new slate and a Webster's blue back spelling book.

Jim had had the advantage of a two months' subscription school the previous year, and he gave me some good advice as to my behavior in school.

"You dassent talk out in times o' books," he said,

"fer the teacher mout whup ye. You don't want to cut up none, caze you'll shore git a whuppin'."

My father had also lectured me as to the importance of good behavior in school, and I was beginning to wonder if the only business of a school teacher was to whip little children.

We reached the schoolhouse long before eight, the opening hour. At eight o'clock the teacher rapped repeatedly with a stick on the facing of the door, as a signal to come in to books. There was a scramble for the door, all trying to get in at the same time.

The building, "Gravel Hill Meetin' House" was a long log house, fronting the big road. It had a large door in front, which always stood open, and a smaller door in back near the right hand corner. At the back was a rostrum with a desk, which answered for a pulpit. In front of the rostrum was a long boxed bench, looking not unlike the casing of a coffin. This was known as the Mourner's Bench in times of the "big meetin's." In front of the Mourner's Bench was a small table, and here the teacher presided.

The house was seated with benches made of undressed lumber resting on, and nailed to, blocks. There were no backrests and no desks in front.

In addition to the two doors the house was further ventilated with large cracks between the wall logs. These cracks were also convenient to spit out through for those who chewed and dipped and wanted to deviate slightly from the usual custom of spitting on the floor. This building was the religious, political and social center of the entire neighborhood.

A school tax was rarely voted in our district. The only source of revenue came from the state per capita apportionment. To have a school we must wait until there was sufficient funds in the treasury.

The annual school election was held on the third Saturday in May. At this meeting, among other transactions, the electors voted for or against a school tax. The school laws permitted a tax to be voted up to as high as five mills on the dollar.

I still cannot understand why the voters in our school district did not favor a school tax. Probably those who paid taxes and had no children of school age voted against it from a selfish point of view, but there were many men who voted against a school tax and who did not pay any taxes at all. I suppose they did not understand the system. They argued that the money had to go through so many hands that the leakage would be too heavy before it got back to the treasury.

The summer I was eight years old, there had accumulated in the treasury to the credit of our district about fifty dollars. This, at twenty-five dollars a month, would hire a teacher for two months, and a Mr. Vincent was employed to teach for three months, the last month to be taught by subscription at a dollar a scholar.

Mr. Vincent was a stocky little man past middle

age, wearing gray jean pants, brogan shoes with no socks, a percale shirt, a celluloid collar stained from long use, and a calico coat that had seen better days. He wore steel-framed spectacles and a brass watch chain.

He came from nobody knew where, but it was said that he had had educational advantages in his younger days. He had been a lawyer, a preacher, and a book-keeper, and had been successful in making a failure of everything he had undertaken. Probably when he became convinced that he was good for nothing, he considered himself eligible for the profession of teaching school.

He spent that first day enrolling, classifying, and assigning lessons. Nearly all had blue back spellers. The larger ones had Ray's arithmetic and McGuffy's readers.

In forming classes in spelling he asked us how far we had been in the spelling book. Some had been to Horseback, some to Baker, and some to Botany. He classed them accordingly.

There were six classes in spelling, four in reading, three in arithmetic, and three in writing. Most all had slates and pencils.

I knew my letters and was put in the a b ab class. There was one class below mine, the a b c class. Jim was put in the spelling class that started with Baker, and he was in the First Reader. Nora's first lesson in the speller was Horseback, and she had a

Third Reader. Lelia started in the speller with Amity, was in long division in arithmetic, and was in the Fourth Reader. Hers was the senior class in the school.

There were about eight in my class. When the time came to say our lessons, the teacher made a chalk mark on the floor. We were required to stand with our big toes right up to the chalk mark, so that we would all be in line. Standing at the foot of the class was Tom Ward, a lanky, gawky overgrown youth of about twenty, nearly six feet tall. He was barefooted and wore home-made cotton pants much too short and a shirt that had once been white, but was colored from long wear without washing.

We began spelling out and pronouncing the words in our awkward way. It came Tom's time to recite, and the teacher said, "You may recite, Thomas."

"Whadje say, Mr. Vincent?" Tom asked.

"Just go ahead and say your lesson," Mr. Vincent said.

Tom, with a droll, loud voice, began, "A b, ab; a b, ab; a b, ab." There was a shifting of bare feet and suppressed laughter.

"Looky hyar," said Tom as he turned around. "I've come to this school to git a little book larnin', an' youens kin lafe if you wanter, but I've sot in to git a edication an' I'm goin' ter git it, an' I kin whup any uv youens that's lafed at me."

As he said this, he wiped a tear from his eye with his shirt sleeve.

"Order, order in the school rum," the teacher said as he repeatedly rapped the table with a hickory switch. "Thomas you may go to your seat."

Then he addressed the school.

"We are not here to fight, neither are we here to laugh some at the others. It may be that some of you have had better school advantages than has Thomas, but that would be nothing to laugh at, and the determination that this young man shows and the interest he is taking make me think that the laugh may soon be on the other side."

He instructed Tom privately, until he was as far as Baker; then he was permitted to come to the class.

Nearly every day for a week new students were enrolled. The Liveslys came from across Bear Creek, the Crosses lived up in Greasy Valley, and the Faulkners came from across Bull Mountain. Some of these children had as far as seven miles to walk, and across mountains. Students kept enrolling until there were over forty of us all in one room.

The summer days were intensely hot, and crowded as we were, we often thirsted for water. When many of us were snapping our fingers at the same time, a bucket was passed around, and we each took a drink of cool spring water from a gourd dipper; then put the dipper back into the bucket.

At the noon recess the children of each family went off by themselves and sat on logs or stumps to eat their dinner. The dinner usually consisted of cold biscuits and molasses. The molasses was poured from a small bottle into the lid of the tin pail, and the biscuits were sopped in it. After dinner, we scattered over the playground. There were shocky-headed youths with pockets bulging with apples and peaches, grownup girls with black gum tooth brushes in their mouths, and children of all ages. Nobody wore shoes except a few of the marriageable young women, who came barefooted, carrying their shoes in their hands until they came within sight of the schoolhouse.

We had few studies, but we recited often, thereby going right on through the books. Friday afternoons were given over to exercises such as spelling matches, recitations, and readings. Everyone had to make a speech or make a bow.

"Twinkle Little Star" and "See, O See The Shining Thing" were favorites among the little folks. The larger boys recited "The Boy Stood On The Burning Deck," and "Somebody's Darling" was a favorite among the young women. The little fellows who could not memorize a piece would sometimes recite a meaningless rhyme such as:

"Had a little dog, an' his name wuz Rover
When he died, he died all over."

Or:

"Old John, big John, old John Bailey,
Had a wife an' three little babies.

One in the corner, one in the cradle,
One in the soup pot eatin' with a ladle."

The mountain people have a dialect and pronunciation of their own. For instance they say "far" for "fire" and "fair"; "fur" for "far"; "fer" for "for," and "hit" for "it." For the plural of you, they say "youens," not "you all" as some think.

I remember once, when the Second Reader was reciting, how Bill Babb, an overgrown, gawky boy read as follows:

"I'm glad toe see you little bird,
Hit wuz yore sweet song I hyeard.
What wuz hit I hyeard you say—
Give me some crums toe eat toe day."

The teacher called this correct, and if usage controls the pronunciation, then it was correct.

We would also fall into the habit of reading our verses in a sing song way. When Miss Etta Whittaker read, it sounded as follows:

"I met a little COTTAGE girl,
She was eight years OLD she said.
Her hair was thick with MANY a curl,
That clustered ROUND her head."

In this and all other schools in the mountains the punishment was inflicted by whipping. The offending boy or girl was marched out on the floor in the presence of all and was whipped over the back and shoulders with a green hickory switch, sometimes until the blood came. This was expected of a teacher. His qualifications were often judged by his willingness and ability to inflict punishment.

School closed at five in the afternoon, and in July the sun was then still high. I remember coming home one afternoon and finding Bob Massey and Dick Simpson, two neighbors, at our house. They were eating watermelons, sitting with my father under a tree.

"Hello thar, little Wamie," Bob said. "How many whuppin's did ye git toeday?"

Then turning to my father, he said, "How do you like the new teacher, anyhow, Ben?"

"Purty far," my father said as he nodded toward me and smiled, "cep'n he don't whup Wayman enough."

"Wal, he don't whup nobody enough," Bob said. "Why nary one uv my chilluns is cotched a whuppin' yit."

"Lemme tell you somep'n," said Dick after he had drawn a long slice of melon across his mouth until the meat had vanished, "ef this hyar sun gits much hotter, I'm a-goin' to haf to go arter my little gal ever evenin' an' let 'er ride behine me on my hoss. Hits jist too hot fer her to come home in the heat uv the day, thisaway."

"You better come a whistlin'," said Bob. "He otter

stay an' teach them scholars tul night. A day's work is not a day's work tul the sun goes down."

"Now talk about a whuppin'," said Dick. "When I war a chap an' went to school to ole man Eubanks, he jist tuck a big hickory switch aroun' with him all the time, an' when a boy didn't behave hisse'f, he shore giv 'im the elbow grease. Why I've seed 'im wear out two hick'ries on one boy. That war a rail teacher."

"You better come a whistlin'," said Bob. "When I went to school, I had to stay thar all day an' study my lessons, an' I had to know 'em too. I don't believe in thishyar high falutin' way uv teachin' nohow. The teacher fer me is one that'll take up books at seb'n an' let 'em out jist in time to git 'em home by dark. An' if a boy looks cross-eyed, give 'im a good whuppin' an' then you've got 'im."

Among the long list of rules that the teacher read to us every morning, one read, "No fighting." We little fellows often fought, but we squared things up by taking a whipping, and it was all over. I remember one day when two grown young women got into a fight. Miss Jennie Bostic and Miss Sallie Neuby became involved in downright combat. It seemed that Sallie had made some remarks about the way that Jennie was dressed at the meeting the previous Sunday. Jennie demanded that she swallow her words and apologize, but Sallie stood firm and took back nothing. The fight was on, Jennie being the aggressor and Sallie fighting back in defense. They fought like wildcats for several minutes before they were separated.

The teacher immediately called books. We all marched into the house and with solemn faces took our seats. There was not a sound or move except that of Jennie as she gently sobbed, while holding her face in her hands. With great anxiety we waited for the next move.

The teacher rose and said:

"I am very sorry that this trouble came up on the playgrounds between two grown young women. I think that Miss Sallie fought only in defense and that Miss Jennie started the fight and kept it up all the way through. However, I admire any young woman who has the pluck to protect her character. Both the law and society will accord her the right to defend herself against any slanderous talk. Yet it would be impossible to permit this incident to go unnoticed and those partaking to go unpunished. I do not feel equal to the occasion and shall not attempt to deal with this case alone, so I will have the board of directors meet at the opening of school tomorrow morning, and we will then decide on what steps to take."

The matter was soon settled, however, for Miss Jennie had signaled her brothers and sisters and they all had their books gathered up. When the teacher took his seat, they all marched out of the schoolhouse on their way home, not to return.

One day William Frayser and Clint Henry got into

a dispute over a ball game, and the result was a big fight. When we went in to books the teacher told the two boys to come forward and take a whipping for fighting. Frayser took the floor to receive punishment, but Clint grabbed his hat and leaped to the door saying, "I'll be dad burned ef I'm agoin' to take no whuppin'," and made off for home.

Clint was not interested in his studies; but he loved to play ball, and he now felt nettled that he was out of school, and seemed to feel a hatred for the teacher and the school in general. One day he came by the schoolhouse riding an old raw-boned gray horse. He slowed up as he was passing the schoolhouse door, looked in and with a grin yelled, "school butter." Then by kicking and whipping he urged old Gray to a trot.

The word "school butter" meant an insult to the school, and it was the custom all through the mountains, when anyone passed a school and cried "school butter," for the whole class to run out and catch the offender and duck him in a hole of water. If no water was convenient, they rode him on a rail. If, however, the offender escaped, all was well, as they could not bother him afterwards.

"He hollered 'school butter,' Mr. Vincent," said Bill Babb.

"Well, he is gone," the teacher said.

The next day at about the same time Clint again came by, and reining old Gray a little nearer the door, he looked in and cried out in a little louder voice, "school butter." As before, he lashed old Gray until he was in a run.

"Must we go git 'im now, Mr. Vincent?" asked Bill Babb.

"You couldn't catch him," replied the teacher. "But that's all right, he will be back tomorrow."

We all strongly suspected that Clint would come by again the next day. The entire recess was taken up in discussing ways to catch Clint. It was agreed that Jim Sawyers and Bill Babb should post themselves on top of the hill, and when Clint passed, they would run down on the other side and intercept him.

Sure enough, at about the regular time, we saw Clint coming. He was barefooted, wearing home-made cotton pants much too short and held up by hickory bark tied around the waist. He had on an old straw hat with broken places in the top where locks of his shocky blond hair protruded. In his left hand he held the bridle reins, while in his right he carried a heavy hickory switch. He reined old Gray near the schoolhouse door, and with a defiant grin, yelled as loud as he could,

> "School butter, chicken flutter,
> Rotten aigs fer the teacher's supper."

He then began kicking old Gray in the sides, and with body bent forward, he lashed the horse first on one side, then on the other, till, as little Buster Green said, "Ole Gray jist far'ly flew."

The boys on the hill were signaled, and they ran down the road and caught Clint as he came along. The whole school turned out, and we took Clint to the swimmin' hole, which was a half mile away. We pitched him, head foremost, into about ten feet of water. The girls took as much delight and interest in the proceedings as the boys.

Clint came out shaking his fist, crying and declaring that he could whip the whole school; but nothing else was done, and he was allowed to go his way.

All too soon to suit any of us the free school term came to a close. Lelia and Nora continued on, attending the subscription month.

It was now the first of September, and my father was very busy getting in his fodder and hay, and he thought it best for Jim and me to stay at home and help him. He was planning to go to the river bottoms to work that fall, and wanted to get his corn gathered and all work about the place done, so he could get off early.

CHAPTER IV

SOME OF OUR NEIGHBORS

"WELL, Wayman, I guess I'll leave you about Wednesday. I'm going to the bottoms to work."

This was spoken by my father one night as we sat around the fireplace. The light of the flickering pine caused the shadows to dance upon the log walls, and I had been dreaming.

"Let me go with you," Jim said.

"If Jim goes, I'm a-goin'," I quickly spoke up.

"A lot of good youens could do," my mother said. "Ye haint big enough to cut timber and make rails."

"I wuz jist thankin'," my father said, "I could take a load of apples an' they could go along an' help peddle them out. Then we might pick cotton an' make a little money."

"Well, I don't keer," my mother replied. "If they can make enough money to buy some shoes fer them an' the girls."

I was so excited over the prospect of making the trip, that I had to be scolded several times that night before I could get off to sleep. I wanted to go somewhere. I wanted to see the "furriners," and hear them talk, and see the funny clothes they wore, and the funny houses they lived in, all jammed up close together, I had heard.

We loaded our wagon with choice red apples and covered it with a sheet stretched over bows. Wednesday morning we hitched the two oxen, Jolly and Brandy, to the wagon, and were on our way to the bottoms. We took with us some old quilts, some camping utensils, a lot of cooked food, and some corn for the oxen.

When we struck the cotton plantations, my father cut a green stick with four prongs and fastened it to the front of the wagon. He put a large red apple on each of the prongs. In passing houses or where people were at work, we hollered, "Ap-poles, ap-poles, fine ap-poles."

We soon disposed of the apples and obtained employment on a farm near Conway. We camped in a small vacant house and picked cotton at seventy cents a hundred pounds.

One Saturday, when it was too wet to pick cotton, we went into town. We were standing around the stove at Frauenthal's store with a lot of other country people, when someone shouted, "The train! The train is coming!"

There was a scramble for the door, and my father rushed Jim and me over to the depot to see the train. It was so wonderful, so powerful, so terrifying, that my knees knocked, and I trembled as the monster slowly moved away. If the engineer had blown the whistle, I think I would have fainted. Later, when we were telling Nora about our experiences and described the train to her, we asked her to guess how many horses pulled it. She said she didn't know, but guessed there were a good many. We then laughed and told her there weren't any.

I got to see a good many "furriners" that trip, and they were too funny to laugh at; but their way of talking was not so different from ours.

When the weather became too unfavorable for cotton picking, we went back home, taking with us money enough for the family's needs.

Jim and I were large enough now to go around the neighborhood and visit other boys. Once we were at the home of Parvin Waymac, playing around with the children, when Clint and Tilda got into a fight. Clint picked up a piece of corn bread that had been thrown out for the hogs, and let go of it, striking Tilda on the jaw, and she fell. Stansel, their brother, called as loud as he could, "Paw, Paw, come yare quack! Clint's knocked Tildy down with a pone o' brad."

I can still remember Mr. Waymac's house. It was a small log house of one room, with one door and no windows. The old clay chimney leaned over so that it had to be propped with a pole. Old quilts were stuffed in the walls where the clay had fallen out.

Bill Osburn, another neighbor, lived on Bull Creek. Bill lived in a small log shack surrounded by two or three acres of cleared land. I never did know how Bill's house was ever built, or how the land was cleared, as he was never known to do a day's work. He was too lazy to bring in a stick of wood when he was cold, or to fetch a bucket of water when he was thirsty. He left all such drudgery to his wife. However, in hunting, fishing and trapping, Bill was over-industrious. When preparing to go hunting, he rose long before day and climbed the hills and waded streams until dark drove him home. Few men could keep up with him when he was following the hounds, and the severest weather never kept him back. By hunting he kept his table well supplied with meat, and by swapping turkey or venison for work, he got his land tilled, which yielded sufficient corn for his bread.

One day Jim and I were down on the creek fishing, and we came up to Bill's house. Mrs. Osburn met us at the gate and minded the dogs until we got in the house. We found Bill down on the floor molding bullets. Making bullets was nothing new to me, but the dexterity with which he handled the bullet molds was interesting. With a ladle of melted lead in one hand, and the molds in the other, bullets were discharged and rolled on the floor almost as fast as I could count them.

There were no chairs to sit on. Our seats consisted of split logs set up on legs. There was a greasy goods box on which were two tin plates and a broken case knife. This was their table. By the fireplace were a frying pan, a skillet and lid, and a tea-kettle, and in the back part of the house was a scaffold made of unbarked poles, on which rested a mattress that was made of straw. There was nothing else to indicate that the house was occupied, except an old banjo that hung on the wall.

We asked Bill to play for us, and he seemed willing to accommodate. He seized the banjo and struck up the tune, "Molly Hare." Mrs. Osburn sat on the bench and kept time with her foot.

I have often thought of Bill Osburn and his wife living there alone, far removed from the financial and social problems of the world, and have wondered if theirs was not the greater happiness.

The most outstanding character in our neighborhood was old man Everet Howard. The mountain family is usually large in numbers, and in this respect old Everet's family was no exception. He had a lot of grown up boys.

One day Everet was hunting his hogs and rode by the back of Bud Lipscumb's field, where Sal Saucer was cutting cornstalks. Everet stopped and asked about

his hogs, and this led the way to a conversation. Sal told him that she was from up in Greasy Valley and was working for Mr. Lipscumb for her board. Old Everet expressed a sympathy for her and promised to try to find her a better home.

Every day for a week Everet went off to hunt his hogs and always made it a point to go by where Sal was at work.

Sal Saucer was a homely looking, dull appearing woman, but she was about thirty years younger than Lou, Everet's wife. The old man became insanely infatuated with her and wanted to marry her, but there was Lou in the way.

After several clandestine meetings with Sal, he finally arrived at a plan whereby he could get free from Lou. He became melancholy, had nothing to say, answered questions only in monosyllables, took no interest in the affairs about the place, and began sleeping off in the kitchen with some of the children.

Lou noticed his strange behavior and called his attention to it, asking him to explain. Well, he said that he was in serious trouble. Something had taken place that was bothering him, and it concerned her as well as himself. Lou's curiosity was highly aroused, and she demanded that he tell her all about it. He said that it would break his heart to tell her, but much as he hated to do so, he would have to impart to her the sad news.

He then told her that the Lord had appeared to

him and told him that they were unlawfully married, and that they were, in the sight of the Lord, living in adultery. He had demanded that Lou be sent away, and that Everet go and marry another woman in accordance with the law. This shocking disclosure took Lou off her feet. She went to the boys and told them about what their father had said. The boys talked to the old man, but he was firm in his story and told the boys that their mother would have to leave.

Old Everet's melancholy grew worse. Occasionally he would refuse to eat, and sometimes he sat up all night.

News travels with great rapidity among the mountain folk, and in a very few days everybody in the entire settlement knew about the strange revelation that came to old Everet Howard. It was discussed at length, not only in our home, but in every other household and upon every occasion where people met. Some few people believed in the truth of old Everet's story and began searching the scriptures to learn whether or not it was biblical. Others argued that the old man only wanted to get rid of Lou, and marry a younger woman. My father said it was nothing but downright meanness in him. Some even thought he had lost his mind.

When Everet and Lou married, there was no such thing as a marriage license in Arkansas. It would be hard for the courts to go back thirty years to prove that this couple had been legally married. Hence it was thought that the matter could best be straightened out by the church.

Parson Yates, the local preacher, called a special meeting. People came from all directions. Many came from neighboring localities. The house was full and the yard was full. Our whole family was there.

After reading a few verses, a song and a prayer, Parson Yates rose and said, "My dear bretherin an' sisterin' an' frien's, we come here today on a powerful strange mission. I'm gittin' purty ole, an' I been servin' the Lord a mighty long time, but I have never yit been called to a meetin' sich as this. Brother Everet Howard says that the Lord visited him an' tole him to send away his wife, Sister Lou, an' go out an' marry him a nother wife. Now, the business of this meetin' is to decide whether or not Brother Everet shall be allowed to divorce his wife an' marry a nother. I'll 'pint Brother Ed Battenfield to argy fer him and Brother Jim Hardin to argy agin him. These two bretherin will please come forward."

The two men came up, Mr. Battenfield seating himself on the right, while Mr. Hardin took a seat on the left.

"Now, Brother Howard, you come forward," said the moderator.

Old Everet rose, took a large chew of tobacco out of his mouth and threw it out through a crack, went to the water bucket and took a sup of water, washed out his mouth, and spit out at the door. He came on down the aisle with his home-made straw hat in his hand. He was full six feet tall, wearing home woven cotton pants that were cut plenty long, but had drawn up until the bottoms of his pants and the tops of his wool socks barely met. He wore a white cotton shirt. That is, it had been white once upon a time. Across his shoulders were a pair of bed ticking suspenders. His hair was shocky and uncombed, and his long beard would have been gray had it not been stained amber color with tobacco juice. He was directed to take a seat near the moderator, facing the congregation.

"Now, Brother Howard," said the moderator, "jist tell all you know about this here case o' yourn."

"Wal," said Everet, "one night four week ago, come nex Thursday, when all uv my fambly wuz up on Possom Trot, tendin' the big meetin', I wuz at home asleep, an' I hyeard a voice callin' my name, 'Everet, Everet, Everet,' jist lak that. I thought it wuz somebody a callin' me outside, an' I got up, I did, an' looked outside through the crack an' thar warn't nobody out thar, an' I knowed they couldn't be nobody in the house, caze the door wuz shet an' propped tight. I laid back down, I did, an' jist as I got good an' sound asleep, I hyeard the same voice again, jist lak before, a callin' my name three times. I riz up in bed, easy lak, an' I seed somethin' that looked lak a eengel, an' I said, 'Speak, Lord, an' don't be afeared, fer it's me.' I got up, I did, an' lit a piece o' pine an' thar warn't nobody in the house, an' the door wuz still shet an' propped tight.

"I wuz skeared an' went back to bed. Hit wuz a long time 'fore I hyeard the same voice a callin', 'Everet, Everet, Everet.' I says, says I, 'Speak, Lord, an' don't be afeard, fer it's me.' Then the eengel, hit says, 'Everet, that womurn that thou callest thy wife is not thy lawful wife, an' thou hast been livin' in adultery fer thirty year in the sight an' 'bomination uv the Lord. Git ye up an' send this womurn Lou away, an' go out in the world an' up an' down hit, an' fine thee a nother wife an' marry her accordin' to the law. Thus sayeth the Lord.' Then the eengel hit jist vanished, an' I hain't never seed hit no more."

Ed Battenfield rose and said, "Friends an' Brother Moderator, I b'lieve ever' word this good man has said. I know Brother Howard to be a truthful man, caze he wunst tole me whar they wuz a flock uv turkeys. I tuck my gun an' went over to whar he said, an' thar wuz the biggest flock uv turkeys I ever seed. An' I know him to be a honest man. I wunst lent him a jug o' 'lasses, an' he paid me back. He paid me back in as good a 'lasses as ever went down yer throat. I thank we would be doin' our dooty to 'low this good ole brother to git this yere devorce o' his'n."

Jim Hardin then rose and said, "Brother Moderator an' fellow church members, I don't b'lieve a word ole Everet Howard said. I thank he is either stone crazy or it is jist pure hard down meanness in 'im. Why didn't the eengel go to Sister Lou. Jist thank uv it. This good womurn has lived an' starved with ole Everet fer thirty year. She's raised him a big fambly. She's done all his washin', cookin' an' sewin'. She kyeared the cotton, spun the thread, weaved the cloth an' made them breeches he's got on. She made that 'ar shirt he's got on. She knit them socks he's got on. Yes, sot up 'way in the night an' knit 'em while ole Everet wuz asleep, a dreamin', mebbe, how to git rid uv 'er. An' now, send her away? Naw, not by my say so, he won't. I say we ought to send him back to his fambly an' make him stay thar an' behave hisse'f. An' if he don't behave hisse'f, take him out an' give him a good whuppin'."

It was noticeable that Hardin's speech had made an impression. But Battenfield was a foe that was not to be reckoned with too lightly. He rose and, with a pious and solemn look, said, "Friends, Bretherin an' Sisterin, an' Brother Moderator. We mus' be mouty keerful how we flout the Lord. If the Lord told Everet Howard to git this divorce, then we mustn't keep 'im from it. Yes, I say we mus' be mighty keerful how we meddle with the Lord's business. I move, Brother Moderator, that we 'low Brother Everet this divorce."

"I second the motion," said Zack Griffin.

"Hits been moved an' seconded that we give Brother Everet Howard his divorce," said the moderator. "All in favor uv it stand on yore feet."

Five or six people, fearing that there might be a

possibility of incurring disfavor with the Lord, stood up. Others, seeing them stand, stood also, and so on until nearly everybody was standing. The motion was carried, and Everet Howard was free from any matrimonial bonds.

The next morning old Everet saddled his gray mule, put a saddle on the sorrel nag, and rode to Bud Lipscumb's, where Sal Saucer joined him. They went up to Bear Creek to a justice of the peace and were married. He took his bride home, and the family had to make room for her.

This hasty action on the part of old Everet and Sal set people to talking and asking questions. Bud Lipscumb came over to Gravel Hill and told the people that Sal had confided to his wife how she and old Everet had conspired to get rid of Lou, and that the angel story was originated for that purpose. This little spark soon fanned into a flame, and the flame into a conflagration. People dropped their work and began gathering at each other's houses and talking. Another meeting at the church was called. This meeting was at night and was for men only. I was too young to go, but I heard all about it afterwards.

Fifty men, armed with shotguns and rifles, rode to Everet Howard's house. They were met by a pack of savage dogs. "Call off yore dawgs," said Bill Ward, "fer we air a comin' in." There was no response. A rifle ball through the head stopped the advance of one of the dogs, and the others ran under the house. The men dismounted, and while about ten men held the horses, the others advanced upon the door.

"Open the door," said Ward, "or we'll break in."

"If you do," said an excited voice on the inside, "you'll git shot."

Six men seized a large log and drove it, end forward, against the door. The door was thrown clear of its fastenings, and struck old Everet, who stood with his gun in his hands. The gun was knocked upwards, discharging, the shot going through the roof. Don Phillips wrenched the gun from old Everet's hand and struck him a blow, which felled him to the floor.

Lou was on her knees crying.

"We ain't a goin' to hurt you, Sister Lou," said Jim Sawyers, "but we air a goin' to whup that ole man o' yourn an' that womurn. Whar is she?"

"Look under the bed," said Ward. At the same time he seized Sal by the foot and dragged her out from under the bed. Three or four men lifted her to her feet.

"Stan' up thar," said Ward. "We air goin' to larn you to go aroun' marryin' other women's husbands."

Sal fought, bit, kicked and screamed, but she was powerless in the hands of these men. Two men held each arm while Bill Ward whipped her back and shoulders with a hickory switch. After he had whipped her for some time, Lou ran up to him and said, "Don't whup her no more. You'll kill the womurn."

"She needs killin'," said Bill Ward.

But Jim Sawyers said that she had been whipped enough, and the men let her go. She fell crumpling into a faint.

"An' now fer the ole man," said one of the men. But old Everet was lying sprawling on the floor, either unconscious from the blow he had received, or else he thought it was a good time to play 'possum. The men decided to leave him alone.

"Now, Sister Lou," said Ward, "you tell this womurn not to let the sun set on her in these diggins tomorrow night. You tell her to git out an' stay out."

The next day old Everet threw some plunder in a wagon, and he and Sal drove out of the country, up about fifty miles further north. In about a year, Lou and the boys followed them, and I heard that they all lived agreeably together as one family.

Another character that I well remember was old man Bolden, who lived a couple of miles from us. He wore his hair long, and claimed to be part Indian. He claimed that he knew where four bushels of gold were buried in the Indian Territory, and was always talking about what he was going to do with it when he could get money enough to go there to get it.

Mr. Bolden's family consisted of himself and his wife. These two old people lived in a secluded section on a little place known as the Bobbs Place. Years before old man Bobbs had homesteaded there, but for some cause had left the country, and nobody seemed to know his whereabouts. Bolden and his wife had moved on to the place simply because it was vacant and deserted, and nobody seemed to know or care about it.

One day old man Bolden happened to pass our house, and we invited him in to eat dinner. After much persuading, he came to the table, claiming that he was not in the least hungry. When his coffee cup was empty, my mother would say, "Have some more coffee, Mr. Bolden."

"Jist a sup, ma'am, jist a sup," Mr. Bolden would say. By counting the times Mr. Bolden would pass his cup for a sup, I noticed that he drank seven cups of coffee.

"Wal, I would ax youens to come to see uz," the old man said, as he was preparing to go, "but I guess we'll haf to git out from thar."

"Why?" my father asked.

"Wal," Bolden replied, "the sheriff war out at my house last week an' he said a womurn owns the place an' wants ter move on it."

"Who is the womurn?" my mother asked.

"Ole man Bobbs's daughter, I thank."

"I know," my mother said. "She was jist a little gal when they left here."

"I don't see how no womurn can make a livin' on that place," my father said.

"I know hit's been mighty hard fer me to make a livin' on it," Bolden replied. "Wal, hit's her'n, an' all I can do is to git out an' let her have it. By the way, Ben, you got any more uv that good manifactered terbaccer, er don't you chaw that kind now?"

My father produced a half pound plug of star navy. After biting off a big chew, Mr. Bolden cut off a small part of the plug. He put the large piece in his pocket, and handing the smaller piece to my father, said, "I'll ketch you without some one uv these days."

CHAPTER V

THE LAMP

"WE seen that new womurn when we passed Boldens', Ma," Lelia said, when she and Nora came in one afternoon.

"How does she look?" my mother asked.

"Looks lak she tries to be proud," Lelia replied.

"Well, I wursh I had a gingham dress lak that'n she had on," Nora said.

"Don't you bother about her dress," my father said. "I'm goin' to buy you an' Lelia both a new dress."

"Lak to know what you expect to buy it with," my mother said. "You haint got a cent of money."

"Well, you heard what I said, didn't ye?" my father replied. "I'll not stop at gittin' them a dress, but I'm goin' to git you one, an' it'll be the purtiest dress that's ever been brought to these mountains."

After talking for a while, my father explained that some cattle men were in the neighborhood, and that he had bargained with them to take all of our surplus cattle. This added new interest to the subject and Lelia and Nora began discussing the kind of dresses they wanted. Before the week was out, the men came and bought all of our cattle that we did not need, and my father had his pocketbook stuffed full of money. Some of the yearlings were claimed by Jim and me, and my father promised to take us to Little Rock on his next trip and buy us some clothing.

Soon after this we loaded the wagon with turkeys and furs, hitched Jolly and Brandy to it, and were on our way to Little Rock. It took us several days to make the trip. We arrived in the city early one morning and put up in a wagon yard. After disposing of our hides and poultry, we put in the day in shopping. Since my father was flush with money, he bought sufficient supplies to last us a year. I remember going to Gus Blass' store and hearing my father tell Mr. Blass that he was a poor man from the mountains and that he wanted to buy goods from somebody that would not beat him. Mr. Blass replied, saying, "Anybody that would cheat you, after you talk that way, is a rascal."

We each got a pair of heavy cowhide boots, paying three dollars a pair for them. We bought several yards of gray jeans, enough to make each of us a suit of clothes. This was my first suit made of cloth that was not woven at home. We bought shoes and several yards of goods for wearing apparel for my mother and sisters, besides other articles that we needed about the place.

That night we took in the sights of the city. Little Rock, the state capital and principal city, was then a place of between ten and fifteen thousand people. Everything was so exciting and so different from what I had been used to, that I gazed at everything so hard that my eyes were sore the next day. Little insignificant occurrences, of which I would take no notice in after years, made a lifetime impression on my mind.

Here I saw, for the first time, a street faker. At the intersection of Main and Markham, then the business center of the city, a man was standing in a wagon under a torch, crying out his wares. He held up a pocketbook, elaborately describing it, setting the price at one dollar. He then picked up a lady's necklace, commenting on this in detail, stating that it was heavily plated and would wear and look like gold. Next he picked up a gent's watch chain and told what a good value it was. He then held up a band finger ring and a pair of ear bobs. He had all these goods priced so that they were worth about twenty dollars. He then dropped the jewelry into the pocketbook, one piece in each pocket, closed the pocketbook and held it out, saying, "Who will give me fifty cents for it?" My father bought three of them, one for each of us.

On up Main Street we came to an auctioneer. After selling several articles, he held up a pair of ladies' black cotton hose. They probably would have sold in the stores for ten cents a pair. He went on to tell what splendid values they were, stating that they would readily sell in all the stores at one dollar a pair. However, he was going to sell them at two pairs for a dollar. No one made an offer to buy them, and he said, "Then, if you have any doubts about this being a bargain, I will make it three," holding out three pairs. Still nobody seemed anxious to buy. He looked around and said, "By the jumping jingoes, you caint outdo me. I am going to sell these stockings. Here I am going to give you five. Think of it! Five pairs of stockings all for one dollar!"

I saw my father reach into his pocket, but he was too slow. The auctioneer jerked up another pair of hose, crying out, "I never saw the back of my neck if I don't give you six." My father could not hold out any longer and said, "Wrop 'em up."

"Wrop 'em up!" repeated the auctioneer. "Who wouldn't say wrop 'em up?"

We went into a variety store and saw some people looking at an oil lamp. It was a small brass lamp, with a handle and no chimney, which burned a little round wick. It seemed to be quite an improvement over the sperm candle and pine torch, and it cost only fifty cents. My father bought it, and this completed our shopping.

When we were nearly ready to leave, we met up with Gov Strickland, who lived across the hills from us. Gov was looking for a way to get out home, and my father invited him to ride out with us.

Gov's habits were not highly commendable, as it was alleged that he bet on horse races and played cards. In fact, it was said that he never worked at all, but made his living by gambling. He wore his hair long and usually had on a coat, presumably to conceal a pistol which he always carried, and he was considered "bad medicine."

As we drove off the bridge across the Arkansas River, we were stopped by a tall, well dressed man with a pleasant voice.

"Good evening, gentlemen," he said. "About how far are you going out this road?"

"Some distance," my father replied.

"I was just wondering if you would mind handing out some circulars in your neighborhood," he said. "I am a tailor."

He then produced a handful of cards on which were tacked tailor's samples.

"Now here is a suit," he went on, "that I can make for fifteen dollars, and——"

We were startled by a voice behind us. "Hullo, hullo. What's goin' on aroun' here, anyhow? What's up?"

The speaker was a youngish looking man, quick

of speech and action, who had appeared unnoticed by us.

"Good evening, sir," the tailor said coolly, and then turned back to my father and continued: "And here's an all wool suit that I can make for——"

"Well, by jabers, I'm from Texas," the new man said. "Yes, from Texas, and I'm flat busted. You see, I was in Old Kate's house last night and they stripped me—tuck ever' cent I had."

"That's bad," said the tailor, seemingly annoyed by the man's presence.

"Oh, that's all right," said the Texan. "I've learned the trick. I'll make it all back when I get back to Texas."

He then held out three cards about the size of playing cards, and went on: "It's a trick called Adam and Eve and the Snake. They have three cards like these. I'll just show you how it's played."

"You will have to excuse me," said the tailor. "I have detained these gentlemen too long already. They probably want to be on their way, and I am a busy man myself."

"Oh, it won't take but a minute," protested the Texan. "You don't care, do you, Mister?" addressing my father.

My father shook his head. Gov had eased down from the wagon and stood by the men.

"Here's the way it's done," said the man from

Texas. He then shuffled the cards a little and spread them out on the wagon with the backs up. "Now, the bet is to pick out the snake. I'll bet you a dollar you can't do it."

"I'll go you," said the tailor as he produced a large roll of bills and peeled off a dollar. The Texan also drew out a big roll and took off a dollar. The tailor picked up a card and turned it over showing the snake.

"You saw me," the Texan said. "You saw me shuffle the cards. I want to try that again."

He then turned his back to us and began shuffling the cards. The tailor leaned over to my father and whispered, "Watch me win. The snake has got one of the corners turned up a little. Watch me win it."

The men seemed to take little notice of Gov, but directed their attention to my father. Gov stood with his elbow resting on the wagon, and his close set, piercing eyes followed every movement the men made. I could not help noticing him, excited as I was over the card trick.

The Texas man then spread the cards out, and we all detected one of the corners turned up just a little. The tailor picked it up, and as we expected, it was the snake.

"I refuse to bet with you any more," said the loser. "You either know the trick, or you are too lucky to suit me. I'll bet with these other gentlemen, but not you."

The tailor winked at my father, signifying that now was his chance.

"Either one of you men want to take a chance?" asked the Texan.

Both my father and Gov shook their heads.

"Oh, well," said the man from Texas. "I'll try you another time, and if you win, I'll quit." He then drew out his money and went on, "I don't believe I've got any change. Who's got change for a five."

"I think I can change it," my father said, and pulled out his pocketbook and began opening it.

Quick as an electric flash, the Texan grabbed the pocketbook and wheeled to run. He was brought to a sudden stop by the muzzle of a blue-steel six shooter thrust just under his chin, while Gov held his finger on the trigger.

"Jist hand back the man his pocketbook," Gov said with a calm voice.

The robber was scared white and speechless. He attempted to stammer, but Gov said in a louder voice, "I say, hand back the man his pocketbook an' be damn quick about it."

The robber reached the pocketbook back behind him, and my father took it from his hand.

"Now," said Gov, "march yourself off and keep yer hands up till ye git back under the bridge. An' ricko-leck, by God, this is Arkansas, an' you fellers better git back to Texas 'fore you git yer damn heads shot off."

When we arrived home, we found my mother and the girls overjoyed to see us and delighted at the many things that we had brought them. When my mother came to the lamp, she made inquiries as to what it was for. My father explained that it was to take the place of the sperm candle and the pine torch. He went on to explain that all he had to do was to fill the lamp with kerosene, light the wick, and it would give a better light than a candle, and it had only cost fifty cents, and a gallon of kerosene was ten cents.

My mother was not favorably impressed with the idea of a lamp. She upbraided my father for throwing away his money for something that was of no value and of no use. She reminded him that the woods were full of good pine an that it took only a little effort to get it. She went on to enumerate several needed things about the place that could be bought for fifty cents. My father looked as if he had been flim-flammed, but he tried to argue his point. He explained how much nicer looking and how much handier it would be than the old method of lighting.

While my father was making his argument in favor of the lamp, Uncle Ben Brady and Parson Yates rode up. They began examining the lamp. Parson Yates picked it up, looked at it carefully, set it down, and said nothing. He shook his head significantly, as if to say that it was not for the best. Uncle Ben said that he knew all about a lamp. He said that he heard of one just like ours on White River which had exploded and killed two people. He went on to tell what a dangerous thing kerosene was, and the best way to deal with it, he said, was to have nothing at all to do with it.

When Uncle Ben and Parson Yates left, we resumed the subject of the lamp. Jim and I took sides with my father, and Jim volunteered to light it and give it a try out. My father would not allow this, but he filled it with oil and took it down into the orchard and set it on a stump. He then went back to the house, tied a piece of pine to a ten foot pole, lighted the end of the pine and went down to the lamp. He reached the pole out to the lamp, standing as far away from it as he could. My mother had gone back to the house, refusing to have anything to do with it. We children stood on the inside of the fence with great excitement, eagerly watching for the fireworks to go off.

My father, fearful and trembling, touched the lighted pine to the wick and, with great haste, ran back and jumped over the fence where we were. The little lamp popped and flickered, the blaze going over to one side and then to the other, and finally burning straight up in a bright blue flame. My father called my mother out, and we all watched the lamp for some time. He then went down and touched it with the pole. The little lamp seemed to be perfectly tame and burned along quietly. He then became more courageous and picked up the lamp in his hands. It still showed no signs of becoming violent, so he took it triumphantly into the house.

CHAPTER VI

LELIA CATCHES A BEAU

WELL, I've hearn about that Bobbs woman," my mother said one evening when she came in from Liza Harris', where she had been to a quilting.

"What wuz it?" asked Lelia.

"Why, that youngun of hern haint got no pappy," my mother replied. "The woman hain't never been married."

"I thought Bolden said her old man went off and got killed," said my father.

"I know," my mother said. "That is what she tells, but Susan Kiker hearn that a man fooled her, then run off to keep from marryin' her."

They talked on for some time, discussing the new woman, and my mother gave strict instructions to Lelia and Nora to have absolutely nothing to do with her, and by all means not to be caught in her company. My mother did not want to be hard on the woman, but she wanted to play safe until a complete investigation of her case could be made.

"Ole Miss Milam says she'll find out," my mother said, "and if anybody can, she can, for she knows all about what's goin' on among the men and women in the country."

"I have heard some news too," Lelia said. "Mr. Glaspy is back here gettin' up another sangin' school, an' I want to go. Pa says he will pay the dollar."

"Don't see how you can go," my mother said. "You cain't go by yourself."

"Wayman has some new clothes," Lelia replied, "and I thought maybe he could go along. Hit won't cost nothin' as he is too little to learn to sang."

The singing school started on Monday, and I was sent along with Lelia for protection. The school opened with fifteen or twenty young men and women, and the only book used was the song book. All the song books which we knew anything about had the character or shape notes. Up to this time Gravel Hill had used a song book having only four notes. At this school the teacher was discarding the four note book and introducing the seven note book. From then on the seven note books were used.

On Friday afternoon several of the neighbors came in, since Mr. Glaspy was giving a little exhibition of the progress of the students. Among the visitors was

Wes McWhorter, a young man about the age of Lelia, who lived beyond our home. On the way home he walked by the side of Lelia.

I became interested in some hickory nuts that had fallen along the way and got behind. When Lelia missed me, she became alarmed. She had no fears that I was lost or that anything had happened to me, but she was shocked at discovering the fact that she was walking along the highway with a young man and no one else in sight. This was an offense of which no decent girl would be guilty, notwithstanding the fact that it was broad daylight.

She kept looking back and wondering aloud to Wes where I could be. Wes had grown up sisters and understood just how she felt, and he tried to pacify her by telling her that I was probably keeping right along with them in the woods near the road, and that I might be looking at them and laughing. He said that that was the way he did when he was little and had to go anywhere with his sisters. I managed to overtake them before we got home, but was mistaken when I thought that this would square things. As was the custom when young men went home with young women, Wes took his departure on reaching the gate.

Lelia went directly to my mother and told her about my not keeping up with them. The offense was so great and the situation so disgraceful that my mother did not scold or in any way chastise me, but waited until my father came in and laid the matter before him, de-

manding that he settle with me. My father asked no questions, but took me out in the yard and cut a peach tree limb. With this he impressed upon my mind the fact that I was expected to keep up with my sisters when I accompanied them anywhere, especially if a young man were along.

I was very glad that this had occurred before the Sunday following. Had it been after that day, my father would have been so enraged that I would probably never have survived the punishment.

That Sunday afternoon Kittie Nelma and a young man, Bob Wilson, came over to our house. With them also came Kittie's brother, Jake. Jake was paying attention to Nora. The four young people played about the yard, jumped rope, and amused themselves as young people of their age usually did. They all went into the kitchen for some water. After drinking, Kittie and Bob stepped out into the yard about six feet from the kitchen door, which stood open.

Jake noticed a white coonskin hanging against the wall, and as a white coon was rare, he began examining the hide and asking questions about it. They had been standing there discussing the white coonskin for four or five minutes, when my mother came down into the kitchen. She gave Nora a look of warning which Nora well understood, and the young people hurried out of the room to join Kittie and Bob.

When the company had gone, my father called Nora into the big house where were also my mother and Lelia, and he asked her what she and that boy were doing in the kitchen alone. Nora tried to explain that they were looking at the white coonskin, and that she had not noticed when Kittie and Bob went out. That explanation did not satisfy my father. He went on to say that he had traveled a great deal and knew something of the ways of bad women, and that for a girl to be alone in a room with a young man in broad daylight and with the door open, was just the same in the eyes of people as if she were alone with him in a room when it was pitch dark with the door closed.

My mother said it was the most disgraceful act which any member of the family had ever been guilty of; and that, too, right after Lelia had had to walk along the big road with a young man and no one else in sight, and worst of all, a bad woman was living within a mile of us.

She feared that the reputation of the family had been ruined. My father threatened to drive Nora from home, and my mother wanted to lock her up in the smoke-house until she came to her senses. They had poor Nora crying and promising never to be guilty of such flagrant indiscretion again. Lelia was sorry for Nora and told my mother she could see nothing so bad about it after all; and she said that she would probably have done the same thing at Nora's age. My father and mother finally quieted down, and Nora went off to bed without any supper.

The following Sunday the singing school was brought to a close with an all day singing. People came and brought their dinners and spent the day either in taking part or listening to the singing.

All of our family were there, and when the singing was dismissed, we started walking home, whereupon Sam Dent stepped up to the side of Lelia and said, "Can I see you home, Miss Lelia?"

Lelia replied, "Yessir," looking straight at the ground. When we arrived at the yard gate, Sam bade us all good-bye and went home.

Sam, in asking Lelia if he could go home with her, was acting in accordance with the customs and manners of the day. When a young man wanted to go with a young woman, he would be at the church or gathering, and when the crowd was dismissed and the people started home, he would walk up to the girl and ask her in such terms as:

"Can I walk home with you, Miss Blank?"

If the girl said "yes" all would be well. But if she said "no," he would turn and walk back to the crowd of boys who were watching him and who were by then laughing at him. When a girl refused to accept the company of a young man, it was said she had "slighted" him.

This was the first time that Sam Dent had ever gone with Lelia. He had talked with her at different gatherings, but had never before asked her for her company. As Lelia was now at a marriageable age, this occasioned something new for my father and mother to speculate upon.

Sam, about twenty-four years old, weighing a hundred and seventy pounds, six feet tall, with a ruddy complexion and sandy hair, was fairly goodlooking. He lived with his parents, was known to be industrious and inclined to accumulate and save. He was acceptable to my father and mother as a prospective husband for Lelia, and it was noticeable that his attentions were not displeasing to Lelia.

One day Jim took a sack of corn to the mill to be ground and saw Sam Dent there. We had to haul our wheat twenty miles to get it ground, but there was a grist mill that ground corn within ten miles of us at the falls upon a prong of Bull Creek. At this place the water went over a bluff precipitously falling a height of several feet. A set of paddles, constructed on a wheel and looking not unlike the paddles of a steamboat, was placed within reach of the falling water, which, striking against the paddles, caused the wheel to revolve. This furnished the power for the mill, which was known as a water mill. The mill rocks were usually in bad order, and when the water was low and the power weak, the grinding was very slow.

The first sack of corn brought in was placed just next to the hopper, and the next sack was placed just back of it, and so on. The miller ground each sack as he came to it, each customer waiting his turn. Probably from this fact a sack of corn was called a "turn of corn."

Sam and Jim got to talking while they were waiting. Sam said that he was coming to see us the following Saturday night. Jim told our folks about this, and they well understood that Sam Dent was coming a-courting. It was the custom, when a young man went courting, for him to go to the girl's house on Saturday night and stay over until Sunday afternoon.

On Saturday Lelia and Nora cleaned off the yard by sweeping it with a broom made of switches tied in a bundle, called a "brash broom." They scrubbed the floor of the big house with a mop made of corn shucks, using sand and soap with the water. They made a scarf for the mantle out of some wrapping paper that they had been saving, and baked some peach pies in the shape of a half moon, and they cooked a lot of cakes the color of gingersnaps but larger. We called them "sweet cakes."

Along about sun-down Sam came riding up. We were looking for him, and my father met him at the gate and invited him to get down. We went down to the lot, and Sam unsaddled his horse and put the saddle in the crib. I turned our mule out of the stable, and Sam put his horse in. Jim brought ten ears of corn and a bundle of fodder, and we fed Sam's horse. We all walked back to the yard and entered the big house where Sam greeted my mother and sisters, who, after a little, went to the kitchen and busied themselves with the supper, while my father entertained Sam. They talked on such subjects as killing deer, trapping beaver, hunting turkey and farming.

In preparing for the supper my mother went to the trunk in the big house and got out a red tablecloth which was used only in case of company. Also she had me climb up to a joist in the kitchen and get a small cloth bag which contained some coarse brown sugar. She emptied some of the sugar in a teacup and set it on the table.

When supper was announced, we gathered at the table and my father asked the blessing. On the table were a plate of fried chicken and a dish containing slices of fried ham floating in red gravy, also a plate of hot biscuits. The pies and cakes were saved for Sunday. My mother asked Sam if he took sugar in his coffee, and when informed that he did, she put a spoonful of sugar in his cup and poured the coffee over it, and after stirring it, tasted it. It was not sweet enough, and she added a little more sugar and passed the cup to Sam without the spoon. There was no need of a spoon, as the custom was to pour the coffee out into the saucer and set the cup on the table; and then to take up the saucer and blow the coffee until it was cool enough to drink.

When supper was over, my father, Sam, Jim and I all went back into the big house, while my mother and sisters remained in the kitchen. When the dishes were washed up, they joined us. We sat around the fire for a while, my father, mother and Sam doing nearly all the talking. Lelia joined in occasionally, and Nora would laugh when anything came up that was funny.

After some while my father got his hat and said something about going out to separate the cows and calves. Sam and Jim followed him, and when they went out, my mother and sisters fixed the beds. Lelia drew out the trundle bed and told me to sleep in it, as Sam would sleep in the big bed with Jim. There was only a straw mattress on the trundle bed, and every time I moved the straw would rattle. Lelia scolded me, and my mother threatened to whip me if I didn't lie still. They didn't want Sam to know it was a straw bed. When the men folk came back, my mother and Nora were in bed, and Lelia was sitting near the fire on one side of the wall. My father told Sam that he was tired and would have to lie down, and that whenever Sam felt like lying down, he could sleep up there with Jim. Sam took a seat by the fire opposite Lelia, and Jim lay across the bed with his clothes on. For about a couple of hours, Sam and Lelia had the pleasure of talking with each other without being interrupted by others of the family. They talked on such subjects as the latest socials and gatherings, the prospects of the marriage of certain young couples, and matters concerning the immediate neighborhood.

Now these two young people were really courting. Sam poured out his love to Lelia in the most glowing terms, yet he never spoke a word on the subject. Sam's love-making was well understood by Lelia, and she quickly responded with favor which Sam was able to understand; yet there was nothing spoken that would indicate it.

Somebody has said that before there was any language, people conversed with each other very freely and with great satisfaction and understanding, and that language was invented for the purpose of deceiving. There may be some grounds for this, as such belief is greatly strengthened in the manner of courtship of the mountain people. They must do all their talking in the presence of others, and their love-making is done by thought transmission assisted by looks and actions.

When Lelia thought they had sat up long enough, she woke Jim and told him to get off his clothes and to "go to bed right." Sam said something about going out to look after his horse, and Jim went with him. When they got back, Lelia was in bed, and Jim covered up the fire, which made the room dark, and then he and Sam went to bed. The next morning my father called Jim and told him it was time to get up and make the fires. Sam got up with Jim, and after the fires were made, they went out to the lot and fed the stock. When they got back, we were all up, the beds were made, the house swept, and my mother and sisters were in the kitchen cooking breakfast.

In the afternoon, when the dinner was all over, Nora suggested that we go gather some chinkapins. Jim got the axe, and we all walked about two miles to

Half-Way Hill, where there were several chinkapin trees. We selected one that was well loaded with nuts that seemed to be ripe, and Sam cut it down. The forest was so vast and the chinkapin trees so numerous, that it was not considered wasteful to cut one down.

We were all laughing, talking, and getting the nuts out of the burrs, when we heard a strange noise among the rocks near the place where Nora was standing. We all recognized it to be the sing of a rattlesnake. Sam shouted to Nora to get out of the way, but Nora did not wait to be told. When she heard the rattlesnake's sing, she leaped instantly from where she was standing, and as she did so, the reptile struck, missing her foot by a hair's breadth.

Sam ran at the snake with the axe, but it had drawn itself into a coil, and Sam knew enough not to get too close to it. He got a pole and touched the snake with the end of the pole. The snake struck at the pole, and as it did, Sam ran up to it and severed its head with the axe. It was a powerful snake and was what we called a diamond rattlesnake. They were looked upon as very poisonous and dangerous, and it was said that, when they struck, they struck at one's throat. This snake had seven buttons on its rattle. Sam said each button indicated a year in age. The rattlesnake always gives warning by singing before it strikes and it can strike only when it is in a coil.

An encounter with a rattlesnake was not an uncommon occurrence in the mountains, but owing to the alarm of Nora's close call, Lelia insisted that we abandon the chinkapins and go home. It was then late in the afternoon, and Sam saddled his horse and rode for his home.

CHAPTER VII

LELIA IS ENGAGED

ABOUT a month after the close of the singing school Mr. Glaspy, according to promise, came back and gave a day's instruction to his class free. Lelia went and I had to go along for company. When the day's exercises were over and we were getting ready to go home, I came out into the yard and saw Sam Dent and his little brother Wayland, who had apparently happened by just by chance. Sam was driving his horse Ceilum hitched up to a small open buggy, called a buckboard. "Git in an' ride, Wayman," Sam said to me. "I am goin' right by yore house. Git in the back thar with Wayland."

Sam seemed to be in no hurry about driving off, and when Lelia came across the yard starting for home,

Sam said, "Mout as well git in an' ride, Miss Lelia; hit's a right fur piece to walk an' taint none outer the way fer me to go right by yore house."

Lelia stopped and stammered, indicating that she would accept; and Sam leaped down and, with the grace of an ox assisted her to a seat in the buggy, saying, "The chilluns is in the back an' I guess you will have to ride up thar with ugly me."

After discussing the singing class awhile as Ceilum trotted along, Sam remarked, "Jist been gittin' out boards to kiver my new house, an' hit shore has been hot today."

"You buildin' a house?" Lelia asked. "You must be goin' to git married."

"Hit takes two to make a contrac' lak that, Miss Lelia," replied Sam. "Haint never found no purty gal what'd wanter be starved to death yit."

"Oh," said Lelia, "mebbe she wouldn't haf to starve. She could bake bread, an' I guess you could pack water."

"Yes," said Sam, "an' I know a mighty purty gal not too fur from me right now that I'd lak to git to bake that bread, too."

Lelia blushed, reached out and stripped some leaves from a protruding twig and said, " 'Pears lak it mout rain," although there was not a cloud in sight.

"We shore do need a rain," Sam said. "That late corn o' mine's tarnin' plum yaller, hit's been so dry."

The buckboard rumbled along, bumping over roots

and rocks, and it was all that little Wayland and I could do to keep from falling out.

For some distance there was nothing said, and Sam broke the silence with, "I seed Miss Addie Cross, when I wuz over in Greasy Valley, an' they air givin' a social at her house nex' Thursday night come week, an' I 'lowed mebbe you mout want to go."

"Haint had no invitation," said Lelia.

"Yes," he replied, "she tole me to fotch you. Reckon you can go?"

"Will if Pa an' Ma will let me," she said.

"I'll stop by an' ax 'em," Sam replied.

Ceilum stopped at our gate, and Sam went in with Lelia. After he had assured my father and mother that there would be no dancing and that the social would be composed of church members only, they consented to let Lelia go.

At the appointed time Sam came by, and Lelia was ready to go to the social. It was understood, of course, that somebody must go along with them, as a young man and a young woman were not supposed to go alone.

Since I was the lightest, it was decided that I should go and ride behind Lelia. Owing to the fact that we had to cross Bull Mountain and Bull Creek, it was best to ride horseback.

When we arrived at Mr. Cross's house, we found young people from all parts of the community, and they were just beginning a game called "Trot Charley." The social was a party similar to the dance, except that the fiddle was left out. Only the "sinners" took part in a dance, but religious people could take part in a social and still be immune from church discipline.

In the game "Trot Charley" the young men chose their partners, and everyone stood in rows, the girls facing the boys with an aisle of about four feet between them. The first couple joined hands and sashayed up and down the aisle, while all sang:

"Come over here, my sweet sugar lump,
Come over here, my darling.
Come over here, my own true love,
And bake a cake for Charley."

Then the couple would start a promenade, while the other couples joined hands and followed, all continuing the song:

"I won't have any of your weavly wheat,
I won't have any of your barley.
I'll take some flour in half an hour,
And bake a cake for Charley."

"Charley is a handsome man,
Charley is a dandy,
Charley is the very lad
That treats the girls on candy."

The same movements were repeated with the second couple taking the lead, and so on until each couple did its part and the game was over.

The young people had gone through with several exercises, in which the boys had the prerogative of choosing partners. It was then decided to engage in a game in which the girls would choose the partners. Lige Smith placed two chairs in the middle of the room and escorted Miss Jeanette Naylor to them, seating her in one of the chairs, while he took a seat in the other one. Ebben Davis and John Gill locked arms and began walking around the couple, singing:

"Hawg drovers, hawg drovers, hawg drovers we air,
A-courtin' uv yore daughter, so neat an' so fair.
Kin we git largin' here, O here?
Kin we git largin' here?"

Then Lige sang:

"This is my daughter that sets by my knee,
An' no hawg drover kin take 'er from me.
An' you cain't git largin' here, O here,
An' you cain't git largin' here.

Then came the response:

"Kyear nothin' fer yer daughter, murch less fer yerse'f,
I'll go to Kaintucky an' better myse'f,

An' I don't want largin' here, O here,
An' I don't want largin' here."

After a whisper with Miss Jeanette, Lige sang as follows:

"This is my daughter that sets by my side,
An' Mr. Bob Jones kin make 'er his bride
By brangin' a nother one here, O here,
By brangin' a nother one here."

With her permission Bob escorted Miss Mary Smyers to the chair, and Miss Jeanette joined Bob in a march around the room. This was repeated until all the girls had chosen partners, and then all played "Chase the Buffalo."

It was customary for parties of this kind to break up about midnight, but since a slow rain had set in, and since many of the guests lived at quite a distance and were either afoot or on horseback, it was agreed to continue the party. The rain became harder and they played on until daylight, but I had become so sleepy long before this, that I went back into the kitchen and went to sleep on the bench.

When morning came, we mounted our horses and were on our way home. Sam's horse was much larger than Lelia's pony, and it was suggested that I ride behind Sam. As we rode over the hills, the sun came out, driving the clouds away, and it was clear and beautiful. The fresh morning air coming over the mountainous woodland was refreshing and invigorating. Both Lelia and Sam seemed to be engrossed in thought, and there was no sound except the rhythm of the iron shoes of the horses striking against the rocky trailway.

Sam spurred up his horse a little and said, "I never seed you look any purtier'n you did las' night, Miss Lelia, an' I thought yore hair wuz fixed awful nice."

"I'm glad you lak it," said Lelia.

"Yeah," went on Sam, "an' I wuz jist thankin'—I've got forty acre uv as good land as ever a crow flew over, an' twenty uv it cleared an' fenced, an' as soon as I git my house done, I'm goin' to ax you a question."

I could see that a sudden thrill had come over Lelia. She seemed to be so excited that she was about to rein her horse off the roadway. She liked Sam and looked forward to hearing him talk like this some day, but it was all unexpected now.

Sam continued, "I would ax you now, but I'm afeard you mout not answer 'cordin' to my wishes."

"Oh, I don't know," said Lelia, appearing not to understand. "You can ax it—I'll not hurt you."

"Wal," Sam said, "I've always lacked you—ever sence I first seed you, an' I wuz 'lowin' that as soon as I git my house done—Oh, hello there! Bull Creek's up an' swimmin'."

We had come to the water where it had spread out over the bottoms. "We cain't cross here," continued Sam. "We'll haf to go aroun'."

"Don't see why," said Lelia. "Hit's jist a mile to our house over thar, an' hit's ten mile aroun' the other way."

"Cain't hep it," protested Sam. "That water is too high. Hit won't do."

"Wal," replied Lelia, "my horse can swim. Cain't yourn?"

"Yes," returned Sam, "but the creek is too swif' an' danger's. We'll git caught in the rapids. Hit won't do. We mustn't go in it."

"You can stay here all day if you wanter," replied Lelia, "but I'm goin' across."

Then before we could detain her, she lashed her horse with her riding switch and urged him into the water. These mountain streams rise and fall quickly, and when swollen, they are exceedingly swift and dangerous. Sam knew Bull Creek. He knew that the chances were ten to one that Lelia would be swept from the saddle and dashed against the rocks. He had not a minute to lose. I was already on the ground, and he told me to hold his horse. He took off his coat and hat and shoes, and plunged into the water. In midstream two large boulders rose high out of the water like the tops of houses, one on each side of the current. This formed a kind of gorge through which the torrential waters rushed with a mad fury. The water coming against the rocks with a powerful force, would shoot up into the air, burst into a white foam, and fall back, causing a heavy mist through which it was difficult for vision to penetrate.

Sam gained the first boulder. Lelia's horse did well until he struck the swift current; then he began to waver and go down. Lelia in her excitement began pulling on the bridle reins.

"Giv 'im the bridle! Giv 'im the bridle!" shouted Sam, but his voice was drowned out by the onrushing torrent.

A heavy piece of timber came down, bobbing up and down, barely missed the horse's head, and shot through the gorge like an arrow. The swift current lifted Lelia from her saddle.

Primitive people learn early to combat danger in all its phases. Lelia battled against the current with assurance and with little fear, but the waters were too powerful. I was standing at the edge of the water, jumping up and down, screaming and weeping. It seemed certain that she was being hurriedly rushed to her death, when Sam, supporting himself on a jutting rock with his left hand, seized Lelia with his right as she entered the gorge and lifted her up on the rock. With Sam's assistance Lelia was able to get back to the shore where I was.

We walked to Bud Quinn's house, where Sam borrowed Mr. Quinn's wagon and team, and took us home, surrounding the high water.

Through all this excitement I had failed to notice what had become of the pony, and we supposed that he had been killed. But the next day my father found him in shallow water where his bridle reins had caught on to the snag of a tree and were holding him. He was swollen and bruised, and showed signs of a struggle.

. Lelia was confined indoors for several days due to the hurts and bruises sustained in the adventure. Sam did not come to our house, but sent his little brother Wayland every day to see how Lelia was. Sunday came, and still Sam did not come.

"Is Sam sick?" asked Lelia of little Wayland.

"No'm," replied Wayland.

"Looks lak he would come an' git you in his buckboard," went on Lelia. "Hit's a right fur piece fer you to haf to walk, haint it?"

"No'm," replied Wayland, "I kin walk it."

Several weeks went by, and still Sam did not come to our house. We heard that he had begun going to Mt. Carmel on Sundays instead of Gravel Hill. I went home with Wayland one Sunday, and heard Mr. and Mrs. Dent talking about Lelia and Sam.

"Looks lak Sam an' Lelia has split up," said Mrs. Dent to her husband.

"I 'lowed they had, seein' as how Sam don't go there no more," Mr. Dent said.

At the supper table Mrs. Dent, addressing her son, said, "Sam, when you goin' to put the kiver on your new house? Looks lak hit would ruin, standin' open thataway."

"Plenty uv time fer that yit, Maw," Sam replied. "Don't know as I'll need it no ways soon nohow." There was nothing more said on the subject.

One afternoon Lelia and I had been in the woods gathering scaley bark hickory nuts, and we were in the big road on our way home. Sam came driving up in his buckboard. Lelia had seen and recognized him. She gave him the right of way by walking to the side of the road. She reached out and picked a wild flower as she walked, giving the occupant of the buggy the same attention she would to a stranger.

"Howdy, Miss Lelia. Howdy, Wayman," Sam said as he reined his horses to a stop. "Youens git in an' ride."

I climbed into the buggy, taking a seat in the rear.

"Git in, Miss Lelia," Sam went on. "Hit's a right fur piece fer you to walk."

Lelia did not look up, but asked, "Do you want me to?"

"I shore do, Miss Lelia," Sam answered, as he leaped out of the carriage to assist her in.

"I thought mebbe you wuz mad at me as you haint never been over," Lelia said, looking straight at the dashboard, as the horse trotted along.

"I haint never been a bit mad, Miss Lelia," Sam said. "I've been in a plum good humor with you all the time."

"Well," said Lelia, "I know I ought to minded you an' not go in the water, but I thought you wuz jist a foolin' me an' the water wuzn't so danger's, an' I guess you got mad at me."

"No, I didn't, Miss Lelia," protested Sam. "You

couldn't never do nothin' that would make me mad at you."

Lelia had drawn a small handkerchief from her apron pocket and wiped her eyes.

She continued, "You said you had somethin' to ax me, an' you never come back an' I knowed you wuz mad at me."

"No," Sam said, "I never wuz mad at you, Miss Lelia, an' what I wanted to ax you wuz jist this: I wanted to ax you to marry me, but after hepin' you outer the water, I wuz afeard you would wanter say 'no,' an' would say 'yes,' jist caze I heped you outer the creek. I'm not goin' to take the upper han' uv no gal an' make her promise to have me jist caze I done her a good turn. An' Miss Lelia, I wuz afeared you wuzn't a kyearin' fer me, but somethin' tells me now that you do, an' I'm goin' to ax you right now. Miss Lelia, will you have me?"

She had her handkerchief to her eyes and was crying and did not speak, but nodded her head.

"That's all right, little gal," said Sam. "I'm goin' to put the kiver on that house an' we'll have a little business with the squar."

CHAPTER VIII

THE WEDDING

IN about a week Sam came to see Lelia, and on taking his leave he asked to speak to my father and mother. He asked them if he could have Lelia. They told him that they had great confidence in Lelia's judgment in selecting a husband, and that they were perfectly willing to have Lelia and him marry. The wedding was set for about a month off. That night my father and mother sat up late and talked in low conversation. The next day my mother and sisters talked earnestly a great deal about things that Jim and I were not allowed to hear.

Lelia was to get married, but it was to be kept a profound secret. Jim and I were cautioned not to tell it to anyone. It was not the custom to announce an engagement, but on the contrary one was denied and kept a secret by the engaged couple until about two days before the wedding. While the secret of Lelia's and Sam's approaching marriage was closely guarded, it was not long before everybody knew it. It was talked about freely by all except the participants and their families.

The wedding was to be at our house, and as the time drew near, great preparations were under way. My mother put up about a dozen chickens and fed them corn to fatten them. My father put in a pen a year-old pig, called a shoat, which he fattened. My mother and sisters spent the week before the wedding in cleaning up and cooking. They baked a lot of cakes, pies, custards, and light bread.

The second day before the wedding my father and Jim got on horses and rode over the settlement, asking people to come to the wedding. Where it was difficult to reach families, they would send them word. The people invited were not in the least surprised. Somehow, in spite of its being kept a secret, everybody knew when the wedding was going to be, and they knew that they were expected to attend. However, two days was plenty of time to prepare for it, as they were not expected to give any gifts. There was no such thing as a wedding present, except between the contracting parties.

On the morning of the wedding Jim and I hitched Red and Star to the wagon and went to Uncle Ben Brady's and Cousin Stark Henry's to borrow their tables, chairs and dishes. When we got back, my father and Uncle Charlie had moved all the furniture out of the big house and had made temporary benches all around the room against the wall.

They took the two tables which we had brought and our own table, and by placing them end to end, made one table about sixteen feet long—long enough to seat twenty people. There was not room in the kitchen for the table, and it was placed in the yard between the kitchen and the big house. It was well shaded by two oak trees.

Aunt Smanthey and Aunt Lou helped get the dinner ready. The chairs were placed around the table as far as they went, and benches were used for the other seats. There were not enough china plates to go around, and tin plates had to be used to piece out. Also tin cups with handles were used in serving milk and water.

We could not grow coffee, and therefore we had to buy it. My father did not feel able to spare the money with which to buy the amount of coffee needed for so many guests, so we substituted sassafras tea, in addition to which we had milk and plenty of water.

They put the dinner on the table. There were plates of fried chicken, dishes of chicken pie, boiled backbones and fried spare-ribs, gooseberry and huckleberry pies, fried pies and baked cakes, custards and lightbread. Prominently displayed on each of the three sections of the table was a boiled ham with the skin taken off and decorated with large round spots made with black pepper. At the end of the table was a pound cake.

When the table was fully set, somebody said that it was time for the wedding to take place. I went into the big house and took a seat by my mother and father on one of the benches. The other seats were occupied by women and girls, and a few men were standing up in the room. Squire Nix came in, followed by Sam and Neut McDill. Sam went to Lelia and took hold of her hands, and she got up and went with him to the middle of the floor. Neut and Alice Smith followed them, Alice taking a place by the side of Lelia, and Neut standing by the side of Sam. Squire Nix stood in front of them.

Sam and Neut were dressed alike. They did not have any coats on, but wore vests. They had shirts made of sea-island domestic, with store-bought false shirt bosoms of a pinkish color. They wore store-bought black jean pants which came down over the tops of their Sunday boots.

Lelia and Alice were also dressed alike. Each had on a calico dress from the same bolt of goods. Each had her hair parted in the middle, plaited, and hanging down behind, tied with a pink ribbon. Each had a red rose pinned on the left shoulder. Their cheeks and lips were well rouged from the effect of fresh air, sunshine and plenty of physical exercise, but there were no cosmetics. Lelia was wearing a silver ring on her index finger. It was made out of a dime. Ned McGhee, who had a blacksmith shop, had a reputation for making rings out of dimes. He had a punch about the size and shape of a ring measure. He would take a dime and drive the sharp point of the punch into the center of it. He then hammered and beat the dime, bringing it farther up on the punch, until it was the size wanted. After the ring was punched out, he polished it with sand and buffed it with buckskin. Sam had taken a dime to Ned and had him make Lelia's wedding ring. Alice was wearing on her third finger a ring, which some young man had given her. It was made out of a black rubber coat button. Such rings were common, and we called them "gutta-percha rings."

Squire Nix, a newly elected Justice of the Peace, performed the ceremony. He mumbled something. I do not think that he knew himself what he was saying, for he seemed greatly agitated. He wound up by saying, "I pronounce you man and wife."

John Parker was in the house with his fiddle, and at the finish of the ceremony, he struck up the tune, "Billy in the Low Ground." Some of the boys began to kick around a little, and Bob Naylor cried out, "Choose yore pardners fer the firs' set." Neut McDill went over to Bob and touched him on the shoulder. There was a whispered conversation for a few minutes, and the music stopped.

My father said something to Parson Yates, and the parson announced in a loud voice, "Everbody come to dinner." Sam and Lelia took seats in the middle of the table and opposite them were seated Neut and Alice.

The other seats were filled with the older and more prominent people who were there. Brother Yates asked the blessing. The younger folk and the children ate at the second table. When the dinner was over, many of the guests went home.

Some of the young people who remained seemed to be quite active, and it was whispered around that there was going to be a dance at our house that night. John Parker had promised to come back, but one fiddler was not sufficient for so important an occasion; and Jim Sawyers and Everett Green got on their horses and went up on Bear Creek after old man Mulligan, who was said to be the best fiddler in the land. Aunt Smanthey came to my mother and told her that they were preparing to dance. My mother's decision was that they could not have the dance in her house. Bill Henry and my father went around back of the smokehouse, and Bill drew from his inside coat pocket a quart flask of red whiskey, and both took several drinks. My father came back looking very lively.

Bob Naylor then came to my father and asked whether he minded if the young people danced a little at our house. My father was in high spirits right then, and he told Bob that it would be agreeable to him if it was to my mother. Then Neut and Bob went to my mother and began trying to persuade her to allow them to dance. My mother was firm in her refusal and said that so far the day had been pleasant and that she would not allow the Devil to come in and mar it. She was crying and declaring that they would never dance in her house, when my father and Lelia and Sam came up. My father said that he did not think there would be any harm, just as long as none of the family danced. Lelia argued in favor of the dance, saying that the young people were all friends of hers and Sam's. My mother finally consented to the dance, provided there would be no drinking or cutting up. Everybody then went home except Aunt Smanthey and Aunt Lou and their families.

A little after dark, the people began coming in for the dance. They came from Greasy Valley, from Bear Creek, from Round Mountain, from Wild Cat Slough and from Possom Trot. Robert Faulkner and Will Baskin brought the two Miller girls, Wes McWhorter and Ed Mathews brought the Cross girls, and preacher Stone's girls came with Charlie Christmas.

It was a moonlit night, and many of the boys stayed out in the yard, some of them sitting on the yard-fence, while the girls all went into the big house. By an hour after dark a good crowd had gathered and they were wanting to dance, but the fiddlers were not there. John Parker had agreed to come back, but he was late. They were fixing to send after him, when somebody said that Mulligan had arrived.

Great activity was immediately shown. The boys began coming into the big house where the girls were seated on the benches around the wall.

Old man Mulligan came in with a fiddle buttoned

up under his coat, with the neck protruding forward. Behind him came Jim Sawyers, holding in his hand two small sticks about the size of soda straws. Mr. Mulligan was given a seat in a corner near the fireplace, and Jim sat down by him, facing the fiddle. Mulligan began thumping the strings and twisting the screws and spitting on them to make them hold. When the fiddle was tuned to his liking, he drew the bow across the strings a time or two, and struck up the tune "Sally Gooden."

As there was no other fiddler to assist by playing the second, Jim Sawyers beat on the base strings with the two little sticks. This was called "beatin' straws." In a short time, the fiddler stopped playing and again began tuning his fiddle.

"Pardners fer the first set," cried Everett Green. Frank Hobbs and Rena Bernard took the floor, next came Robert Faulkner and Addie Cross, then William Frayser and Nettie Strong, and last but not least came Jimmie New and Annie Burton. This completed the proper number for the dance, four couples. Again the fiddler drew his bow across the strings and struck up the tune, "Rye Straw," while Jim beat straws furiously.

Everett Green began, "Honor yore pardner. Lady on the left. Eight han's up an' circle to the left."

Each of the men made a polite bow to his partner, then to the lady on his left, and all joined hands and danced in a circle to the left. John Parker came in, and Jim quit beating straws while John played the second.

The dance was on, and as they danced, the fiddlers played "Sally Gooden," "Rye Straw," "Billy in the Low Ground," "Mississippi Sawyer," "Black-eyed Susie," "Sugar in My Coffee," "Run, Nigger, Run," "Goin' to the Pasture," "Shortnin' Bread," "Cotton-Eyed Joe," "Natchez Under the Hill," "Arkansas Traveler," "Fisher's Horn-Pipe," and "Eighth of January."

When all the figures of the reel were called out, the set was finished and the announcer wound up by saying, "An' the ladies take their seats." At this point, the dancers left the floor, the men going back amongst the men, while the girls found seats as best they could, and the fiddlers ceased playing. While the fiddlers rested their fingers and tuned their fiddles, Everett called out, "Choose yore pardners fer the nex' set," and four more couples took the floor and the dance was as before.

A crowd from Round Mountain, headed by Dan Blackburn and Will Griffin, seemed to want to make trouble. Dan and the Jordan boys had plenty of whiskey, and they, with the Griffin and the Roper boys, would go out where their horses were hitched, drink freely, and come back and stand in and around the door and look on at the dance. Along about midnight this crowd was feeling their whiskey. They had come uninvited, and from this fact they seemed inclined to act ugly.

It was time to choose partners for another set, when Griffin felt like dancing. He went up to Sis Chaney, who was sitting on the end of a bench with a number of other girls, and asked her if she would dance the next set with him. Sis saw that he was drinking, and made excuses. He then asked the next girl, and so on down to the end of the bench, all of them refusing to dance with him. He felt slighted and insulted, and when the next set started, Griffin began running through the set, dancing by himself. Sam went to him, told him that his actions were annoying and asked him to leave the floor. Griffin said to Sam, "By God, I'll dance jist whar an' when I damn please." As he said this, he drew back his fist and struck at Sam.

Neut McGill and Jim Sawyers joined Sam, and they threw Griffin out of the house and told him to leave the place. He went outside the gate followed by Blackburn and the rest of the Round Mountain crowd. They were talking loud and swearing, and one of the Jordan boys passed his bottle around and they all drank. By this time Griffin felt like fighting. He danced around a little and yelled out: "Whoop-ee! Wild an' wooly, raised in the cain an' suckled by a b'ar. I kin whup anything in Gravel Hill Township!"

I saw my father with the shotgun in his hand, running around the house in the direction of the disturbers, with Granville Bruton behind him trying to get him to stop.

Word quickly went through the house that there was a big fight on outside. All the men in the house, including the dancers and the fiddlers, rushed out to see the excitement.

The usual way of ending a dance was to break it up with a fight. It was seldom that a dance lasted all night, for in most cases a fight broke it up before the night had passed.

My father, with the gun in his hand, went up to the crowd and told them in language they well understood that he wanted order.

"Do you hear that, Griffin?" said Dan Blackburn. "The boss says, by God, keep order! Wot in the 'ell you fellers cuttin' up fer anyhow? Hoo-ee! Drunk an' all dressed up, an' no whar to go. I live on Roun' Mountain. I'm all wool, warp an' fillin' a full yard wide, an' I kin whup my weight in wil' cats. Hoo-ee!"

Then he began dancing what we call "knocking the back step." Old man Garrison and Mr. Wooten, invited guests from Round Mountain, had gone to my father and told him to leave it to them, that they would get the offenders away. After these two had talked to the men a while, the latter all rode off.

As it happened, there was no fight, and as the rough crowd had gone, the dance was resumed and kept up until daylight. Then the crowd was dismissed, and all went home.

Sam's house was finished, and he and Lelia moved in that day. My mother gave Lelia a large feather bed and some quilts. My father gave her a cow and a calf. Sam's parents gave several needed things.

CHAPTER IX

THE FOURTH OF JULY

WITH us there were only two holidays, Christmas and the Fourth of July. The former we always observed, and we celebrated the Fourth only when we could go to a barbecue. We never "took" New Year's day, and we had not heard of Thanksgiving Day.

One night about the last week in June the people held a meeting at Gravel Hill for the purpose of making arrangements for the annual Fourth of July barbecue. Frank Stone presided, and the men were called upon to donate animals to be barbecued. Some gave sheep, some hogs, some goats, and some yearlings. My father gave a sheep. In all, there were about twelve animals offered. A few days before the Fourth my mother and Nora began cooking for the barbecue. They baked light bread, pound cakes, pies and custards.

The day before the barbecue there was great activity on and around the grounds. Tom Moore and Jay Vanwinkel hauled undressed lumber and built a platform large enough to dance on. They erected a lemonade stand at one end adjoining the platform. Two other lemonade stands went up on the grounds. Bill Brown owned a swing which he brought and put up. It was about a twenty-four passenger swing, and was propelled by hand and with a lever. My father and Sam assisted a lot of other men in cleaning out two excavations in the ground the shape of ditches, each about twenty feet long. They built fires of hickory and oak wood in these pits, and the carcasses were suspended on poles stretched across the meat hanging just over the coals of fire.

Old man Adams, who had the reputation of being an expert in barbecuing and who lived up on Possom Trot, was sent for and stayed on the grounds all of the night before the picnic, directing the barbecue.

The men built two tables each about fifty feet long. They were made by scaffolding up lumber to about the height of an ordinary table.

On the morning of the Fourth, long before day, we were all up, getting ready to go to the barbecue. My mother prepared some hot water and some lye soap, and Jim and I had to wash all over. Sam and Lelia came by in their buckboard and hauled our tub, in which were packed our dinner and dishes. Our family walked to the barbecue.

When we arrived, people were coming in from every direction. Some of them lived as far as fifteen and twenty miles away, and must have started long before day. People came in two-horse wagons with boards stretched across the wagon bed for seats, they came in ox wagons seated with chairs having cowhide bottoms, they came on horseback, some riding two on a horse. Some rode mules and some rode donkeys. Some came in two-wheel carts drawn by a single ox. Most of the people, however, walked, as did our family.

Soon after we arrived, a man drove up with a wagon-load of ice. We had never heard anything about such an industry as an ice factory. Had a man told us that it was possible to manufacture ice in July, we would have doubted him. There was an old man living up above the shoals who put up ice in sawdust every winter and preserved it for use in the summer. He sold his ice only to people who wanted to make and sell lemonade. I cannot remember of any other purpose for which ice was used. Doctors did not prescribe the ice bag in case of sickness, and ice was not used to cool water. The mountain spring water is very cool, just the right temperature for drinking.

Along about an hour before dinner time, my father and Sam were assisting a lot of men carve the barbecue meat, while my mother and sisters were helping other women in placing the dinner on the table. My father had given me a quarter to spend, and Wayland Dent had a few nickels; so we strolled around the picnic grounds, spending our money and taking in the sights. We went by the dancing platform, where there seemed to be great activity. The dance was on, with John Parker and old man Mulligan furnishing the music. Also Moore's stand seemed to be doing a good business. When a set was finished, the men would turn to the refreshment stand and treat their partners. There was a charge of five cents a set for each couple who danced, and this went into a fund which paid the fiddlers.

Off to the left of the platform, the Gentry boys had a lemonade stand, and across from them about fifty yards was another stand operated by Will Drake and John Journey. Between these two stands was Bill Brown's swing. There was a fiddler playing in each of the lemonade stands, and a man was playing an accordion while occupying a seat in the swing. The fiddler in Gentry's stand was coming down on "Cotton-Eyed Joe," and the one in Drake and Journey's stand, with great writhing of the body, was entertaining the people with the tune, "Old Molly Hair," while the man with the accordion in the swing played "Black-eyed Susie."

Drake would cry out, "Ice cold lemonade, fresh an' fine, one glass fer a nickel an' two fer a dime!" Then would come the voice of Lum Gentry saying, "Right thisaway to git yer lemonade, made in the shade, stirred with a spade, an' the best lemonade that ever wuz made."

As Wayland and I made our way through the laughing, joking jovial crowd, we could hear the squeaking of the several fiddles, the loud strains of the accordion, the constant barking of the dispensers of lemonade, the sonorous voice of Bill Brown, urging the people to ride in his swing, the shrill voice of Bud Strong, who called the dance sets, and added to this, occasionally, we could hear from the bushes the neighing of an impatient horse and the lowing of a discontented ox. It was the Fourth of July.

When dinner was ready, Bill Ward stood on a stump and announced dinner, saying, "Everbody come to dinner! Come one, come all! Any uv youens that didn't brang no dinner, come right on anyhow, fer they's plenty here fer all. Come on ever'body!"

The people gathered around the dinner table, standing on both sides, and we ate until we couldn't. When the people were through eating, the women gathered up the dishes, and as they did so, they took a share of the cooked food that was left. My mother took home enough to do us for two or three days.

At the Fourth of July picnics it was the custom for somebody to make a speech. Dr. Creasy, who lived in another section of the county and who was visiting in our neighborhood, had agreed to be the speaker for this occasion. There had been a small platform erected just outside the picnic grounds and far enough away so that the speakers would not be disturbed by the fiddles and the refreshment stand barkers.

Dr. Creasy mounted the platform, and for some time talked about the Fourth of July and why we should celebrate it. He read from a book a lot of whereases and resolutions, all of which seemed unintelligible to his hearers. We were not in the least interested in what a few people were doing a century back. I was standing by my father and Sam, and they seemed to be bored with the speech. To us the Fourth of July was a day on which we had a picnic and a good time in general. It seemed that the doctor was unable to drive home to us any facts or to give us any enlightenment as to why we were observing this day, as we could not connect the Fourth of July with the activities of people who lived a hundred years before. Everybody seemed glad when the doctor brought his speech to a close, since there were some candidates to be heard.

In nearly all of the counties of Arkansas the Democratic nomination is the equivalent to the election. While some sections of our county were strongly Republican, yet the county as a whole nearly always went Democratic. It seems that there had developed an opposing faction in the Democratic party in our county, and the members of this faction were stoutly bidding for the nomination at the coming primary. Several of the members of this faction were at our picnic to speak in behalf of their candidacy.

The first candidate to take the platform was a man

named Huffaker, who lived on the edge of Greasy Valley. He said he was running for the office of sheriff. He scratched his head all the time he was talking and urging his election. His principal qualifications for the office seemed to be the fact that he lived in our part of the county.

The next speaker was a one-armed man who lived in the southern part of the county. He wanted to be tax assessor, and it seemed that about the only claim which he had to the office was that he was a poor man and needed it. He wanted the people to vote for him, as it would help him out.

The best is usually saved for the last. The last speaker was Newt Shafer, who was a candidate for the legislature. Newt was about forty years old, six feet tall, clean shaven, and he had coarse black hair and wore a long linen duster. He could not read or write, but his natural abilities were creditable to say the least.

He opened by saying, "Feller citizens, an' gentlemun, as youens all know, I'm runnin' for repzentive, an' these two frien's that youens had jist hyeard is runnin' fer sheriff an' assessor, an' you'll be makin' no mistake when you vote fer 'em.

"Before goin' any furder, I want to say a word about the Fourth uv July. I've jist been listenin' to Dr. Creasy's speech on this great and glorious day, an' the Doc is right. Hit is a great day. An' when I wuz listenin' at the Doc, I wuz thankin'—Thar is three reasons why we orter preserve this great day. Firs' hit's about the turnin' pint from sprang to summer; secon' hit's gin'ly a clear day an' a warm day, an' the best day in the year to give our barbecues; an' last, but not least, hit's the day that orter fin' all uv us with our craps laid by an' a hook an' line in our han's an' tellin' the feesh to look out."

Mr. Shafer paused here to take a drink of water. My father and Sam looked as if they were highly pleased at this learned way of explaining why we should observe the Fourth. I heard my father tell Sam that he could stand and listen to that man talk all day.

After drinking a gourdful of water, Newt drew a red bandana handkerchief from his ulster pocket, and wiping the perspiration from his face and hands, proceeded:

"Now, feller citizens an' gentlemun, as I have done told you, I am a candidate fer the legislater, an' as most uv youens know, Cal Johnson, the man that's got the job now, is runnin' agin me. Now, who is this man Johnson? Why he's a upstart uv a lawyer that lives in town an' never done a honest day's work in his life.

"He wuz sent to the legislater the last term, an' what did he do? Why nothin' cep' drank whiskey an' play kyards an' galavant aroun' with furriners.

"Now, gentlemun, here is a few thangs he wants to do. He wants to build a new court house. Thatar ole court house is a better house than I'm livin' in. Hit's better'n you air livin' in, an' hit's good enough fer many a year yit.

"He wants to build a ar'n bridge acrost Devil's Fork. Now listen here, men. I've swum that ar creek on my hoss a many a time. My father swum it before I was born; my grandfather swum it; an' my boys can swim it arter I'm gone. Nex', he wants to enlargen the free schools. Listen here, fellers, the Devil has never quit laffin' yit at gittin' the free schools in Arkansas. Now, feller citizens an' gentlemun, all these thangs that Johnson wants to do means spendin' money. Hit means more taxes an' bigger taxes fer you to pay. If you send this man back to the legislater, hit won't be long till this county will be dreened uv ever' loose dime in it."

Here the speaker paused for more water.

Shafer's reputation as an orator had preceded him, and he was not in the least disappointing. My father and Sam, both of whom had been standing with their mouths open, drinking in every word that the speaker said, looked at each other and nodded approvingly. It was noticeable that Shafer's speech was making a favorable impression on the audience. Here and there, out through the crowd could be heard, " 'Raw fer Shafer! 'Raw fer Shafer!"

The speaker continued: "Now, gentlemun an' fellers, if I'm elected, an ' I'm shore to be elected—there hain't nothin' that can keep me frum it—here is a few thangs I'm a goin' to do. I'm goin' to do away with all the free schools uv Arkansas."

There was not much demonstration at this, but the audience stood at attention.

"Nex'," went on the speaker, "I'm goin' to lessen all the taxes in this county."

A few more shouted, " 'Raw fer Shafer!" and the speaker went on "Men, listen to me. The corn that you work an' raise in your own field is yourn, hain't it? If you take that corn an' grind it into meal an' make bread outen the meal an' eat it, hit's yourn, hain't it? If you feed that corn to yore hawg, an' kill an' eat the hawg, hit's yourn, hain't it? If you feed that corn to yore hoss an' plow the hoss, hit's yourn, hain't it? If you make lye hominy outen that corn an' eat the hominy, hit's yourn, hain't it? Now fellers, hear what I got to say. If you take that corn an' make a gallon uv whiskey outen it an' drank the whiskey, why in the name uv God hain't it YOURN?"

At this, there was a great demonstration. Whoops, yells, and cries of " 'Raw fer Shafer" could be heard from many of the bystanders. It was some time before order was restored.

Shafer continued: "I'm goin' to have a act passed makin' it agin the law fer any revenuer to set foot anywhar in Arkansas. Now, men, I hope everybody here is my frien'. If you vote fer me, I know you air my frien', an' if you don't vote fer me, I still want you to be my frien'. I hain't got no grudge agin nobody.

"I hain't got no book larnin'. I don't know how to

cipher. I don't know how to spell. I don't know how to read an' write. But I do know what is right an' what is wrong; an' youens can be shore to know that, when I am elected, I'm goin' to do what is right."

By this time the other two candidates had placed three gallon-size brown jugs on the platform, and the speaker said, "Now men, me an' these other two candidates have got a little mountain dew here, an' we want all uv youens to come up an' taste it. Hit don't make no difference whether you 'ten' to vote fer us or not. We want ever' one uv youens to come right up here an' drank an' be merry."

The women, long since tired of the speaking, had all gone back to the picnic grounds, and the men did not have to be asked a second time to take the jugs.

Every man seemed to get his share of the mountain dew, and judging by the way they acted, some of them got more than their share. The crowd was dismissed with great shouts, yells, screams, and whoops, all for Shafer.

When the Fourth of July had passed and the barbecue was over, we began arranging and planning for the next and biggest event of the year, the "Big Meetin'." It was seldom that a summer passed when Gravel Hill did not hold the big meeting. Great preparations had to be made, and we had much to do before time for the meeting to start.

One Saturday night Brother and Sister Bradberry came to our house to stay all night. It was always a great pleasure to have company on Saturday night, but I hated to see these two old people come, for I knew that I would have to go back down in the field and cut more green corn to bring up to feed their horses.

After supper we all got our seats out in the yard in the moonlight, and my mother got some chewed black-gum tooth brushes and a bottle of snuff, and passed them to Mrs. Bradberry. My father did not smoke, but he had some good tobacco which he gave Mr. Bradberry. Mrs. Bradberry did nearly all the talking, and about all Mr. Bradberry could do was to sanction what his wife had said.

"Brother Yates war at my house tother day," she said, "an' he say he wants the big meetin' to start week come Sunday. He say we must all git to prayin' an' try to make this the biggest outpourin' uv the Sperrit that Gravel Hill has ever had. Arter he left, I got to thankin' about it, an' hit jist 'pears to come to me all at onc't that the Lord had called on me to visit ever'body in the settlement an' git 'em to prayin' an' gittin' ready. That's why I come over hyar tonight. I want youens to git down to prayin' an' git yerselves ready fer the Lord's work.

"The great trouble is we don't have the brotherly feelin' fer each other we orta. We must visit more among our neighbors, an' when they air sick, set up with 'em an' wait on 'em. An' when they air in trouble, pray fer 'em.

"Another thang, we gotta git red uv all bad examples in the settlement 'fore any good will come uv this meetin'. Now look at that Bobbs gal over at ole Bolden's. I went to Square Nix yistidy an' I said to him, 'I say, Square, you air the jestice an' hit's yore place to make that ar womurn at ole Bolden's leave the country.' An' do ye thank? He had the ordacity to ax what the womurn had done."

Good brother Bradberry took advantage of his wife's pause to take a fresh dip of snuff, and said, "Oh, mebbe the womurn hain't so bad arter all."

"Now you jist shet up," his wife said. "That's jist lak a drotted man. Let a ole strumpet uv a woman come stragglin' through the country an' ever' man is ready to take up fer her. Wal, she'll not be thar long. That woods colt o' hern is about to die, ef hit hain't already dead. Ole Miss Milam says they hain't got nothin' t'eat and they air all about to starve to death."

I went off to bed and left good old Sister Bradberry still talking. The next morning our company went home early, as they had to get back to attend to the cows. When they had gone, I noticed that my mother seemed to be worried about something. Soon I heard her call my father.

"Ben," she said, "I am goin' over to Bolden's today."

"I knowed it," my father replied. "I knowed you would go, an' I will go with you. These folks may git sick an' die, but I'll see to it that they don't starve to death."

They walked over to Bolden's, and my father soon came back. He hurried me over there with some sweet milk and biscuits. The baby was sick, old man and old lady Bolden were both down in bed, and the young Bobbs woman was trying to wait on all of them. They had not had anything to eat for three days except parched corn. The woman had been trying to pulverize the parched corn and soak it in water to feed the baby. My mother fed the baby some milk with a spoon. It was so desperately hungry that in its eagerness it would grab the spoon with its little hands, thereby spilling the milk before it reached its mouth, and my mother had to hold its hands so she could feed it.

My father had also been busy that day, and before we left he came with Sam and Lelia and Bill and Liza Harris. They brought a sack of meal, a middling of meat and some chickens, besides a lot of cooked food. When we went to leave, the young woman followed my mother to the gate. She was crying and said that she did not know how to express her appreciation for what we had done.

Late that night I heard my father and mother talking. They both said that they felt much better prepared for the meeting now than they had before.

CHAPTER X

THE CAMP MEETING

THE first Sunday in August was set as the time for the "Big Meetin' " to begin, and until then we were busy making preparations. We put up some chickens to fatten, and the week before the meeting my mother cleaned house. We finished hauling in our fodder, so that we might have nothing to do during the time of the big meeting.

The weather was dry and warm, and it was decided to erect a bush arbor and hold the meeting under it. My father and Sam went to Gravel Hill and assisted the other men in cleaning off the grounds and scaffolding up some poles. They cut bushes with green leaves and placed them over these poles, close enough together so that the sun could not shine through. They placed rows of logs about eight feet apart under the arbor, and with the lumber from Tom Moore's dancing platform they laid planks on these logs, to serve as seats. They erected a small platform at the rear of the arbor and brought the pulpit from the church and placed it on this platform. They also brought the mourner's bench and put it just in front of the pulpit and platform.

The meeting proper was to start on Sunday, but on the previous Saturday a business meeting was held in the church house and was attended by church members only. About the only business they had to transact was to turn out members who had violated the rules of the church. The church clerk had a small day book in which he had the names of all the members. He called off this list of names, and the moderator asked if there were any charges to be preferred against any of them.

Harmon Harrold rose and called the names of eight, who, he said, had danced out of the church. Six of them were absent and had their names scratched off. The other two were Sam and Lelia who had danced the night of their wedding. They were allowed a chance to defend themselves, and both said that they were sorry and that they had asked the Lord to forgive them and felt that He had done so. They were allowed to remain in full fellowship.

The moderator asked if anybody else had any charges to prefer against any of the other members. Jim McCann rose and said that he had been told that Dan Amous was drunk the previous Christmas. Mr.

Amous was absent, and his name was scratched off. Again the moderator asked for further charges. There was a pause; and then Harmon Harrold rose for the second time and said that he was about to forget it, but he had reliable information that John Gentry had been seen at a horse race over in Greasy Valley the previous spring. Mr. Gentry's name was ordered taken from the list of church members. The moderator waited for more charges. Old man McCone got up and said that he hated to report it, but felt that it was his duty to say that he had seen Ed Honley with a deck of cards. This was good evidence that Mr. Honly had been guilty of playing cards, and he was turned out of the church. This seemed to be about all, and the meeting was about to adjourn, when Harmon Harrold for the third time asked to be heard. He said that he didn't intend to say anything about it, but it would not be serving the Lord right if he did not report it. He said that he was at Lum Gentry's house, and Lum was saddling a horse. The horse stepped on his foot, and Lum said "Damn." Lum was turned out of the church for cussing. This closed the business session.

All differences between members had been settled at special meetings of the church. It was seldom that church members took their troubles to the courts. They usually settled them in the church. I remember once Bill Cummings and a man named Harmon had a falling out about Harmon's hogs getting in Cummings' potato patch. They had a fight and were carrying guns for each other, when they were cited to a church meeting. It took about three days to get the matter settled, and get Cummings and Harmon on friendly terms.

Now that all offenders against the church discipline had been eliminated, they were able to start the big meeting with a clean slate. In bringing new members into the church they had four sources from which to draw. First, there were the hardened sinners, those whom they had never been able to move; second, those who had arrived at the age of discretion since the last big meeting. Children were not admitted into the church and were not allowed to kneel at the mourner's bench. They must be about eighteen years old before they were considered old enough to use their own judgment in such matters. Third, there were the mourners left over from the last meeting. It took all the way from one to four years at the mourner's bench before conversion. Of course, spontaneous outbursts of the Holy Spirit were not uncommon, even to those who had never knelt at the mourner's bench. But religion coming to those who had sought it at the mourner's bench was considered more consecrated. Fourth, there were the backsliders—those who had violated some rule of the church and had been turned out. As a usual thing the backsliders, one and all, went back into the church.

Few of us had a clock or any kind of timepiece. Therefore, we expressed the time of day by the position of the sun. For instance, when we said that the sun was "an hour high," it was about one hour after the rising of the sun. When we said it was "an hour by sun," it was about an hour before the setting of the sun. An hour before dinner time would be about eleven o'clock. We used such expressions as an hour before day, and an hour after dark, etc.

Sunday morning when the sun was about three hours high, we were on our way to the meeting. When we arrived, quite a number were there and others were coming. They came from all the neighboring regions, and as some of them lived quite a distance, they brought provisions and cooking utensils and camped on the ground. They slept in their wagons and on quilts spread on the ground. We lived within walking distance, only three miles, and we walked there and back twice a day. On account of our nearness to the meeting we had company nearly every night.

About an hour before dinner time a large crowd had gathered, all ready for the opening day of the big meeting. There were old men with bed-ticking suspenders, home-knit wool socks; young men with high top boots and paper collars; aged women with their heads enveloped in huge bonnets; young women with sailor hats and shoes that buttoned up the side; tired mothers with cross babies and children with clean clothes and clean faces.

The people took seats in the arbor as they would in the church house. There were benches on the left side of the pulpit, and this was called the "Amen Corner."

Here sat the aged men and those who could not hear well. On the other side of the pulpit were seated the aged women. In front of the pulpit, to the right, sat the women, and to the left sat the men. The young people who "cut up" sat in the rear. The mothers usually took charge of the children, except for the larger and more unruly ones, who sat with their fathers.

The meeting was conducted by Brother Yates, the local pastor, assisted by Brother Larkin, who lived up on Wild Cat Slough. When it was time for the services to open, Brother Yates arose and announced that they would sing "Amazing Grace." He had a short but very thick hymn book, containing the words without the music. Each song was marked either "L.M." or "S.M." or "C.M.," meaning long meter, short meter, or common meter. The preacher lined the song in this manner:

> "Amazing Grace, how sweet the sound
> That saved a wretch like me."

The congregation followed by singing. Then the preacher continued:

> "I once was lost, but now I'm found,
> Was blind, but now I see."

The congregation sang after him. When all the song was lined and sung, the preacher read a chapter from the Bible and called on Brother Jim McCann, a very prominent member, to lead in prayer.

Jim McCann was a prominent member, not because he was in the habit of dropping large checks into the contribution box, not because the church boasted of his membership on account of his wealth or social standing, not because by some political trickery he had been elected to a high office of trust. He was a prominent member because he was always up and about the Lord's business. When there was serious trouble of any kind in the neighborhood, Jim McCann was usually the first to be on the scene. When there was sickness, he visited those stricken and soothed them with his kindly attentions. He gave liberally of what he had to those in need.

After the prayer Brother Larkin arose, and from a small thick Bible read his text. He then started off something like this:

"Bretherin an' sisterin, I feel that this is goin' to be the greatest meetin' that this holler has ever had. I feel that before this meetin' closes that ever' sinner is goin' to come an' jine the church, an' that we air goin' to run the devil clean outen this whole settlement.

"Rickoleck though, my good frien's, the devil is not idle. He knows what's goin' on an' you can see his works ever'whar. When I went to mill yistidy, I seed two young men a settin' under a tree a-playin' kyards. I heard two ole men a-talkin', an' they cussed about ever' other word. I seed a young womurn an' ever'thang about her wuz pride. Pride in her walk, pride in her talk, an' pride in her looks.

"Yes, my frien's, the devil has got this world by the

tail with a downhill pull. He's here, he's thar, an' he's ever'whar.

"Onc't, a long time ago, a man said he had a dream. He drempt he went to a meetin' an' he seed devils at the meetin' house. They war in the corners, under the banches, an' all over the house. Then he went to the hoss races. The men war a-cussin' an' playin' kyards an' bettin' on the hoss races, an' he seed jist one little sickly, weakly, pale an' puny devil. Then he drempt he seed the chief devil, the big devil of 'em all; an' he sez, sez-ee, 'Mr. Devil, I see you have a lot of fine looking devils at the meetin' house, an' jist one little no count devil at the race track. Why is that? Is the race track a better place than the meetin' house?'

"The chief devil laft long an' loud, an' sez, sez-ee, 'Why them 'at's at the race track belongs to me anyhow, an' they air doin' what I want 'em to do, but them 'at's at the meetin' is a-workin' agin me, an' I have to send my best lieutenants thar to take up fer my cause.'

"Frien's, we mustn't let the devil git the upper hand uv this meetin'. We must rout him. We must labor in the Lord's vineyard, an' we must work an' pray."

Brother Larkin talked along this line for about an hour and a half. He was about fifty years old, had long black whiskers a little streaked with gray, and wore a long blue calico coat, brogan shoes, and a hickory shirt.

Mr. Larkin was what some people might call ignorant. He had not been schooled at an expensive and fashionable seminary. He expounded the gospel in the absence of any long drawn-out theological education. He did not have access to voluminous commentaries explaining what this or that in the Bible means. He had only the Bible to read, and he interpreted it as it is written. He believed, as did his mountain ancestors for centuries back, that God wrote the Bible, and that every word in it means exactly what it says, or He wouldn't have written it thus. But the honesty and sincerity of this good old man was not to be doubted.

It was about two hours after dinner time when the meeting was dismissed, and it was in the middle of the evening when we arrived home and had dinner. Jim and I went to the field and cut green corn and brought it up to the crib to feed the horses. We cut and brought enough for another horse, as it might be that we would have company that night.

We ate a cold supper and walked back to meeting. There was a large congregation, and the prayers and sermon were long. It was about an hour of midnight when we got back home. It was dark, and we lighted our way with pine torches.

On the second night of the meeting, after a lengthy sermon, the preacher called for mourners. Pink Jones was the first to come. This was Pink's fourth year at the mourner's bench. Next came Bud Dent. This was also his fourth year. The preacher, encouraged by this start, urged the congregation to continue singing, while he went on:

"Come right on up, young man, young womurn,

come right on up! Come to the Lord! He is a-waitin' fer you."

The congregation kept up singing a song that started off like this:

"I have a Saviour gone to Glory,
I have a Saviour gone to Glory,
I have a Saviour gone to Glory,
On the other shore."

They continued this song, substituting for Saviour mother, father, sister, brother, uncle, aunt, nephew, niece and friend. After each verse they sang the chorus:

"Bye an' bye I'll go an' see him,
Bye an' bye I'll go an' see him,
Bye an' bye I'll go an' see him,
On the other shore.

"Won't that be a happy meetin',
Won't that be a happy meetin',
Won't that be a happy meetin',
On the other shore?"

As they sang, the preacher continued: "Sinner, turn yore back on the devil, an' come out fer the Lord. Won't you come? Hit's nothin' but the Devil that's a-holding you back. Won't you come? Young man, turn yore back on kyard playin' an' horse racin'. Young womurn, turn yore back on dancin' an' come to Jesus while hit's not too late. Sinner, the Devil's a-goin' to git you. He's a-goin' to git you, shore's you're born. He's arter you. I can see his horns, his hoofs. I can hear his chains a-rattlin'. Look out! Sinner, the Devil's standin' behin' you, an' he's a-goin' to grab you an' drag you down, down, down to Hell!"

A couple of girls were sitting in a corner at the edge of the arbor. They looked behind them into dark, and they heard the trace chains on a pair of horses rattle. The girls thought that they would feel just a little safer closer up, and they lost no time in getting up and advancing toward the front, looking for a seat nearer the pulpit. Everybody, of course, thought that they were coming to the mourner's bench.

"God bless you, young womurn," said the preacher. "And God bless you, young womurn."

Jim McCann seized one of the girls, Ashly Thornton took hold of the other one, and they ushered them right on up to the mourner's bench. The girls could not now back out, so they knelt.

Suddenly there was an outburst of screaming from a woman. She was crying and shouting, "Glory be to God, my sisters—my two lost sisters. They air comin' to Jesus!" The two girls were her sisters.

The congregation took up a good old song that ran something like this:

"O turn, sinner, turn;
May the Lord to help you turn.

O turn, sinner, turn,
Why will you die?"

Pink Jones shouting, "Glory, Hallelujah!" leaped into the air and fell kicking and knocking. It took eight men to hold him. Bud Dent, the other four-year mourner, rose from the bench laughing and shaking hands with everybody, and saying that the Lord had forgiven him his sins.

Converts kept coming to the mourner's bench, and the choir, which was the entire congregation or all those that cared to sing, turned to another good old song that ran this way:

"On Jordan's stormy banks I stand,
And cast a wishful eye,
To Canaan's fair and happy land
Where my possessions lie."

They followed each verse with the chorus

"I am bound fer the promus' land,
I am bound fer the promus' land,
O who will come an' go with me?
I am bound fer the promus' land."

There were now about three or four women and two or three men shouting. I was in the back and heard Nora Perry and Melissa Journey talking to each other. Nora said to Melissa:

"Le's go up an' show 'em how to shout."

Then they took their tucking combs out of their hair and handed them to Nora's mother and asked her to hold them, as they might otherwise get broken. The two girls went up to the front where there was the greatest activity. Melissa struck out with her hands and arms shouting, "Glory, Hallelujah! I'm so happy!"

Nora held her handkerchief to her nose and screamed continuously. By this time there were twenty or twenty-five people shouting. The onlookers, sinners, and those who took no part in the meeting stood on the benches and watched the proceedings. Some of the mourners were screaming, some were crying, some were jumping up and down, some were shaking with laughter, and some lay on the benches and moaned. I heard the preacher say, "Keep on, brother; keep on, sister. God's in this arbor. He come right down through the top. He's in this arbor now!"

The meeting held on late. It was about an hour after midnight when we got home.

There was one character in this meeting whom I shall always remember. He was John Kiker. John was a lanky, gawky fellow and was known as a "shoutin' member." He came across the mountain riding a donkey so small that John's feet almost dragged the ground. The weather was warm, and he was dressed in a two-piece suit, consisting of a shirt made of home woven cloth and pantaloons of the same material. He was barefoot and had no underwear. As I mentioned, he was outfitted in a two-piece suit.

John would usually wait until the shouting was well under way, and would then leap into the midst of the crowd, knocking and kicking and shouting. He would get down on the floor and roll and kick and yell in a tone of voice something like that used for calling hogs. He would roll around on the floor, his shirt-tail would come out, and his pants would come unbuttoned; but he seemed entirely unconscious of his predicament, so filled was he of the "Holy Sperrit."

The women began complaining about John's behavior, and several of them refused to take any further part in the meeting. A committee of men waited on John and explained to him that his actions during the shouting were perfectly ridiculous and his behavior obnoxious. They demanded that he change his manner or stay away from the meeting. John was furious. He went out to get on his donkey and go home. Sam was out seeing about his horse when John passed him, snapping his pocket knife and talking to himself. Sam heard him say as he passed, "By Gawd, they can jist go to Hell with their God damn meetin'! I've got as good a right to shout as any uv 'em has."

The meeting lasted for about ten days, when everybody seemed to be completely worn out. There was talk of closing, but the preachers could not decide. There were only four mourners left. The others had all been converted. Mr. Larkin put it up to the four mourners. Two of them voted to close, and the other two to continue. However, they closed the meeting, as the women wanted to get busy with their cutting and drying of fruit, and the men wanted to save their late corn fodder.

There had been no collections at this meeting. There was no money asked for and none given. None was needed. The meeting was conducted without any expense. Even the candles that lighted the arbor were home molded. We did not pay the preacher, and he did not want pay. I remember that once, when our preacher was in hard circumstances, my father gave him a ham of meat and my mother gave him a pair of wool knit socks that she had knitted.

A few days after the meeting closed old man Bolden came to our house and told my father that he wanted to work for him, in order to pay for the assistance we had given them when they were all sick. When my mother saw that he was there, she put on the coffee pot. My father would have no pay for what he had done, but invited the old man to stay for dinner.

"Air you an' the Bobbs woman gittin' long all right?" my mother asked.

"Oh, yes," he replied. "Gittin' long fairly well. Ye know her ole man's thar now."

"No," my mother said, "we had not heard he was here. We thought he was killed."

"Wal," Bolden said, "she thought he wuz, caze she couldn't hear from 'im. But he war out in Collyrady somewhar, an' he said all the letters he writ war sent back to 'im, an' he said he jist had to come back an' hunt 'er up. He's goin' to build them a new house, an' he wants me an' the ole lady to stay on with them; so I guess we'll be thar the balance uv our lives. Jist a sup, ma'am, jist a sup," as he passed his cup for the sixth time.

CHAPTER XI

THE YEARS ROLL ON

TIME went on. Five years found Lelia and Sam with two children, Smanthey and Lou. Smanthey, the older, was four years old. I was then nineteen. Age was telling on my father and mother. Their hair was turning gray. My mother had to wear spectacles in order to see how to sew.

I had had such educational advantages as were offered the average mountain boy. The idea of the free school was gaining favor, and hardly a summer passed that we did not have a public school of two or three months. In addition to that we often had special schools. Once a Mr. Hambright came through organizing an arithmetic school and offering to carry his class through the book in ten days. His charges were reasonable, only a dollar a scholar, and I attended.

True to his promise, he took us right on through the book by the time the term of two weeks had expired. In addition to our regular lessons we were taught how to add two columns at the same time, and shown a quick method of multiplying by eleven, also many other short cuts through the arithmetic.

We dwelt but a short time on Common and Decimal fractions, and the pages that we found difficult we were allowed to skip, as they were considered of little importance anyway. When we got into Interest, Percentage, Proportion and Equation, the teacher read the definition of each term and put a few examples on the blackboard and worked them, showing us how it was done; and on the last day of school, we finished the book. We had been through the arithmetic, and in our opinion we knew all about mathematics that was worth knowing.

Besides the arithmetic school and the singing school, we often had a writing school. Writing teachers were numerous, and when they came into the settlement, they usually tacked up papers on the schoolhouse and on trees showing specimens of their art in penmanship, and giving the date when the school would open, the length of term, and the price of tuition.

One such teacher, a Mr. Welch, came into our midst, and Jim and I attended. He taught for two weeks at two dollars a scholar. He did not board at any certain place, but just stayed around with his pupils. Jim soon showed signs of unusual aptitude in writing and attained a high art of penmanship, such as drawing a bird, writing the Lord's prayer on a space the size of a dime, making highly shaded and flourishing capitals, and performing other feats with the pen that only those well schooled in the art of penmanship could accomplish.

Mr. Welch spent considerable time at our house. He was very friendly with Jim and suggested that he qualify himself to teach school. Jim was well pleased with the idea, and Mr. Welch loaned him a Harvey's grammar and a Barnes' History of the United States. He advised Jim to study through the summer and enter a good school for the year in the coming September; and by the following summer, he would then be able to obtain a third grade teacher's certificate. He explained that each county granted three grades of licenses, all of which were good only in the county in which they were issued. The first grade lasted for a period of two years, the second grade one year and the third grade six months. Anyone aspiring to teach, even though with a limited education, could get a third grade certificate. He went on to say that there was also a state license good for life in any county in the state. That was usually granted only to those who were able to show a diploma from a reputable teacher's college.

That summer Jim studied the books which Mr. Welch loaned him and kept up his practice in penmanship. One day my mother was admiring some specimens of Jim's penmanship when she expressed a regret that she was not able to write. My mother could read sufficiently to consult the almanac and read the Bible, but she could not write. Jim said that he would teach her. He gave her something to copy and asked her to follow his instructions. My mother began tracing the letter as he had directed, and it was not long before she was able to write a legible hand.

Jim was much enthused over the idea of going off to school and becoming a school teacher; but when he envisioned himself a teacher, he did not stop there. In his imagination he kept climbing until he was of the great rulers of the land. One day I came across Jim in the woods mauling rails. As we did not particularly need any rails right then, I could not imagine why he was making them, and asked him what he was doing.

"I have just been reading the history of Abraham Lincoln," he said, "and when he was a young man, he made rails. If I ever amount to anything, I want it said that I had in my life split rails."

My father and mother wanted Jim to go off to school, but they were unable to give him any financial assistancc. However, Jim laid claim to several head of cattle and a good horse, all of which he sold for a good price and got together a little money. We had some friends living at Quitman, and he decided to attend the school at that place. Quitman is an inland mountain town, and in it was located Quitman College, a school under the auspices of the Southern Methodist Church.

I drove Jim to Quitman and we found our friends who lived there, and he arranged to board with them at eight dollars a month. There were only two of us now left at home with our parents, Nora and myself. I stayed around home that year assisting my father in the field and in trapping for fur. The mast was good that fall and the indications were that we would have several head of hogs to kill. Our smoke-house was old and decaying and about to fall down. We therefore decided to build a new one. My father and I chopped down trees of the right size, cut them into the proper lengths and snaked them up to where we wanted to build.

Then in order to get the smoke-house erected, we had to give a house raising. My mother had about two quilts ready to quilt and she decided to give a quilting at the same time. We set the time of the house raising and quilting at about a week off, so that we would have plenty of time to arrange for the dinner.

I got on my horse and rode over the settlement, inviting the men and women to come to our house the following Thursday, the men to the house raising and the women to the quilting. That was one way we had of getting along. Every man stood ready to assist his neighbor in doing something that he could not do alone. There were twelve or fifteen men at our house that morning, and every man had brought his wife, daughter, or sister.

We began on the smoke-house by laying two logs about fourteen feet apart. With axes we cut notches in the ends of the logs; then built on up to the height we wanted. There were men on hand who were very proficient in notching the ends and keeping the corners even, and while the process was slow, we had the walls up before night.

On occasions like this people expected something a little more pleasant than hard work. My father had supplied himself with a gallon of whiskey, and when we went in to dinner, he brought out the jug, and every one of the men took a drink. My mother also looked out for her friends. She had obtained two bottles of Garret's snuff; and as the women quilted, they passed around the snuff bottle often and all would take a dip. For a toothbrush each procured a small green stick, preferably black gum, and chewed one end of it until it was soft. They would dip the mop end of the stick into the snuff and put it into their mouths.

When the walls of the house were up and the quilting finished, the people all went home; but most of them came back that night, for it was the custom on such occasions to give either a social or a party. We gave a social for "party" was just another word for dance.

We had all the improved land we could work, but a tract of about five acres was worn out. It was so old and worn that it would not produce corn or wheat, and when land got that way it was fit only for pasturing.

Hence, we abandoned that tract of land, and cleared and fenced new ground. We never thought of fertilizing land except the garden. We were not skilled in any of the arts of agriculture and knew but little about restoring worn-out land to a productive state. The idea of a school to teach people how to farm would have sounded ridiculous to us. We considered that we knew all that there was to be known about farming. My father farmed as did his father, and his father as did his, and so on back for a century. Then why should we go to the trouble of restoring worn-out land anyhow? Land was plentiful and cost little or nothing. Therefore, when our land had aged to a state of unproductiveness, we abandoned it and cleared new ground.

As the spring drew near, it was time to roll logs. During the fall and winter many trees had fallen in the field, and they had to be piled up and burned. We did not cut them up for fire wood, for timber was too plentiful. My father and I went into the field and chopped the logs into toting lengths, and we invited our neighbors in to a log rolling. About fifteen men came bringing handsticks with them. We shoved handsticks under the logs, and the men would take hold of the handsticks—a man at each end of the stick—and pick up the log and tote it to the spot where we decided to make the log heap. When the logs were all gathered into piles, we could then set fire to them and burn them up.

Log rolling offered a mighty good way for men to

compare strength with each other. Two men would be toting together, each lifting up on the same handstick with all his strength, whereupon the weaker would of course "give down." It was then said that the other one had "pulled him down."

Along in the evening, when almost all of the logs had been piled up, about a half dozen of us were standing around with nothing to do. Among us were Ed Honly and John Kiker. Ed had his dog with him, a half-starved brindle cur; and John also had his old spotted dog along. When the dogs faced each other, they began growling and showing their teeth.

"Better call off yer dawg, Honly," said Kiker. "He mout git whupped."

"Wot ye mean 'mout git whupped?' " countered Honly.

"Don't yer see," said Kiker, "they air about to git in a fight?"

"Oh no," replied Honly, "thar won't be no fight. My dawg will jist eat up yourn, that'll be all."

"Yeah, an' by God, mine will be at the eatin'," said Kiker. "My dawg kin whup yourn; ef he cain't, I kin whup his owner."

"What's that?" asked Honly.

"You hyard me," said Kiker. "I don't chaw my terbacker but onc't."

"Wal," said Honly, "ye better tarn it over an' chaw it on tother side, er by God I'll make ye."

The dogs seemed to share the ugly feelings of their

masters and went to it. Kiker's dog was getting the best of the fight, when Honly picked up a stick and struck Kiker's dog a hard blow which ended the dog fight.

"Hol' on thar," said Kiker. "You'll take a whuppin' fer that, er you'll whup me."

"Wal, I'll not take the whuppin'," replied Honly.

The two men clinched. They scuffled around for a while and fell to the ground, with Kiker on top beating Honly in the face. Honly managed to get out from under Kiker, and they rose to their feet. They clinched again, this time falling with Honly on top. Honly's finger happened to get in Kiker's mouth, and Kiker clamped down on it.

"Tarn loose," shouted Honly. "You air bitin' my fanger off."

The two men rose to their feet, and Honly reached for his hat, indicating that he was ready to quit. Kiker also looked as if he were well satisfied.

Of course, all of this was fine sport for the rest of us. It was always fun to see a dog fight, but it was much more exciting to see two men fight. However, when at home that night, I thought over this seriously. These two men had fallen out and fought over absolutely nothing. They had no grievances against each other. Neither had wronged the other in word or act. Exactly like the dogs, they met; one growled at the other, the other growled back and the result was a fight. The men acted literally like dogs; or shall we have it just the other way and say that the dogs were acting like men?

Our planting was soon finished, and it was beautiful to see the corn after it had come up in the hills formed at the intersection of the crossed furrows. In any direction I looked there was a straight row of corn. It was a pleasure to plow and work this cornfield.

One day Sam came to our house and said that Smanthey was sick; he asked my mother to go to his house and see if there was anything she could do for the child. The healthfulness of the Ozark Mountains is not to be questioned. I have seen people well along in years who had never experienced abnormal temperature. We had but little need for a doctor, as our ills were few and we had learned to treat ourselves. We gathered herbs from which we concocted medicines, and we had a remedy for nearly every ailment. Ginseng grew wild on the hillsides, and we gathered it in plentiful quantities. Also there was another herb that we called "Sweet Anise," which was considered very healing. We gathered lobelia, mullein and peach-tree leaves. However, people sometimes got sick, nevertheless, and as everywhere else they sometimes died of illness and not old age.

When my mother reached Lelia's house, she found little Smanthey seriously sick. Other women were sent for, those of age and experience. They gave doses and applications, but the disease seemed to be obstinate and would not yield. After two or three days of uncontrollable fever, it was decided to have a doctor.

The nearest doctor lived fifteen miles from us, and

I went after him. On his arrival the first thing he did was to look at Smanthey's tongue to determine the condition of the liver. He then held her wrist between his thumb and finger and counted the pulse beats. By this he measured the temperature and guessed at the degree of fever, since he had no fever thermometer. The doctor then placed his pill bags over his knees and opened them; with a long-blade knife made especially for physicians, he measured several doses of powders. The doctor stayed over night and went home the next morning.

The neighboring people were very good about coming in to "set up." There was a crowd every night, and the company of course had to stay in the house where the sick child was. There was no other place for them. When her fever was high, they walked on tiptoe and talked in whispers. In spite of the close attention which we all gave her and the frequent visits of the doctor, little Smanthey continued to grow worse and on the afternoon of the eighth day breathed her last.

Some of the men brought in a large, wide board, and took it to the back part of the house, where each end of the board was placed on a chair. The women laid little Smanthey on the board, folded her arms on her breast and placed coins on her eye-lids to hold them closed. They then spread a sheet over her.

People from all parts of the neighborhood came to "set up." They sat around the fireplace until daylight and talked in low tones and with reverence.

Lelia and Sam were grief-stricken and almost prostrated; my father, mother and Nora were all worn out; and it was left with me to arrange for the burying. Granville Bruton went to Mr. McCullough's, and Mr. McCullough and he made the coffin. I rode to the nearest store, which was fifteen miles away, and bought some white goods and a pair of white stockings and some black velvet. The coffin was lined with the velvet and brought to Sam's house. With the white goods the women made the shrouding and put it and the stockings on Smanthey. They then laid the little girl in the coffin and placed it in Granville Bruton's wagon.

When we arrived at the graveyard, several people were there, and some of the men were digging the grave. It was not quite finished, and we had to wait. When the grave was completed it was sundown. They placed the coffin alongside the grave, but owing to the lateness of the hour, it was not opened to allow us a last look. There were no flowers. To no one had ever occurred the thought of bringing flowers. Brother Hooker, the new preacher, was on hand. He offered up a short prayer and spoke only a few words, among them, "Jesus wanted her, and He took her home to Him. She is with Him now."

They lowered the coffin, and the men began shoveling the dirt into the grave. We walked out of the graveyard and started home.

To permit some of the women folk to ride, my father and I walked. The yellow moon came up over the mountain, and it seemed to add loneliness to that sad October night. My father and I, as we walked over the hills, said not a word to each other.

When Jim's school was out, he came home and began looking around for a school to teach. Squire George, a friend of ours who lived up in Greasy Valley, was a school director, and he promised to contract with Jim to teach school in his district provided he could get a license. Jim took the examination and was granted a third grade certificate.

The school opened at the usual time, and I attended. The distance from our house was nine miles, and we stayed at home and rode horseback to and from the school. Jim gave me his books, and I studied and recited from them as he had been taught at school. I was in a class consisting only of myself, and to make up for the time that Jim spent teaching me, I heard some of the younger classes in spelling.

When the term was out, Jim began planning to go back to school. It was agreed that I should work and assist him to get through that year at school; and that he should stay out of school the next year and help me go to school. My father, to assist us, agreed to allow me all I could make with that arrangement in view. After taking Jim back to school, I began looking for some kind of employment at which I could earn some money.

CHAPTER XII

THE GOLD MINE

IT was now about time for cotton to begin opening, and many of the people were preparing to go to the bottoms to pick it. Bud Lively came over to our house and said that the Gee families were going to the Arkansas River to pick cotton. He wanted me to join him in going along with them. I needed employment and decided to go.

There were three families of the Gees, and they went in two wagons which were loaded with bedding and cooking utensils. There was enough room in the wagons for the women and children to ride, but the men and boys walked. When we came to a steep mountain, we got behind the wagons and pushed, as the teams were small and weak. We camped out at night, always stopping near a spring or a creek, so that we might be supplied with water. We built log fires, fried bacon and baked bread, and slept on quilts made down on the ground.

When we got to the bottoms, we obtained employment on a farm and were allowed to occupy two small houses, such as are usually reserved for cotton pickers. Old man Gee and Henry, with their families, took one of the houses; and John Gee took the other one. John took Buddy and me to board with him, charging us twenty-five cents a day each. The two of us picked cotton there for a few days when we met up with Tom Boman, a man whom we knew back in the mountains. He was older than either of us, being something like thirty or thirty-five.

Tom had heard that gold had been discovered near Hot Springs, and he was talking about going over there. One day he met up with a Baptist preacher, who lived on the south side of the river in the direction of Hot Springs. Tom asked him about the gold, and all the preacher knew was what he himself had heard. He said that he had been told that they were digging and were finding gold, and that they were employing a great number of men, and at high wages. That was enough for Tom. He decided to go at once and wanted Bud and me to go with him. As it was almost too early for cotton to be well opened, we decided to go.

We gathered up the few articles of wearing apparel which we did not have on, put them in flour sacks, crossed the Arkansas River, and were on our way. The distance was sixty or seventy miles across the country to Hot Springs. The way was rough and rugged. It was over a mountain, then through a valley, crossing a stream, then over another mountain, through another valley, and so on all the way.

Late in the afternoon of the second day out we stopped at a house and asked if we could stay over night. A grown boy was there and said that his father was not at home, but that it would be agreeable to his mother to have us stay, as they took in travellers. He showed us water and said that we could wash and get ready for supper, while he went down in the field and brought up some corn to feed his stock. As he went to the field, he hallooed and sang as mountain people often do, as they have all out-of-doors and there is no danger of disturbing anybody. And as he hallooed, he yodeled. In a few minutes I saw Tom and Buddy in a serious conversation, and Tom motioned to me.

"Git yer thangs an' le's git out from here," he said.

"What's the matter?" I inquired.

"We air in a den o' thieves," he said. "Didn't ye hyar that holler'n'? That's a sign to other robbers that they's travellers hyar tonight. We'd better git from hyar."

By this time the boy had come back with his feed. Tom stepped up to him and said, "Say here, feller, we've 'sided to not stay all night. So good day."

We all turned and walked off. The fellow seemed so surprised that he did not say a word. He stood with his mouth open, staring at us as we left.

As we walked on, Tom assured us that he knew what that peculiar way of "hollering" meant. He said it was a signal to other robbers, and he thought that Buddy and I ought to be thankful that we had a man with us who was so well experienced in travelling. We walked on until after dark without coming to any more houses. At last we began going up a mountain which was very rough, with large rocks right in the roadway. We walked up the mountain for three or four miles with no sign of a habitation. We came to a bench—that is, a level place on the side of the mountain—and decided to stay there until morning. We lay down on the grass, using our sacks of duds for pillows, and covered ourselves with our coats.

Far in the night, probably a couple of hours before day, Buddy shook me and whispered, "Wake up." He and Tom had been awakened by footsteps coming down the mountain toward us. We sat up and listened until the sound seemed within about thirty feet of us, and judging by the noise made in walking, we took it to be a man.

"Halt thar, an' tell who ye air!" Tom cried out.

His voice was shrill and loud and rang out through the stillness, echoing back from the hills. The sound of the footsteps instantly ceased. We waited a few minutes, listening for some sound, but we could hear none.

Buddy picked up a rock and threw it with all his force up the road. We heard the rock strike against the road and bounce off, but could hear nothing else. We concluded that the mysterious intruder was a fugitive criminal, who hid out in the daytime and travelled at night. I never could understand how he got up the road or to the side of it without our hearing him.

We were aroused now, and gathering up our sacks, moved on. It was way up in the morning when we got over the mountain and came to a house where we could get breakfast. The man there told us that it was fifteen miles back to the last house which we passed. He laughed and said it was a good thing we had come over the mountain after dark, for it was so rough that we would never have made it in the daytime.

We got to Hot Springs that afternoon, tired and weary. Walking along the street, we came to a row of nice chairs on the sidewalk. Supposing that they were put there to sit in, we all took seats, letting our sacks of duds rest on the pavement by our chairs. Bud and Tom drew out their cob pipes and proceeded to fill them preparatory to a good smoke. Tom's feet were tired, and he pulled a chair around in front of him and rested them on it. A young man, bareheaded and wearing a seersucker coat, came up and began explaining that the chairs were reserved for guests of the hotel. We didn't understand much of what he said, but we did gather that he meant for us to move on. We went to Barnes' wagon yard, where there was a small camp house for the accommodation of customers, and got permission from Mr. Barnes to sleep there that night.

The people of Hot Springs seemed to be greatly agitated over the gold discovery. Capitalists from every part of the United States and from Europe were there investigating the gold report. Several different omnibuses were making daily round trips to Bear City and Silver City, the principal points of interest; but the thought of walking did not bother us in the least.

We headed for the gold fields. When we came to Ouachita River, we pulled off our shoes, rolled up our pants legs, and waded across. About ten miles out, we stopped at a small store to rest. Presently we heard the blast of a bugle. A man sprang from a bench on which he had been lounging and ran out into the lot, where he quickly harnessed a span of horses, driving them around in front of the store. An omnibus came up loaded with people and drawn by a couple of horses, panting and in a lather of sweat. The man with great speed removed the horses from the bus and hitched the fresh ones in. The driver popped his whip and they were off.

As we went on, we found great excitement among the natives. Farmers had abandoned their crops and had gone into the mountains to prospect for gold. We noticed that several of them had actually turned their stock into their fields to eat up the matured crops. We stopped at a house and asked to get dinner. While we were waiting for the dinner to be prepared, a wagon drove up with four or five men in it. All of the women and children went out to meet them.

"Come kiss me, Sallie, come kiss me quick," an old man said to an old woman, as he crawled out of the wagon. "By gosh, we air rich now!"

He then drew from his pockets some rocks about the size of hen eggs, and went on, "Looky hyar! Thar's gold up in themar hills! We've got the purtiest claim inywhar in the mountain."

They all gazed at the rocks, and the girls and children danced around with glee. There seemed to be no chance of our getting dinner at all soon, so we shouldered our duds and were again on our way.

The road was full of men going to and coming from the mines. We met many who looked disappointed and dejected. We were stopped by a man wanting a match. He was a middle-aged man, carrying a bundle tied up in a red bandana handkerchief suspended from a stick which he carried on his shoulder. Tom asked him the distance to the gold diggings.

"T'ey's not any coldt," he said. "T'ey toldt you a lie—a cot tam lie. You are a tam fool if you go up t'ere!"

"Wal, mister," said Tom, "we want work. Do you thank they will give us work?"

"Tey gif you not'ing," he said. "T'ey got no work. T'ey got no coldt. It's all a cot tam lie!" Saying this, he walked on.

We went on to the places of activity. There were refreshment stands, small stores and boarding houses which had recently sprung up here and there. Diggings in different localities were under way, and we saw a smelter in operation. It seemed that results had been anything but satisfactory, and we were unable to meet any encouragement as to employment of any kind anywhere.

We came upon a couple of men frying strips of bacon by running the sharpened point of a stick through them and holding them over a fire. They boiled their coffee in an oyster can. They told us that they were from Texas and had been attracted there by reports that there was plenty of work. Tom began telling them how we happened to come. Tom, footsore, tired, broke and mad, felt just like the rest of us. He carried a big hickory stick which he used as a walking stick.

"I jist wush I could see that goddam Babtis' preacher that tole me that lie," he said, as he shook his stick at the skies. "I'll whup him so bad his wife wouldn't know 'im when she seed 'im. I'll know 'im! I'll know 'im ef ever I see 'im, an' this is the way I'll do 'im." As he said this, he gave his stick a swing, as if he were hitting a baseball, and struck with such force that it turned him around twice.

I do not think that the diggings ever proved profitable, and they were all abandoned. But I regret to think how those mountain farmers, who had given up their crops, expecting riches within an arm's reach, managed to get through another year.

This effort toward gold mining was probably a revival of an interest that was created three-quarters of a century previous. It is said that a little after the beginning of the nineteenth century an expedition of gold hunters was directed to this section by friendly Indians. It is claimed that they dug and found ore rich with gold, but were set upon by a tribe of hostile Indians and were forced to flee and abandon the mines. At about that time the present site of the city of Hot Springs was a wilderness. It was a hollow containing a great number of springs, some of which were steaming hot. The place was visited only by savages.

With no prospect whatever of getting any kind of honest work, we hastily decided to go back across the mountains to the river and begin picking cotton where we left off. That we might be well rested for the trip, we engaged a room for the night.

Somebody told us there was going to be a free show at a refreshment stand near by, and after supper we went to it. The operators of the stand had erected a platform and were giving a free entertainment to attract patronage. One feature that greatly impressed me was "The Arkansas Traveller." It was the first time that I had ever seen that world-famous tune and dialogue played. "The Arkansas Traveller" originated in the southeastern part of the state, near the Louisiana state line. From what I have read and heard, the origin of this well-known tune and dialogue was as follows:

There lived on the Mississippi River Colonel

Faulkner, a cotton planter. One day he was riding through the swamps and got lost. Finally he came to an old man's place, and it so happened that the old man and Colonel Faulkner were acquainted. The former was sitting on a barrel in front of the door, playing the course part of a tune on a fiddle. He was very witty, and when Colonel Faulkner made some inquiries about the roads, the old man in jest gave him some simple answers. Colonel Faulkner caught the idea from this, and originated the dialogue of "The Arkansas Traveller." Colonel Faulkner was a violinist, and on his trips to New Orleans he would play and recite "The Arkansas Traveller." From this beginning the skit quickly swept around the world, and it was played and acted on stages, in school entertainments, and in many other places of amusement.

It takes two properly to play the Arkansas Traveller, the traveller and the squatter. The scene shows the squatter seated on a barrel, sawing the course part of the tune on an old fiddle. The traveller appears and the dialogue begins:

TRAVELLER—Hello!

SQUATTER—Hello yourself!

T.—Can you tell me where this road goes?

S.—It's never moved a step since I been here.

T.—How long have you been living here?

S.—Do you see that knot on that tree? Wal, it was thar when I come here and it's thar yit.

T.—Have you got any spirits?

S.—Plenty of 'em. Sal saw one down by the ole holler gum t'other night an' it like to skeered her to death.

T.—I don't mean that kind of spirits. I am cold and want some liquor. Have you got any liquor?

S.—Had some yistidy an' old Boss he got in an' licked outen the pot.

T.—You still do not understand. I don't mean pot-likker. Have you got any whiskey? I am wet and want some whiskey?

S.—Oh, whiskey! Yes, I had some, but Dick, the damn skulkin' skunk, he drunk it all up.

T.—I am hungry and want something to eat. Have you anything to eat?

S.—Hain't a bite in the house. Not a mouthful of meat nor a dust of meal.

T.—Well, can't you feed my horse?

S.—Hain't got nothing to feed 'im on.

T.—How far is it to the next house?

S.—Don't know, stranger; I hain't never measured it.

T.—Do you know who lives here?

S.—I do.

T.—Then what might be your name?

S.—It might be Jim and it might be John; but it likes a damn sight of either.

T.—Well, if you will let me sleep in your house, I will tie my horse to that tree and do without anything to eat.

S.—The house leaks. Jist one dry place in it, an' me an' Sal has to sleep in that. An' you can't tie your horse to that tree, caze it will shake all the 'simmons off. Ole woman 'lows to make beer outen them.

T.—Why don't you cover your house?

S.—It's been rainin'.

T.—Why don't you cover it when it's not raining?

S.—Caze it don't leak then.

T.—I am puzzled to see how you make a living here. How do you do here anyhow?

S.—Purty well, thank you; how do you do yourself?

T.—Why don't you play the balance of that tune?

S.—Hain't no balance to it.

T.—Yes, there is another part to that tune.

S.—Stranger, can you play the fiddle?

T.—I can saw a little.

S.—Wal, if I was goin' to kill a fiddler, I would never shoot at you; but you can take the fiddle and try. (The stranger takes the violin and plays all of the tune. The squatter leaps to his feet and begins dancing.)

S.—Stranger, take a half a dozen churs an' sot down. Sal, stir yourself round like a six-mule team in a mud hole an' git me an' this gentleman some supper. Go out to the pond whar I killt that buck this mornin' an' cut some of the choicest slices an' fotch an' cook it. Til, drive old Boss outen the bread tray and climb up in the loft an' git that rag that's got some sugar tied up in it. Dick, take the gentleman's hoss around under the shed, an' give him some fodder an' corn, all he can eat.

Tom, look under the head of the bed an' git that old brown jug an' bring this gentleman some whiskey. Play on the fine part of that tune, stranger.

TIL.—Dad, thar ain't enough knives to sot the table with.

S.—Whar's big butch, little butch, ole case, cob-handle, Granny's knife and the one I handled yistidy? That's 'nuff to sot any man's table. Damme, stranger, you can stay as long as you want to an' I'll give you plenty to eat an' drink. Will you take coffee?

T.—Yes, sir.

S.—I'll be hanged if you do. We ain't got none, but jist keep on playin' stranger.

T. (after three hours of fiddling).—Can you tell me about the road I will get out of here tomorrow?

S.—Tomorrow! Stranger, you won't git out of these diggin's for six weeks. But when it gits so you can go, you see that big slew over thar? Wal, you haf to crost that, then you take the big road up the bank, an' in about a mile you will come to a two acre corn patch. The corn's mitely in weeds, but you needn't mind that, jist ride on. In about a mile and a half, you'll come to the damndest swamp you ever seen. It's boggy enough to mire a saddle blanket. Thar's a fust rate road about six feet under thar. Wal, about a mile from thar, you will come to whar's two roads. Take the right hand an' go it for about a mile an' you will see it run out. Then come back an' take the left han', an' when you go it about two miles, you will come to whar they ain't no road. Then you will think yourself mighty lucky if you can git back here whar you can play that tune an' stay here as long as you want to.

After the end of "The Arkansas Traveller" we went back to our room, as we had to get an early start the next morning. We made our way then across the hills back to the cotton farms, where I spent the fall in picking cotton. When the weather became too unfavorable for profitable cotton picking, I went home, taking with me fairly good wages for that fall. I had learned that fur was bringing a good price, and I planned to trap through the winter.

CHAPTER XIII

THE PANTHER

THERE were several fur-bearing animals in our locality, such as the raccoon, the mink, the skunk and the beaver. I bought a lot of new traps and put in the winter trapping. As beaver brought a better price than anything else, I gave close attention to catching this animal. I followed the creek bank, and wherever I saw signs where beavers had been sliding in and out of the water, I set a trap. First I drove a stick in the water and fastened the end of the trap chain to the bottom of it. Then I set the trap in the beaver trail just under the water. When the beaver was caught in the trap it began swimming, trying to get away; and of course it necessarily had to go around in a circle which wound the chain around the stick. The beaver kept going round and round, until its head was drawn under the water and it drowned. Unless I contrived to drown the beaver, it would gnaw its own foot off and make its escape.

One morning I was making the rounds of the traps, several of which I had set along the creek, and as I followed the water's edge, I came to a bend in the course of the creek. As I had no traps set in the bend, I decided to cut across to a point where there was a trap, thereby eliminating the bend and saving time. To do this, I had to go through a canebrake, a place where the cane was tall and thick. I was following a kind of cow trail, when I came to where a log lay across the path. I noticed a rabbit lying on the log, and on examining it I saw that it had just been killed. This aroused my curiosity, and I stood for a few minutes turning the rabbit over and wondering what could have killed it and how it happened there.

I shouldered my gun and started to go, and as I did so, I saw a couple of eyes peering at me just over the forks of the log and about fifteen feet from where I stood. The first thing that came to my mind was that it was a wolf. I could not see the animal's head, but just the two eyes staring at me. Whatever it was I decided to kill it. My gun was a muzzle-loading rifle and shot only once, but without any fear, I aimed between the eyes and fired. Then, with the instinct of the trained hunter, I reloaded my gun before moving from my tracks. I walked up to the forks of the log and saw that my aim had been true and I had killed the creature. It was a large panther.

The panther was the most dreaded and the most hated of all the wild animals with which we had to contend. I well remember the first time I ever saw a live panther. One day, when I was about ten years old, I had been over the mountain visiting the Stanley boys. When on my way home about sundown, I saw something coming through the woods in my direction, which at first resembled a large gangling dog. It was of a brownish-yellow color and had a long tail and a head shaped like that of a cat. I stood still with fear, my eyes riveted on the beast; but before it reached me, it sprang up a tree, climbing the way a man would except with greater speed and activity. I turned to run back down the mountain, when I heard the sound of dogs barking. I stood for a minute and soon saw a pack of hounds approaching, with a crowd of five men following on horseback. Breathlessly I related to the men what I had seen, and they soon located and killed the panther.

The men took me home, and after supper they and my parents sat around the fireplace and talked for several hours, the conversation being about panthers, while we children listened.

"Onc't up on Wild Cat Slough," said Lee Sparks, "the people war at a meetin' an' a painter war hid under a banch, an' when they all knelt down to pray, the painter grabbed a baby outen a womurn's arms an' run out at the door, an' they never did ketch it nor find the baby."

"Ole Crosseye Larkin," said Henry Tanner, "say when he war a boy he war a ridin' along one day and a painter jumped outen a tree and missed him and lit on the hoss' back jist behine the saddle, and hit scared the hoss and it run jist lak a streak o' greased lightenin' and fer a mile they went with the painter a-settin' up behine ole Crosseye and the hoss a-goin' lak hell a beatin' tan bark till they got to a field and the painter jumped off."

For several hours I listened to the terrible deeds of the panther, and the narrow escapes that people had had from it, until I was as badly scared as if I had been listening to as many ghost stories. However, the panther was no phantom. Too often it had furnished physical evidence of its existence, and we regarded it as a grim reality.

Originally panthers could be found anywhere in America, from the Hudson Bay to Patagonia, and were known in different localities by different names, as cougar, puma, mountain lion and panther. In Arkansas it was called panther, and the mountain people pronounce the word "painter." In the early days it lived in every section of the state and lingered in the northern hills long after it had been annihilated in the lowlands. Equally as dangerous and deadly as the lion or the tiger, it is by far the most ferocious beast in North America, and excepting the jaguar of South America, it is the most deadly animal on the Western Hemisphere.

Here in some sections of the Ozarks, among the crags and cliffs, the panther, as do even yet the bear, the wolf and the wildcat, found life particularly inviting, since he could make his home in the thickets and caves miles distant from any human habitation and where the isolation and inaccessibility offered him protection.

Many were the nights when I would be in our own yard and hear the squall of the panther, presumably as he was on his mission of conquest. The animal is sneaking, treacherous and cowardly; yet it has been known to fight to the death when escape would have been easy. Its padded feet, its highly developed sense of seeing, hearing and smelling enable it to surprise its victim. A favorite way it has of capturing its prey is to secrete itself on a limb that projects out over the roadway, and when anything passes under, to spring down upon it. In this way it killed sheep, goats, pigs, calves, and sometimes human beings. It is claimed that the panther does not kill every time simply because it is hungry, but often kills only for the gratification of killing.

When I think of the painter, I am always reminded of an incident that occurred in our family before I was born, and of which I have often been told. When Jim was a young baby, my father went away from home one morning and for some cause was unable to get back that night. He had taken the gun with him, as was the custom when men made any kind of a trip. There was one dog on the place, Tige, a very large and strong animal.

Late in the night, somewhat after midnight, Tige began barking and growling as if something or somebody where approaching. The dog seemed to be greatly agitated, and he barked and growled in such a way that my mother knew he was defying something which was right upon him. In a short while, she could tell by the noise, the dog was engaged in a combat. She thought that it probably was a wolf or perhaps another dog, and she felt that Tige would be able to defend the premises. After fighting had continued a short time, it seemed as if the intruder had left, for the dog quieted down. But in a little while she could tell by the actions of the dog that the thing had reappeared, and soon again Tige was in a desperate struggle with something.

My mother became alarmed, and she had Lelia see to it that the door was fastened and well propped. Lelia was six years old, Nora was two, and Jim, the baby, was only five days old. My mother had not been out of bed since he was born, so everyone in the house was really helpless.

After fighting for a while, for the second time the thing seemed to have retreated, for the dog again quieted down. But not for long. Soon again the dog was apparently in a desperate struggle. In a few minutes the thing seemed to have freed itself from the dog, and it sprang up a tree which stood near the house, for my mother heard it light on top of the house as it leaped from the tree to the roof.

My mother was very much frightened, but she said nothing to Lelia. She lay, listening to the thing as it walked over the roof, seemingly in search of an opening through which it could enter. Suddenly, pieces of clay, of which the chimney was made, began falling into the fireplace. The cold fact dawned upon my mother that the creature was actually coming down the chimney. She leaped out of the bed and with a case knife ripped open a straw bed and began piling the straw into the fireplace where a small fire was burning. The straw quickly ignited, and the blaze shot up through the chimney. The beast gave a fearful squall, and she heard it as it sprang from the roof to the ground. It went away and did not return. They smelt scorched hair, which would indicate that it actually had been in the chimney.

When my father returned the next morning, they told him about it, and he said that it was a painter and that it was after the baby. He went out to look for Tige, and after searching for some time, found him way up under the house. The dog could hardly move. My father dragged him out and found that he was badly lacerated and torn, and both his eyes had been put out. Good old Tige! He was tenderly cared for as long as he lived.

Another incident that I will always remember happened in our county. Ben Coats lived in an isolated section, far out of hearing and sight of any neighbors. He lived in a one-room house with his wife and a two-year old baby. There were no windows and only one door. As it was warm weather, they had drawn the bed out in the middle of the floor so that they might take advantage of the air coming in at the door. Mr. Coats was sleeping on the inner side of the bed, away from the door. Mrs. Coats slept next to the door, with the baby sleeping in front of her on the outer edge of the bed, its head resting on her arm.

Deep in the night the mother felt the baby slipping, as if it were falling off the bed, and she awoke. As she did so, the baby screamed, and she saw something run out through the door. Mr. and Mrs. Coats jumped out of the bed and ran out into the yard. It was dark, and they could not see anything; but they could hear the spasmodic screams of the baby as it was carried hastily through the bushes.

Both, hysterically terrified, ran on foot two miles to the nearest neighbor and gave the alarm. Here two men saddled horses and rode in different directions, rousing the people. When my father and I heard the news, we quickly saddled horses and rode to the Coats' home. When we got there, several men had arrived and the dogs were on the trail. We followed the dogs, and the trail led over a hill, up the bed of a dry creek, and on up the side of a hill to a place where there was a large rock with the ground extending about eight feet up under the rock. The dogs discovered a hole leading under the rock, between the rock and the ground. This hole was about the size of the opened end of a flour barrel, or large enough for a good sized man to crawl through.

Two men carefully shoved the barrel ends of their guns into the hole, while a third man, holding a lighted piece of pine out in front of him, poked his head inside, his chin resting on the two gun barrels. With the torch he surveyed the inside. The passageway led straight for about six feet, and then made a turn. The opening was about two feet across, and a man could not get through without crawling. Nothing could be seen beyond where the passage turned.

It now was a question as to how to proceed. It would not do to put the dogs in the hole, for the beast would tear them to pieces. It would be equally fatal for a man to enter the cave. In the meantime, the men felled a tree in front of the cave and about fifteen feet from it, on which guns were rested to guard the mouth so that the animal would have no chance to escape.

The news of this occurrence spread rapidly. People came from all over the country, and some who came lived as far as fifty miles away. The next day there were at least two hundred people on the ground. Two old experienced hunters who knew well the ways of the painter, took charge. Watch was kept all day and all night.

Their plan was to keep watch on the mouth of the cave until thirst and starvation drove the painter out, for painter we took it to be. They said that a beast of prey would take its chances on fighting its way to liberty rather than starve. They began selecting men to guard the cave! Twenty-four men, two at a time, to keep watch for two hours. They preferred experienced men, those who had in some way encountered the painter; and because I had killed a painter alone, I was among those selected.

Our duties were to lie behind the log, with our shotguns resting on it and trained on the hole under the rock—and to shoot when the painter appeared. We were instructed not to expect the painter to try to sneak out. They said that it would be sure to come out, and when it did come, it would shoot out of the hole like a rifle ball and would destroy anything that stood in its way. They selected, among the many guns, four of the best double-barrel shotguns that were there, and these were heavily loaded with buckshot. We were each instructed to hold a gun trained on the cave and to keep another gun lying by our side, as there might be more than one painter. We lay for two hours with guns trained on the cave, and did not take our eyes off the mouth of the cave for an instant. The men, in relieving us, would first get into position and pick up the guns that were lying by our sides, and get them trained on the cave before we removed our guns. In that way there was not a fraction of a second that the cave was not watched. During the night other men kept pine torches going which lighted up the front of the cave.

The crowd was requested to move back from the cave so that silence could be better maintained around the entrance. Hence the space was cleared of all except those on duty, those who had to keep watch and those who kept up the fires at night. The crowd moved about a quarter of a mile down in a hollow accessible for horses and wagons. There were something like three or four hundred people on the ground all of the time. Many of them brought provisions and camped, as the weather was warm and dry.

The greatest desire of all my life was that I might be on duty when the painter came out. Mr. Battenfield, a middle aged man, was my watch partner. Early on the morning of the fourth day, when I had been on duty for about fifteen minutes, and when it was strong daylight, but just before sun-up, I saw something's nose appear just over the lower rim of the cave. Battenfield nudged me, and I nudged back, indicating that we had both seen it. I placed my finger on the trigger, with both hammers of the gun pulled back. I was almost breathless, and my heart jumped with great expectancy. I thought it would be a century before the creature came out. Then, without any further warning, and with a hideous squall that rent the early morning air, and with the terrific force of a cyclone, the beast sprang through the hole and into the air. Four muffled shots rang out, and the painter turned somersault and lit on its back with its head towards the cave. It was dead, its body having been perforated with bullets from head to tail.

The people in the camps were aroused by the report of the guns and came running up to the cave. When they saw the painter, children cried, women wrung their hands, and men gesticulated and talked excitedly. They would not permit Mrs. Coats to view the painter. Mr. Coats saw it, but became so hysterical that he had to be led away.

The cave was then explored. The dogs were put through first, as it might be that there was another painter inside. The dogs came out unhurt, and then several of the men went into the cave. They lighted their way with pine torches and crawled through the passageway which, after it made a turn, entered into a larger excavation about eight feet by ten, and about four feet high. Here they found several bones, but could not tell much about them. However, they did find the fragments of a little dress, the cloth of which was the same as that which the Coats baby was wearing.

It is said that painters locate babies by scenting the milk from the mother's breast. About a year after Lelia and Sam were married, Sam had to be away from home a few days, and I went with my father to bring Lelia and her young baby home with us until Sam's return. On our way back we were passing through a three-mile stretch of dense woods at about dark, when we heard a terrible squall in the thickets resembling somewhat the outcry of a woman in great distress, a frightful scream dying away in a gurgling sound.

"What was that, Pa?" Lelia asked.

My father said nothing but whipped up his horses. Soon again we heard the fearful cry and this time a little closer than before. Again Lelia asked what it was, but my father, as before, only whipped and urged on his horses. For the third time the dreadful noise was heard. Lelia was alarmed and demanded of my father what he thought of it. My father lashed his horses and soon gained the opening of our field. Then he turned to Lelia and said, "That was a painter, and it was after the baby."

CHAPTER XIV

OTHER ANIMALS

HAD we been able to eliminate the painter from our midst we still would not have felt safe in the woods alone and unarmed. Other ferocious beasts denned and roamed about us, among which were the wolf, the wildcat and the bear. However, they were not considered dangerous like the painter, and it was seldom that man was aggressively attacked by any of them. Probably one explanation of this is that the mountains abounded plentifully in smaller game on which they could more easily prey. Then, too, these vicious beasts, like the painter, had been very unsuccessful in their attacks upon man. These attacks had so often resulted in destruction that the surviving beasts had long since learned instinctively to flee at the approach of man.

Our firearms were rude and primitive; nevertheless, such as they were, we learned to use them effectively. Our guns were muzzle loading, and having no shells or cartridges, we bought our lead, shot, powder and caps separately. The rifle shot but once, and in loading it, I first measured and poured down the required amount of powder, then rammed down a bullet wrapped in a piece of cloth and beat it with the gunstick. After this, I pulled back the hammer and placed a cap on the tube, and the gun was ready to fire. In loading the shotgun, I poured in the powder as in the case of the rifle, then rammed down some paper wadding and then poured in the load of shot. Then I rammed down some more paper wadding and beat it only tight enough to hold the shot in. After placing the cap on, it was ready to shoot.

This operation of loading a gun required some little time, but I have seen men so well practiced that it took only a few seconds to load one. As the rifle shot only once and as it took some time to reload, it was always important that we shoot true to aim. If we did not, our game would have a chance to escape; in an encounter with a dangerous beast bad marksmanship was calculated to result in serious consequences. Hence when we drew bead on anything, it usually meant destruction of the thing aimed at.

The mountain man, wherever he goes, usually takes his gun with him. When he went around the field, across the hill to a neighbor's, to mill or to town, he had his long-barrel gun with him. Thus armed, he was not only prepared to protect himself against any wild beast that might see fit to dispute the right of way, but always had the chance of shooting game, which was a favorite dish. Even men at their work always kept on the lookout for game that they could kill.

The wild animals which roamed our woods were not only dreaded as a menace to ourselves, but were destructive to our fowls and small domestic animals. The wildcat stole our geese, ducks, chickens and young pigs. This animal, also called the catamount and the bob cat, is about half the size of the painter, and while not so powerful, it could easily kill a man. It is of various colors: yellow, gray, reddish, and I have seen some that were white. Owing to its short, thick tail, if seen on the ground at a distance, one might mistake it for a medium-sized dog. It is not a house-cat gone wild, nor is it a kind of wild house-cat. There seems to be no connection between the species. It dens in caves, hollow logs and hollow trees. Like the painter, it is a beast of prey and depends on capturing its own food.

One night I heard a disturbance among the geese, and calling my dog, I ran out quickly to catch the cause of the trouble, thinking it was a fox. The dog was young and had always conquered everything it had ever attacked. It located the varmint in the corner of the fence and at once attacked. I could tell that the wild animal was putting up a fight, for the dog soon began crying as if he were badly hurt and came running back to me. It was dark, but I could see something as it ran up a tree that stood nearby. I called to my father, and he came and brought a gun. I took a torch and moved it up and down and around until my father caught sight of the thing's eyes. By shining its eyes, he fired at it and killed it. It was a white wildcat.

Another night, I was out hunting with Tom Chaney for such game as rabbits, 'possums and 'coons. The dogs treed several rabbits, and we caught them by twisting them out of hollow trees. We cut a hickory switch, split the little end of it, and ran the switch up the hollow of the tree until we felt the rabbit. Then we began twisting and the hair of the rabbit would get in the split of the stick; and as we continued to twist, the rabbit's skin would twist around the switch sufficiently to hold it, and we would pull the rabbit down far enough to reach it with our hands.

After hunting around for a while, the dogs treed something in a hollow stump. The opening into the hollow was at the ground, and Tom began feeling around the hollow with his switch for the rabbit. It seemed that the hollow was large and extended down under the ground. Tom felt around a little and remarked that he had found it, but that it was not close enough to reach with his hand. He had twisted a minute or two, when something sprang out of the stump and on to Tom's head and back. Here the dogs interfered, and the thing left Tom, jumped on one of the dogs, and was then off into the woods.

It all happened so suddenly and so quickly that we could not realize what was going on or what the animal was. I was holding a torch in my hand, and I saw that Tom was bleeding badly. We went home, where we discovered that his neck and the side of his face were badly gashed. Also, the dog that the thing attacked was badly cut on the side. The light was dim, but from the best I could make out, it must have been a wildcat.

The most hated animal in our midst was the timber wolf. These beasts were numerous, and in packs or in pairs prowled about, making the nights dreadful by their hideous howls. The howl of a wolf starts off with a muffled yelping and ends with a long wailing coarse howl, like that of a dog. The howling of a pack of wolves, however, is easily distinguished from the barking of dogs.

The wolves committed great depredations among our sheep, calves, pigs and goats. We had to see to it that our sheep came home every night, for unless they did, the wolves were certain to get them. I have known wolves to come up close enough to the yard gate for us to hear the snapping of their teeth, and we could disperse them only by firing into them. Our dogs would not attack a wolf, but they would bark at his approach, thereby giving us warning; and we would lose no time in bringing the gun into play. In a fight the dog is really no match for the wolf. Armed as he is with powerful jaws and long teeth, the wolf has been known to kill a dog at one snap. Wolves have always retreated when dogs were on their trail, for experience has taught them that men with guns are usually keeping up with the dogs.

Wolves are carniverous and will eat any kind of meat in any kind of condition. They are great scavengers and would readily eat up our animals that died and were hauled off. They are sneaking and cowardly, but will sometimes put on a bold front. I remember one night, when I was on a fishing trip with a crowd. There were about six of us, and we did not take any dogs, as we wanted to fish. We took with us quite a lot of cornbread and grease and a frying pan. We struck camp on the banks of a creek, and since the fishing was good, we caught a great many fish that evening. Some of the boys killed a couple of squirrels, and they were thrown near the camp fire. That night we ate all the fried fish and corn bread we could hold.

We sat around the camp fire and swapped yarns until late in the night. When we got sleepy, we lay on the ground, and as one of the boys remarked, we used the stars for "kiver." Some time before day I was aroused by a gun fire right at me. We all jumped up and saw a big wolf lying before us dead. Bill Ward, one of the boys, said that he was awakened by a noise, and when he opened his eyes, he saw by the moonlight a wolf standing right amongst us, chomping on one of the squirrels. Bill's hand was resting on his six shooter, and he carefully raised the gun and fired at close range.

The next morning Bill proceeded to scalp the wolf. I asked him why he was doing it, and he said that the scalp was worth two dollars and a half. Since the wolves had been so destructive, the county was offering a reward for the killing of them. This reward was afterwards increased to five dollars, which had a lot to do in thinning them out.

It is not likely that wolves will attack people; yet a pack of hungry wolves will not hesitate to attack anything, and I never did consider wolves very pleasant company. When I chanced to see one, it was likely to be on the run. If circumstances did not warrant the wolf's running, I ran myself.

One cold winter evening I was riding across the mountains on my way home, when I saw and shot a young deer. I threw the fawn across the horse behind the saddle and tied it on. It was nearly dark, and I had several miles to go over a rough and rocky trailway. As I rode, blood dripped from the fawn's wounds.

A little after dark I discovered that the wolves were on my trail. I spurred up my horse, as I had no desire to be overtaken by a pack of hungry wolves. I could tell by the howling that they were gaining on me, and within another half mile they had overtaken me. I could get a glimpse of them as they skulked in the bushes near by and could hear them snap their powerful jaws, in the way a wolf does when it is hungry. One large wolf snapped at my horse's foot. My first impulse was to shoot, but after thinking a little, I decided that that would not be the best thing to do.

My gun was a rifle and shot but once. I would have been certain to kill one wolf, but that would not stop the pack, and it would be difficult to reload while riding the horse. So that I might quickly satisfy the wolves, I untied the strings holding the fawn, and let the carcass fall to the ground; and while this occupied their attention, I hurried on over the trail. The wolves, maddened by hunger and cold, soon devoured the deer; and before reaching home, I could hear their hideous howling and knew that they were on my trail again. But I gained the opening ahead of them, and they did not come any further.

Arkansas is known as "The Bear State." It gained this name owing to the great number of black bears which roamed the woods in the early days. Not only were they numerous in the mountains, but in the swamp lands as well. Great numbers of bear lived in the mountains of the Ozarks, where we lived, and they usually lived in caves. We did not fear the bear, however, as we did the painter. The bear is not likely to attack anyone, unless it is molested or angered.

The bear is omniverous and stole many of our pigs, but he was most destructive when he got in our cornfield. He loved roastin' ears, and he was not satisfied with only two or three, but tore down several rows when he made a raid. There were lots of wild bees in our section, and they built their homes in the hollow of trees, high up. It was a favorite sport of the bear to climb the bee tree and rob the bees of their honey, for they were fond of sweets.

We hunted the bear not only for the depredations he committed, but because we liked bear meat. The meat of the bear is dark, but it tastes very good. When anyone killed a bear, it was divided around among the neighbors, and everybody had bear meat for a day or two.

In hunting the bear we had to have specially trained dogs. Not only can the bear bite and scratch with destructive effect, but it can slap with its paw with a force equal to the kick of a mule. Also it crushes its opponents to death by hugging when in a close-up fight.

One summer, when I was about fifteen years old, some animal was tearing down and destroying our corn, and we could tell by the tracks that it was a bear. The bear makes a track almost similar to that of a man. It is so nearly like it that, at first glance, it reminds one of the footprint of a man with very large toes.

Jim Sawyers had two well-trained bear dogs, and we got Jim to help us trail the bear. Uncle Tommie Wilson had two pups that he wanted to train for bear hunting, and he went with us, taking his pups so that they might have the advantage of the experience.

One morning at about daylight we took the dogs to the cornfield, and they were soon hot on the trail. They overtook Bruin within about three miles and brought him to bay. We came up within good shooting distance and stood watching the fight. It was interesting to see how the dogs were able to fight the bear and still take care of themselves. One of them would run up, snap at the bear, and jump back. As the bear slapped at this one, the other dog would run up on the other side, and snap and jump back. The dogs were on the job every second of the time, and allowed the bear no time to slap them with his paw or hug them in a close-up. The pups at first were satisfied to stay at a safe distance and make a fuss by barking savagely. But one of them got a little too brave and ventured up within reach of the bear. The bear caught him off guard and slapped him, killing him at once. Uncle Tommie, partly out of revenge, and partly in fear that the other dog would get killed, fired and killed the bear.

The hunter, in addition to carrying a true shooting gun, was always armed with a very strong knife. In fact, every man and boy carried a knife at all times. About the first thing that a boy wanted his father to buy him was a pocket knife, and when he got it, it was more than likely to be a Barlow. That was considered the cheapest knife on the market and suitable for little boys. As we grew up, we all procured good strong pocket knives, and I still feel at a loss without a knife.

My father owned a mighty good knife. The handle was made out of a deer's foot, and the blade was nearly nine inches long. It was over an inch wide near the rivet, and the end tapered to a very fine point. It lay loose in the handle and could be opened with one hand, simply by slinging it. When open, however, the blade was rigid and could not be closed without shoving in on a spring. This knife was probably a form of the bowie knife. It differed in that the bowie knife was two-edged. The knife which my father had was known as the Arkansas Toothpick and had often been used with destructive results in the early days of Arkansas by men fighting with each other. The reputation of the state suffered great injury by the notoriety occasioned by the use of this weapon.

My father could use his famous knife with great dexterity. One day when I was very small my father was in the woods and came upon a couple of very young bears. He looked around, and not seeing the mother bear, picked up the cubs and started home with one under each arm. He had not gone far when he heard the old bear coming tearing through the bushes after him. He dropped the cubs and leveled his rifle, and waiting until the bear was within shooting distance, he fired. The ball took effect in the shoulder, but it did not stop or turn the bear. My father dropped the gun and drew from his pouch the knife. Maddened by the pain of the rifle ball, the bear came with an increased fury, and just before reaching my father, reared up intent on tearing him to pieces. My father, young and active, quickly jumped out of the way, and the bear lunged forward on all fours. Before it could turn, my father drove the dagger to the hilt in a vital place.

Despite the fact that he had fought with a bear single-handed and overcome him, my father did not feel that he had anything to boast of. He had killed a bear, and that was no news for the settlement. Had the bear killed my father, then that would have been news.

Smaller game abounded. Deer could often be seen in herds. I have seen whole flocks of turkeys when riding through the woods. I remember one summer the wild turkeys were so destructive to our peas that we had to go to the pea patch two or three times a day and shoot into them. Also the squirrels were very destructive to our maturing corn. We often went around the field of a morning and shot them as they were eating the corn. So plentiful was such game as deer, turkeys and squirrels that a great many shiftless people were able to supply their tables at all times of the year with such meat.

CHAPTER XV

THE DEBATING SOCIETY

I CLEARED some money that winter trapping. When spring came, Sam rented a small place about a day's ride south of us, where the people scratched around on the hillsides and in the creek bottoms, and raised a little cotton. Sam wanted to move down there and raise cotton that year, in order to make a little money, and as I would not be needed at home I arranged to join him. He had two mules, and I owned a horse. We moved to a place he had rented, and put in nearly all of the land in cotton, as we wanted it to be a cash crop.

Along in the spring, a man came through organizing an order called the Brothers of Freedom. Sam and I joined, as did almost every other farmer. We held our meetings in the schoolhouse and met every Saturday afternoon. While the object of the association, as well as I can remember, was to promote the welfare and best interests of the farming people, I do not recall that any of us ever discussed any subject connected with better farming. We said nothing that would give any enlightenment on such subjects as how to reclaim worn-out land, or how to cultivate the land so as to obtain a better yield of crops, or how to care for the live stock to the best advantage. We were supposed to know all about such things already.

It would seem that our particular lodge developed into an order, the object of which was to oppose the town people, especially the merchant. The merchant, although necessary, was looked upon as a common enemy, and under the miserable system of business and farming which prevailed, the people had some grounds for complaint. The merchant sold supplies to the farmer, such as food, clothing and implements, in the spring of the year, to be paid for when the crops were gathered in the fall. As security for the payment for such supplies as were thus advanced, he took a mortgage on the homestead. Where the farmer was renting, as in the case of Sam and me, he took a mortgage on the stock and growing crop. We called this system buying and selling on credit.

The credit price of goods was about one-half more than the cash price. If side-meat sold for ten cents a pound cash, the credit price was fifteen cents. If a so-called ten pound bucket of lard sold for cash at one dollar, the credit price was a dollar and a half. I remember once calling for a bottle of liniment that was put up in fifty and twenty-five cent sizes. I told the clerk I wanted the twenty-five cent size. He said they were out of that, but that they had the thirty-five cent size which he could let me have. Of course, it was the twenty-five cent size, but the extra ten cents had been added because it was sold on credit. One man said that his merchant charged him ten cents a pound for coarse stock salt which retailed regularly at one dollar a hundred pounds.

The cost attached to giving a mortgage was twenty-five cents as a notary fee and for the blank on which it was written, but in opening an account, the first item charged against the customer was one dollar for the mortgage. The mortgage system was an evil and remained an evil until it was properly combated.

As we held our meetings weekly, we soon grew tired of lambasting the merchant and other people who wore store clothes, and we began holding our secret and business meetings once a month. However, we held open meetings on Saturday night and let our lodge drift into a kind of literary or debating society. At these open meetings all were invited, whether they belonged to the lodge or not. Women and children attended, and our programs consisted of readings, recitations, speeches and debates.

The debate became the chief atttraction at these

meetings, and nearly all of the time was allotted to it. Two champions would agree on a subject and choose their colleagues, alternately, until there were about four on each side. The principal speeches were made by the champions. The others said only a few words, making a "pint" out of whatever they could think up. We discussed various questions, among which were, "Which is the more powerful, the Sun or the Wind?" "Which is the cause of more evil, Women or Money?" "Which is the more useful to mankind, the Broom or the Dish-rag?"

Barney McCoy was the brag debater in our neighborhood, and we were all glad when we were chosen on his side, since we knew we would win. Barney had the reputation of never having lost a verdict, and we claimed to have the greatest debater in all the land. The same claim was made, however, for Larkin Smith by the people of the Hogeye settlement. Larkin also had never lost a verdict.

We grew tired of hearing the Hogeye boys boasting of having the best debater in the county; so we challenged them to debate, and the two giants were pitted against each other. The subject was, "Which is more attractive to the eye, Art or Nature?" Larkin affirmed that it was Art. The little popguns all went off first, and the two big guns were saved for the last. When it came time for Larkin to speak, he rose and said:

"Gentlemen an' Honer'ble Jedges an' Mr. Churman: the question tonight is, which is the most attractin' to the eye, Art er Nature. I'm on the 'firmative side an' I will prove beyond a shadder uv a doubt that Art is more beautiful than Nature."

Larkin was graceful, fluent and eloquent. He talked for some time, illustrating the beauties of the artist's work, finally coming to his "big p'int."

"Onc't, when I wuz workin' down on the Arkansas River," he said, "a big crowd uv uz war a standin' on the bank uv the river, a-watchin' the water as it come a hurryin' by, makin' its way onward to the sea. Acrost the river wuz Pettit Jean Mountain, liftin' itself heavenward with its peaks a-kissin' the blue sky. Thar wuz a big crowd uv uz, an' we all stood a-lookin' at the river an' the mountain an' the tall trees an' the runnin' vines an' the blossomin' flowers. Hit war awful purty, an' we couldn't thank uv nothin' that could be purtier. But look! Thar come a steamboat down the river. Ever'body tarned an' looked at it. On it come, a-belchin' forth barrels uv smoke from its powerful pipes, an' with a wheel uv paddles as big as this house. Who wuz lookin' at the river an' the mountains then? Not a one! Ever' eye wuz on the steamboat, an' they gazed at it tul it got out uv sight. Now Honer'ble Jedges, I believe you will agree with me that art is more beautiful than nature."

When Larkin took his seat, there was long and loud applause by the Hogeye crowd. Young men kicked heavily against the floor with the heels of their cowhide boots, and old men pounded repeatedly with their large

hickory walking sticks. The Hogeye boys all went out to take a fresh drink, but the rest of us sat with our eyes downward. It was conceded that our society had lost the verdict. Poor Barney! We hated to see him take the floor, for there seemed nothing he could say that would save the day. But when order was restored, Barney rose and began:

"Mr. Churman, gentlemen an' Honer'ble Jedges: I'm on the negative side of this question an' I'm goin' to prove that nature is more attractin' to the eye than art. Yes, I will go furder an' make my opponent, Mr. Larkin Smith, own up to it hisself, before I git through."

Barney was not as eloquent as was Larkin, but he was more forceful and convincing. He talked on for a while and came to the climax.

"My opponent tells you about seein' a steamboat," he said. "I would lacked to o' seed that boat. I know hit must a been a awful purty sight. I rickoleck I war down on the Arkansas River onc't myself. I went to a meetin' one time thar, and all of uz men war on one side of the meetin' house, and a passel of womurn war on t'other side. The womurn war all dressed up in purty shoes and purty hats and purty dresses with a blue ribbon here and a red ribbon thar, and they war awful purty. The womurn wuz nature and the close wuz art, and it war mouty hard to tell which war the purtiest.

"Now, Honer'ble Jedges, s'posen them womurn had a-pulled off them ar close. 'Course they didn't do it, but I say jist s'posen they had. Yes, sir, jist sposen they had a-pulled off they close, ever' rag uv 'em, and hung 'em on the wall. Then which would the men be a looking at, the womurn er the close? Honer'ble Jedges, which would you a-been looking at? Mr. Larkin Smith, answer me this. Wouldn't you a-been looking at the womurn?"

This brought down the house. Even the Hogeye crowd cheered. The judges were not long in bringing in a verdict for the negative, and our Barney's reputation was saved.

I vividly remember the tragic ending of our debating society. One night Dan Dubarry was on the floor talking, when Roy Mulligan, who was sitting in the back part of the house, cried out in a coarse, loud voice, "Who's that speakin'? Is that Colonel Fletcher?"

Colonel Fletcher was a well known lawyer and orator in that part of the state. Dubarry appeared not to hear Mulligan and kept on with his speech. When the meeting was adjourned and the people had all come out in the moonlight, Dubarry stepped up to Mulligan and said, "If you've got anything to say to me, say it now, an' be damn quick about it."

Just behind Dubarry stood his brother Amos, and at Mulligan's heels were two young men, his cousins, Pink and Bob Mulligan. Everybody knew the desperate character of all the parties concerned, and they were given plenty of room.

"I hain't got nothin' to say to you cept'n you air a damn fool," Mulligan said.

As he said this he let fly a rock which he held in his hand behind him, striking Dubarry on the shoulder. The two men then closed in on each other with their pocket knives. Mulligan's cousins and Dubarry's brother joined in the fray, and the five men fought with all the savagery with which a human being could be possessed since the days of the Neanderthal men. With curses, groans and shrieks, they fought like demons.

When the battle was over, the principals, Roy Mulligan and Dan Dubarry, were dead; Pink Mulligan was mortally wounded and died within a few days; and Bob Mulligan and Amos Dubarry were disabled for life. This desperate fight was the culmination of a feud that was of over fifty years' duration. Its history, as told to me, was as follows:

On one side of the mountain there lived a family that I shall call Mulligan, and on the other side lived another family which I shall call Dubarry. Long before the Civil War some kind of trouble had come up between these two families, probably a fight or a killing—the people did not remember which. Anyway, the two families were at outs and never spoke to each other. When the Dubarrys went to church, if they saw the Mulligans on one side of the house, they took seats on the other side, and vice versa.

When the Civil War broke out, John Mulligan joined the Union Army and was known as a Federal, while Will Dubarry espoused the cause of the Confederacy and was known as a Rebel. Both of these men were young and had families. When peace was established, both men came back home and settled down with their respective families, their hatred of each other increased by wartime passions.

One day at a gathering Dubarry accused Mulligan of being a party to the Jay Hawkers' depredations against Dubarry's parents. This Mulligan resented, and the men came to blows, which greatly intensified the bitter feeling between the two families. But matters smouldered along for a few years without any other outburst of violence.

One day John Mulligan was found dead in the road. Will Dubarry acknowledged killing him, but claimed self-defense. Among the children that Mulligan left were two boys, Dave and Roy. Their mother was a coarse, sunburnt woman, homely in her appearance and deadly in her vengeance. Her only prayer, she said, was that her boys would grow up to kill Dubarry. As they grew up, the older one of the boys, Dave, won the reputation of being a bad character.

On one occasion Will Dubarry's colt was missing, and somebody told him that Dave Mulligan had it. Dubarry got on his horse, and taking his gun with him, rode over to Mrs. Mulligan's. He asked to see Dave, and the old lady told him that Dave was not at home; whereupon Dubarry said he had heard that Dave had his colt, and he had come after it.

"Yore colt ain't hyear," the old woman said. "You can sarch the stables. My Dave didn't steal yore colt."

"Wal, he ain't none too good to," replied Dubarry as he rode off.

That night, when the boys came in, their mother told them about Dubarry, and she told Dave that he was not the son of his father if he didn't kill him. So the next day Dave loaded his shotgun with buckshot and went to the field where Dubarry was plowing corn. Without warning he shot him down. He then rode on up to the house, and pointing his gun at Mrs. Dubarry, told her in very abusive language that her old man was down there in the field dead, where he had killed him, and he stated that he would kill every one of them if they fooled with him.

Dave was arrested and brought to trial, and he claimed self-defense. There were no eye-witnesses, and he got off with a sentence of ten years. His mother said that the thing which she regretted most was that he hadn't killed the whole family while he was at it.

By the time Mulligan had served his sentence and come home, two of the Dubarry boys had grown up. He had not been home more than a year when he was found dead in his home. The finger of suspicion pointed to Dan Dubarry, the oldest of the Dubarry boys. He was arrested and brought to trial, but for lack of evidence was acquitted. This was the last act of violence on the part of either family until the outburst of savagery on the night of the lodge entertainment. This was, as far as I know, the ending of the feud between these two families.

The feud, along with the Elizabethan language and old world superstitions, is an inheritance belonging to the mountains. It dates back to the thirteenth century, when Rudolph I acknowledged the right of private warfare. However, the feud is not engaged in by the people of the Ozarks to anything like the extent that I hear it is by the people of the Tennessee and Kentucky mountains. It may be that our ancestors before coming to the Ozarks had reached the point in education where they had learned to discontinue such practices; or it may be that they were not far enough advanced in civilization to know enough to engage in them. Anyway, because the Ozarks are not notorious for feuds, we have missed a great deal of publicity, through books and the screen, which our cousins of the Cumberland hills now enjoy.

But we were not in the least lacking in brawls. Men would fall-out and fight over very trivial matters, such as the ownership of a dog, or the debt of a bushel of corn. Sometimes whole families would get into a fight, one family against another. People were suspicious and quick to accuse each other of some wrong. The mountain people are very clannish, and sometimes the inhabitants of one settlement would be at outs with those of another settlement. Particularly was that the case when most of the people of one settlement were Baptists and those of the other Methodists. Sometimes a community would boast of having the best singing class or the best fiddler. When such claims were disputed by the people of a rival section, the disputants would very often come to blows.

Sometimes a settlement would boast of having the strongest man in the country. It was youth's one desire to become a great man physically; to be called the best man in a community was an enviable reputation. A man possessed of great physical strength was always in prominence ahead of his fellows. Sometimes two men would get into an argument as to which was the best man and fall-out and fight, thereby bringing it to a test. I remember of witnessing the tragic end of such a case when I was a small boy.

Josh Scrimpsher lived in Center Hollow. He was a large man, six feet and two inches tall, and weighed about two hundred and seventy-five pounds. It was claimed by the people of Center Hollow that Scrimpsher was the best man in the surrounding country. Over on Bear Creek lived another large man by the name of Sam Guffy. He was hardly as tall as Scrimpsher and weighed less, but the people of Bear Creek boasted of having the best man in all the country. One day they met at a log rolling, and friends of each urged that they tote together, so that they might see who was the best man. The men got under a heavy log, each at the end of a handstick, and began pulling against each other. Scrimpsher gave down, which was evidence that Guffy had pulled him down and was the better man. Scrimpsher accused Guffy of cheating by getting more than his share of the stick, thereby having more lever power. This Guffy denied, and the men got into a dispute and would have fought, had not Parson Yates prevailed on them to keep the peace. After this the men were enemies: whenever they met, they would have some kind of insulting remark to make to each other.

On the Saturday before Christmas I went with my father to a small cross-road town which boasted of two stores and a dozen houses, all unpainted. Each store had a grocery. When we said "store," we meant a place where they sold general merchandise. When we referred to a grocery, we meant a place where whiskey was sold. Men came to town that day from all parts of the mountains to buy Christmas whiskey for themselves and firecrackers and candy for the children.

We were in Gregory's store warming ourselves by the stove, when Sam Guffy and some friends came in and ordered sardines and crackers. They were in the back of the store, standing at the counter and eating the sardines and crackers, when Josh Scrimpsher and four or five of his friends arrived. Josh walked up to the stove, removed his home-knit gloves and, rubbing his hands, looked over at Guffy and said, "Wal, Guffy, you air eatin' sardines, air ye?"

"Hit would seem that a way to anybody cep'n to a bline man," Sam replied, looking up from his sardines.

"But, you see, I ain't bline," Josh answered.

Sam Billings had just bought a bottle of whiskey, and he pulled Josh's sleeve and showed him the bottle and they all drank freely. The two giants and their friends were all drinking, and I heard some of the men talking to my father, saying that there would be trouble before the day was passed.

After a while Sam and his crowd were standing around the stove in Babb's store, when Josh and his friends came in.

"Goin' to eat some more sardines, Guffy?" asked Josh.

"Will ef I wanter," replied Sam. "Don't see nobody in hyar wot's big enough to keep me from it."

"Mebbe not," said Josh. "I hearn ole Tommy Wilson offered you a mule to come over an' whup me. Jist want to say I'll give you another soon as you do, an' then you'll have a pair."

"Don't know nothin' 'bout no mule," said Sam, "but ef I wan' to whup ye, I'll whup ye."

"You'll know some'n 'bout a whuppin', though, never'n you try it," said Josh. Sam then went on out of the store, followed by his crowd.

They went over to Gregory's store again, and a little later Josh and his crowd entered. I did not want to miss any of the excitement, so I went over too. I saw Sam and his friends all drinking from a bottle. Then Ed Bostick bought a bottle of whiskey and, removing the cork, passed it to Josh. Josh looked over at Guffy, who was just drinking the last of a bottle's contents. Josh said, "I ain't a-goin' to drink in hyar as long as that polecat's a-drankin'."

At this Guffy let go his bottle, aiming it at Scrimpsher's head. Scrimpsher ducked and the bottle passed him, crashing into the mirror behind the counter.

The men clinched, and everybody knew that the battle was on and got out of the way. They fought furiously for a while, and when it seemed that Josh was getting the better of Sam, his friends would shout with joy; and Sam's friends would yell encouragingly when Sam scored. Scrimpsher was a little the heavier, but Guffy was younger and more active.

Suddenly Scrimpsher threw Guffy backwards over the counter, and clutching his shirt collar with his left hand, he held high with his right a dagger with which he was aiming at Guffy's heart.

"Onfar! Hit's onfar," shouted Henry Smith. "He's got a knife."

But before any one could interfere, Guffy with herculean strength threw his antagonist backward, and gripping Scrimpsher's right wrist with his right hand, held in his left a dagger which he wielded with fatal results. Scrimpsher, infuriated by the wounds inflicted by his opponent, with set eyes and teeth drove his dagger also true to aim. Guffy went down, but not until death had also gripped his foe. As Guffy fell, he shouted, "God damn, I died lak a man!" As he spoke, the blood spurted from his mouth.

CHAPTER XVI

I GO OFF TO SCHOOL

IN June I sold my interest in the crop to Sam and went back home, where I joined Jim, who had returned from school. We began making plans for the summer's work, as I was expected to attend school the following year. Jim's old school in Greasy Valley was offered him, and I rode with him to the county seat, where he intended to take the examination for a teacher's license under Dr. Aikin. We found the doctor in his office conversing with a stranger, and as we entered, he said, "There's the man you want to see," indicating Jim. The gentleman then explained that he had come up from Little Rock in the interests of a school book concern and that he was inquiring for a young man with some education and the ability to travel and present his school book proposition to the mountain districts.

The book man's proposition looked flattering to Jim, and he accepted it. He bought a new top buggy on time, arranged with my father for one of his horses, and was ready to enter upon his new field of work.

This left the Greasy Valley school without a teacher. Jim assured me that I was qualified to teach it and urged me to do so. We went to see Squire George, and he agreed to give me the school, provided I could get a license. We then went to Dr. Aikin and explained matters to him, and I took the examination. Among the questions the doctor asked me was, "What is a pronoun?"

"A word that stands fer or instid of a noun," I answered.

"Is that the way you would teach your pupils to pronounce?" he asked. "Would you teach them to say 'instid'?"

I blushed but could not say anything, and he was kind enough to make no mention of the "fer." After the examination, he lectured me a little, urging that I study up on my subjects, and granted me a third grade certificate.

My school opened with a splendid enrollment, and the attendance was good throughout the session. The children seemed to learn rapidly, but I believe I knew as little about my subjects or how to teach them as any one could know and pass for a teacher. I was young to have charge of so large a school. I knew that settled men were preferred as teachers throughout the mountains, as sometimes young men started a courtship with one of their young woman pupils. It was always detrimental to a school to be called a "courting school." I tried in every way I could to appear old; and I stayed in and read during the recess hours in order to maintain my dignity.

As a precaution against any courting gossip, I made a speech to the school, telling them that I had not come amongst them as a wife hunter, that I wanted it distinctly understood that I was not teaching a "courting school," and that I was not a courting man. Nevertheless, I fell before the school was out.

One Sunday Bill Bostic persuaded me to go with him over into the Hall settlement to visit his uncle, Major Russell. I knew of the Major. He lived in a hewn-log double house, which was white-washed, and had a good farm well stocked and well fenced. He marketed a number of young mules each year, and his family were known as "rich folks."

Soon after arriving at the Major's home I understood why Bill wanted me to come with him. He was expecting Miss Dean Massy to be there and wanted me to entertain the Major's daughter, Miss Gertie, so that he could pass the time with Miss Dean. Miss Gertie was about my age, had a soft voice, a pleasing manner, and I found her very entertaining. She had in her front room a carpet on the floor, upholstered chairs, and a cottage organ. She sang and played several religious songs, and as her small white hand manipulated the keys of the organ, I noticed a ring on her finger which I imagined was real gold. She seemed more beautiful than any fairy princess of whom I had ever read.

All too soon to suit me Bill and Miss Dean returned from their buggy ride, and it was time to go. When we were leaving, Miss Gertie invited us to call again and seemed to indicate me. I decided to take her at her word and call again, for I thought I was in love, desperately in love. Two weeks was about as long as I could go without seeing her, and on one Sunday afternoon I made an informal call. Miss Gertie was as pleasant as when I first met her, and she did most of the talking. She asked me what college I had graduated from and what class. I answered the best I could, and told her that I had not received my degree. She talked a great deal about her schoolmates, and stressed the fact that she had an uncle who was a lawyer in Fort Smith. I saw her two or three times after that before the closing of my school, and she was always talkative and friendly. She never failed to mention something about her rich relatives in the city. She seemed to treat me patronizingly, but I took that to be only characteristic of "rich folks." I was fully convinced that she was the girl for me.

When school was out, I met Jim at home, and we held a council to devise ways and means for both of us to attend school that year. He had done well with the book people, and had earned enough money to pay his way in school. During the summer my father's sister and her husband visited us. Their home was in a town south of the Arkansas River, in the lowlands. My uncle was a cattle buyer, and his work required his absence from home a great deal of the time. When they learned that I wanted to go to school the coming year, they said that there was a splendid school in their town, and begged me to go and stay with them and attend it. My uncle said that, if I would stay with my aunt and the children, it would give him a chance to be out at his work more. They offered me free board, and all I would have to do was to make fires, feed the stock, and so on. The proposition was attractive to me, and I accepted it.

I bought a Prince Albert suit of clothes and a derby hat, and Jim drove me to our aunt's home in his buggy. Our aunt lived in a town of about two thousand people, and in it was located a creditable high school. This school was the pride of the town. In fact, it was about all the town had that it could boast of. There were no water works and sewerage system in this town, no telephones, no electric lights, no fire department, no ice factory and no public library. The lack of these did not in the least bother me, however, as I was not used to them.

There was no stock law, and people had to have picket fences to keep the cattle and hogs out of the yards. Several cows slept on the ground under the windows of the church, and some hogs slept under the floor. There was a slimy small creek which ran through a part of the town, in which dead hogs and other carcasses could often be seen. They had a marshal, but his duties seemed to be to play checkers on week days, and on Saturdays to arrest country boys who came to town and cut up.

There was another thing which the town boasted of, and that was its newspaper. This was a small weekly edited by a promising young lawyer. He claimed to be a well-informed gentleman, and I remember once reading one of his articles in which he said that, when in doubt about the meaning of a word, he always consulted "Daniel Webster's big dictionary." This paper went in strong for local news. It devoted space to the birth of a calf or a litter of pigs, when the stock belonged to influential citizens. If any of the élite visited as far as five miles away, prominent mention was made of the fact; and should they visit places distant as far as Little Rock or Hot Springs, the write-up occupied a whole column.

Jim went with me to the school on the morning after our arrival, and we found that Professor Abernathy, the principal of the school, was a very pleasant and agreeable man. He seemed more than pleased at having a pupil from so far beyond the limits of his own county. He gave me good credits for Jim's tutoring, and my home studies, and I was able in some studies to enter the second year. The cost of tuition was five dollars a month, and we advanced him twenty-five dollars. I got the list of required books and was ready to start in.

My aunt saw fit to make some little corrections as to my personal appearance. She made me discard my home-knit wool socks, as they were not worn there; I went uptown and bought a pair of ten-cent cotton hose. She also had me get a shoe-brush and a box of Mason and Dixon's shoe-blacking, and I had to black my shoes every morning before going to school.

The student body was composed of about a hundred young men and women, from fifteen years of age up to about twenty. Most of them lived in the town, and the others were the sons and daughters of the better-to-do farmers who lived out in the country. By close application to my books, I managed to keep up with my class. Some of the subjects were difficult: I had never seen a textbook on algebra before, and it took me some time to understand it.

I got along splendidly with my classmates and schoolmates, and had I been able to disguise my pronunciation, I would have passed only for a country yap. But that telltale drawling articulation gave me away. It was always a great treat to have a country ignoramus in that school, but the satisfaction of having a real mountain greenhorn with them was a pleasure never before dreamed of. My outlandish pronunciation was the occasion for much fun. A snicker went down the class when I said "thar" for "there"; and they all giggled when I pronounced "fetch" "fotch." The boys began referring to me as "Hit" and "Youens."

One day Dee Hamm asked me to lend him my pencil. He then drew from his pocket a piece of paper and wrote the letters "t-o-o-k," and asked me, according to the rules of pronunciation, what those letters spelled. "Took," I said. "Then," said he, "why do you insist on calling it 'tuck'?" I told him that I really did not know, that I had not thought of it in any way.

"Probably," he said, "they laugh at you because they know you know better. Give this matter a little thought and learn to pronounce your words as your books teach you."

I thanked him and promised to take his advice. I knew that Dee was a friend, and that he was advising me for my own good. However, I could not help wondering why my schoolmates said "laf" and "haf" when the dictionary showed that they were pronounced "lahf" and "hahf." Also, I had to learn to say "you all" instead of "youens." I had never heard the expression "you all" before coming to the lowlands. This was used only in addressing the second person plural. There is not a man, woman or child in the whole state of Arkansas, from the most inaccessible retreats of the northern mountains to the densest jungle lands of the southern swamps, who uses the words "you all" in addressing the second person singular. I hope that some day certain writers of fiction will learn this.

I went to church and Sunday school, and in this way made the acquaintance of many of the older people who later proved to be friends. One afternoon when I came in from school, my aunt told me that there was going to be a social gathering at the home of the presiding elder, and that she had promised Sister Evans that I would be there. She thought it would be great for me to get out and make some worthwhile acquaintances. She hinted that some girls of fine families would be there, and that she wanted their first impression of me to be favorable. She told me to try to look my best. So I put on the best I had and walked over to Brother Evans' home.

I knew Brother Evans, but he was not at home; and I introduced myself to Sister Evans. She introduced me to her brother, Mr. Parker, a young man who was making his home with her. Mr. Parker directed me to a seat and went on looking after other arrivals. I sat on a straight chair and in a conspicuous place, perspiring freely. I had on my long Prince Albert coat and celluloid cuffs, and when I drew my handkerchief from the pocket in my coat tail and wiped the perspiration from my face, the buttons in the cuffs would rattle. I wore a stiff white shirt and a high standing celluloid collar with a white string tie in a bow. But little attention was given to me. If anyone inquired as to who I was, the answer was that I was a boy from the mountains attending the school there. The subject was then dismissed with the proud thought that the school was reaching out so far for patronage.

The guests stood around or sat in pairs, laughing and talking about nothing in particular. The young men wore form fitting coats, white vests and loud linen.

The young women wore their dresses and hair in styles that I had never seen. I was very uncomfortable and wanted to make some kind of a change. I knew something about society, as I had read a book on etiquette. Remembering what my book had taught me to say on such occasions, I blurted out, "Mr. Parker, I would be pleased to have a drink of water."

All eyes were instantly turned on me, not with a snicker, but with an outburst of laughter from all parts of the room. Sister Evans fell back in her chair and laughed hysterically. Mr. Parker came across the room with a dipper of water, shaking so with laughter that he spilled part of the water before reaching me. After drinking, I got my hat and went home.

I explained to my aunt that there were no other students there, and really it was against the rules of the school for the pupils to attend parties on week nights, and hence I thought it best to come back and get my lessons. She was anxious to know if I had made a hit with any of the girls there. I told her that in a way I thought I had.

This was the best thing that could have happened to me at that time. I began to realize that I was green, and that I was there to learn, not to go out and be entertained. I decided to leave off all social functions from then on, and with a renewed determination, I buckled down to my books. My class progress was soon noticeable. I remember one Sunday there was an all day meeting of some kind, and on Monday all the students seemed dull and sleepy. I was about the only one prepared for the day's recitations. That day in passing Miss Tampa Simms and Miss Vera Greer, I heard one remark to the other, "That fool is smart, isn't he?"

I had always admired both of these young ladies. They seemed to be so quiet and dignified. They were so modest that, when I chanced to meet one of them, she always turned her head to keep from speaking to me. I had long since learned that in their estimation I was a fool, but I felt highly flattered to hear that I was a smart fool.

It seemed strange to me that, while I was struggling under unfavorable conditions to obtain an education, there were boys of well-to-do parents who had a hatred for any kind of study. They shirked, copied, and some of them began slipping around to me to get me to solve their problems for them.

Spring of the year came, and everybody seemed to be getting new clothes. I was still wearing my heavy Prince Albert coat. Again my friend Dee Hamm advised me. "Get rid of that long coat," he said. "Go out on the streets and see how many young men you can find wearing a Prince Albert coat. Throw away those celluloid collars and cuffs. They are country."

I had never given much thought to the matter of clothes, but had supposed that I was dressing in up-to-the-minute style. One day I was passing Mr. Harris' store, and he was standing in the door. Mr. Harris had always been friendly toward me at the church, and I went in and told him that I was going to buy a suit of clothes as soon as I could get the money from my brother, and that I would like to see what they were going to cost. He showed me several suits, and picked out one which he suggested that I get. It was a sack coat and the only coat I had ever worn that was anything like a fit. I told him that I would come in and get it as soon as I got the money.

"That's all right," he said. "Take it along and pay me just whenever you get the money."

I bought about twenty dollars worth from Mr. Harris and paid him when Jim sent me the money. My pronunciation was improving, and with clothing such as other young men were wearing I was no longer regarded as a curiosity, and the fame of my peculiarities was fast fading away.

There was to be an all day meeting one Sunday, at Mt. Carmel, about ten miles out in the country, and my aunt asked me to drive her and the children there. We went to the home of Mrs. Breedlove for dinner. I was acquainted with Mrs. Breedlove, as she had come to my aunt's home several times. Among the several people who had come to Mrs. Breedlove's house for dinner was Sister Evans, the Presiding Elder's wife.

As it seemed that the table would be crowded, I held back and did not go in. Mrs. Breedlove made room for me, however, and urged me to come in to dinner. When I finally went to the table, they had all begun eating. I was introduced to Sister Evans. I said,

"Yes, I have met Sister Evans before." Then addressing her, I said, "If you remember, I was at a social at your house early in the fall." Sister Evans was in the act of taking a bite of something. She dropped her fork and let her head fall back in an outburst of laughter. As she tried to compose herself, she managed to say through fits of laughter, "I remember you! I remember you!"

The school drew to a close, and at the examination I made good credits and passed. I prepared to go back home where my old school had been offered me for the summer. As I was passing Mr. Harris' store one afternoon, he called me in and said, "What have you in view for the vacation period, Wayman?" I told him that I was going back home and teach a small school.

"I'm mighty glad of it," he said. "It will be better for you to teach. But if anything should occur so that you do not get the school, don't go without employment. Come back here and I will make room for you in the store."

Jim came after me in his buggy. I was glad to see him, and to hear from home. I had expected my sister Nora and Willie Burton to get married, and I learned from Jim that they had already married, and were living at home with our parents, and that everybody was well at home.

CHAPTER XVII

THE HANGING

JIM had his book samples with him and he suggested that we take about a week in driving home, so that he could try to do a little business on the way. I agreed to do this, although I was anxious to get home and see my father and mother and sisters. I loved my mountain people, and I was homesick and wanted to get back.

As we drove along, I told Jim my plans. I wanted to teach that summer and work around for about a year, and then get married and settle down. Jim spoke disparagingly of my plans, saying that I now had an opportunity to make something of myself, and that if I spoiled it all by getting married, that would be the end of a career that could be made useful. "Why the end of my career?" I argued. My idea was to build a house with dressed lumber and paint it white with green trimmings. I would have carpets on the floor, pictures on the walls and flowers in the front yard, just like so many other homes I had seen. If such houses were so numerous in other sections, why couldn't at least a few of them be built in our native hills?

Jim argued that our mountains offered no opportunities to an ambitious young man. I came back at him with the assertion that I had had to go away from home to learn that our own lands were unsurpassed in fruit and stock and poultry raising, and that the world was a ready market for all our produce. Yes, I would go back and marry and settle right there for life. I would teach my people to take advantage of their environment and to develop the resources of their own hills and valleys.

Of course, the girl whom I intended to marry was Gertie. I had had a few letters from her in answer to mine. Gertie was of a practical turn of mind, and she was not the kind that goes in strong for silly, mushy love stuff. Her letters were always short and sensible. In her last letter, which had been some time back, she stated that her correspondence was getting too heavy, since all of her city friends wanted to write her; and she suggested that I not write her any more, just tell her all when I returned. Of course, this was a hint for me to hurry home.

Jim made known his intentions. He had decided to become a lawyer. In addition to his school books he had been studying law. An old gentleman who was a lawyer at Quitman had given him access to his law library and had lent him a lot of books to study during the summer while traveling. Jim said he was going to get his degree at Quitman and take the law course at Vanderbilt. Every day I listened to him as he defended or prosecuted imaginary people.

On Saturday we crossed Fourche River and came to a county town. Jim inquired for Mr. Adams, a member of the school board, and was told that he was out at the races. We drove to the race tracks, where we found a great crowd had gathered for the horse races. It seemed as if every rag tag of a man in the whole country was there, and they had brought with them every possible kind of an excuse for a horse that could be had. They were spending the time in chewing tobacco, swearing, and swapping horses.

The chief attraction of the day was to be a race between a gray pony, owned by a man they called Ashly, and a big old raw, bony horse owned by Dan Robinson. While waiting for this event, a few races were run by half-starved plugs, on which there was light betting and in which little interest was taken. The most amusing of these preliminary races was a slow race between two mules. Will Journey offered to bet five dollars that he had the slowest mule on the grounds. Charlie Brown took him up and they ran their mules, Journey riding Brown's mule and Brown riding Journey's mule. The mules pranced, went forward, backward and sideways, while the crowd shouted and cheered with great hilarity.

Some time before time for the big race, Ashly went among the crowd holding a five dollar bill in his hand crying, "Five dollars to bet on the gray pony. Who's got five dollars to bet agin' the gray pony?"

"I'll bet you five," said a man, running up to Ashly.

"Only one in a big crowd that's willin' to bet five dollars that the gray pony cain't beat anything put on the track," said Ashly.

"No, no," said the man. "I want to bet on the gray pony."

I passed a crowd of men discussing the horses, and heard one of them ask, "What's runnin' agin the gray pony?"

"That ole hoss of Dan Robinson's," a man replied.

Then the first one said, "Why, that's jist a ole hide."

"Yes an' by God that ole hide can run, too," said another big fellow. "You jist wait till Mart Draper gits here. Hell is goin' to tarn loose here arter while."

From then on they began referring to Dan Robinson's horse as "The Hide." Ashly had got hold of it, and he renewed his canvass for bets, again going among the crowd and crying, "Who wants to bet on The Hide? You fellers wot thinks The Hide can win, put up yer money." Almost everybody, however, seemed to think that there was nothing that could beat the gray pony, and Ashly did not get a bet.

After a while Mart Draper appeared on the ground.

Draper was a horse-race man and made his living by betting on them. His friends abided by his judgment about horses. Robinson and several others gathered around him, and after a short conference, Draper, flourishing a roll of bills over his head, went among the crowd saying, "Whar's all them gray pony men? I'll bet any man any amount from five to a hundred dollars that The Hide, as you call him, can outrun the gray pony. Now you fellers wots been a holler'n gray pony around here, either put up or shet up. Gray pony's got all friends and no money."

But the gray pony's friends had some money, and they began wagering. For a while betting was at a high pitch. Men bet their saddles and bridles, and a few bet their horses. At the finish of the race The Hide came out just a little ahead.

We crossed the Arkansas River at the site of old Louisburg, where once stood a thriving city and port. Louisburg was a close competitor with Little Rock for the state capital, when it was decided to move it from Arkansas Post. We walked around over the deserted place, and there seemed to be nothing remaining of that once busy town except a half dozen vacant old houses, with here and there an old cistern from which the house had been torn down and moved away. We walked up to one of the houses that seemed to have been a schoolhouse. The windows were all out, and the doors had decayed and fallen down. There were no seats, and all the furnishing had been moved. We entered the old building, and Jim walked to the rear, where we supposed the teacher had had his desk.

"I wonder," said Jim, "if General Albert Pike taught school here. He taught somewhere up in this part of the state, and it may be that it was right here."

He stood up as if facing a class and said, "I can see the recitation bench. Over here to the left sat the girls, and to the right were the boys. I wonder where they are now. Where can they all be, those boys and girls who once filled this old building with so much life?"

"Many of them are yonder," I said, indicating the graveyard that we had just passed. "Back yonder."

We drove on up the river and learned that a hanging was to take place at Clarksville on Friday, and we decided to make our way to it. In those days legal executions were public, and people went great distances to see a man hanged. In this case four men were condemned to die for killing a conductor while they were in the act of robbing a train. The hanging of four men at one time made the occasion more than usually attractive.

When we arrived, a great crowd had gathered, and more were coming. They came from every direction and by every mode of travel. A man came through the crowd selling a "History of the Train Robbers," and we bought one. It was a small pamphlet giving a short life sketch of each of the doomed men. From what I gathered in this pamphlet the facts of the crime, for which they were about to pay the penalty, and the incidents leading up to it were about as follows:

Gov Johnson, the leader of the gang, was a man about forty years old. He had been brought up in the mountains, and had been in the toils of the law on several occasions, having figured in numerous cutting and shooting scrapes. He had recently left his home county suddenly, and in leaving, he had picked up a piece of rope while passing a horse lot. That of itself was not so bad, but there happened to be a horse tied to the other end of the rope. In making this trip away from home, Gov wanted somebody to go with him, and he went by the home of Lester, his nephew. Lester was a mountain youth about eighteen or nineteen years old, who had been brought up amid Christian surroundings and had never known anything but truthfulness and honesty. He wanted to go somewhere where he could earn some money, if he could do so in a legitimate and honest way. Gov assured Lester that he could find plenty of work, and agreed to see him through. So Lester went with him, and Gov said nothing to Lester as to how he came by the horse he had. They went up into the Choctaw Nation, where Gov disposed of the horse.

Then they drifted down into Arkansas, where for a while they obtained employment as day-laborers on a farm. Leaving there, they headed South and met up with two more men going in the same direction. The men gave their names as Cooper and Foley. They traveled along together until night, when they came upon a vacant house near the railroad and close to a creek bridge. They had some bread and ground coffee with them, so they decided to camp there for the night. Lester and Cooper washed up some old tin buckets and cans that were left on the place, while Gov and Foley went back to a farmhouse which they had passed and stole a couple of chickens.

They sat around the fireplace eating their supper, while Gov and his two new companions related their hard luck stories to each other.

"Yeah, tha's jis' the way they do a pore man in this country," said Gov. "Now, looky hyar at me. Fer forty year I've worked as hard as any man that ever seed the sun, an' I hain't got money enough to pay fer a night's largin'."

"You ain't by yoreself," said Foley. "You ain't by yoreself. Look at me, fer instance. Fer thirty year I've done nothin' but work like a dog, and I've got no money and never did have none—though I've made money and plenty of it. But what becomes of it? Course, you all know where it goes. The rich get it. The poor man does all the work, and the rich man gits the money."

Cooper joined in and said, "I used to worry over these things, but they don't bother me a bit now. I've got it fixed thisaway. The world owes me a livin' an' I'm goin' to have it. I've always done my part. I've worked like a nigger all my life, an' the rich had always got every dime I made; an' I'm tellin' you fellers right here and now: I'm not goin' to starve as long as anybody else has got anything to eat. If I cain't git it one way, I will another. I may be hung, but I'm not goin' to starve to death."

"Now that's jist the way I look at thangs," said Gov. "But look at Lester thar. He won't tech a bite of them ar chickens jist caze they air stoled. I keep a-tellin' him hit ain't no dishonest ack to take from the rich. Whenev'n you steal from a rich man, you air not a stealin' a tall. You air jist takin' back sump'n that he's stole from the pore."

"Ha, ha!" laughed Foley, and addressing Lester, he said, "Time you git as old as I am, young man, you'll git out of all that kind of foolish notions."

The next morning a passenger train came through. Gov was watching it and noticed that it slowed down before crossing the bridge. An idea instantly came to him. The men were ready to move on, but Gov told them that he was feeling a little badly and wanted to rest awhile before starting. He walked out to the railroad, looked up and down the track, walked across the bridge, walked around in the woods a while, and came back to the house.

"Looky hyar, fellers," he said. "I've jist been a studyin', an' I've got somethin' in my head 'sides nits an' lice. Air youens willin' to work about a half a hour fer a few hundred dollars?"

Lester said nothing, but Gov did not have to ask

the other two men a second time. He then made known to them a plan he had for robbing the train. Both Foley and Cooper readily agreed, and Gov turned to Lester, saying, "What do you say, Lester?"

Lester replied, "I'll do anythang you say, Uncle Gov."

There were only two pistols in the crowd, and after carefully laying and discussing their plans, it was agreed that Lester and Cooper should keep the passengers covered with the guns, while Gov and Foley went through their pockets.

The next morning, when they heard the train in the distance, the four men got on the track and began walking in the same direction in which the train was going. Gov and Lester walked behind Foley and Cooper, with about the length of a coach between them. When the train slowed down before crossing the bridge, the four men leaped on to it. They entered the day coach, Foley and Cooper going in at the front, while Gov and Lester entered at the rear. Cooper, a large man with a coarse, loud voice, brandished a pistol and cried out, "Throw up your hands, every damn son-of-a-bitch of you. We are robbin' this train. Throw 'em up, and by God, keep 'em up."

"Don't look thisaway," cried Lester, "or you'll git shot."

Gov and Foley began hurriedly searching the passengers and relieving them of their money and valuables. The excitement was too straining on Lester, and he was becoming nervous. The conductor, unaware of what was going on, opened the door and came into the coach; whereupon Lester, his nerves at a high tension, threw his gun on him and fired. The shot was fatal. Foley pulled the cord, giving the engineer the signal to stop, and the four men leaped from the train and escaped into the mountains.

They wandered around the hills for a while and finally took refuge in a cave, where they were soon located and surrounded by a posse. They showed fight and were fired upon by officers, a bullet striking Foley in the leg. The men then surrendered. They were speedily brought to trial, charged with the murder of the conductor while in the act of robbing the train. They were held equally guilty and the penalty was fixed as death.

The time of the execution was in the latter part of June, I think about the twenty-fourth, and the sun was mercilessly hot. A scaffold had been erected, made of strong heavy timbers. In the center of the floor of the scaffold was a trap door supported by a new grass rope. The four prisoners, each having had a shave and a hair cut, were marched from the jail through the immense crowd to the scaffold. The county had furnished them with new clothing, and all were very well dressed. The first to ascend the steps leading up to the scaffold was Cooper. He walked with an unsteady step and was white around the mouth, over which there played a sickly and forced smile. Next to him was Gov, frowning and scowling and vengeful. Following him was

Foley, who was wounded and walked with a crutch. He looked pale and sick. Last came Lester. He, too, looked pale and thin and weak. Hesitating at the steps for a moment, he looked over to the right, then slowly he turned his head and surveyed the crowd to the left. He seemed to have seen no one whom he could recognize. His mother was not there nor his father, nor any of his sisters or brothers; not even a friendly acquaintance. His head dropped, and he gazed at the steps. Urged on by the officers, he began ascending the steps. When about half way up, his knees began to shake and he fell backwards, but was caught by two men. They lifted him to his feet, but he had no command of himself. He was in a swoon, and they had to drag him on up the steps to the scaffold, supporting him, one under each arm.

A minister ascended the steps with a Bible in his hand. He opened his Bible, read a few verses, and started singing that good old song, "There is a Fountain Filled with Blood." As he sang, thousands of spectators joined in and sang the song through. The minister then offered up a short prayer, and after shaking hands with the doomed men, came down.

They strapped the men's hands behind them and drew black caps over their heads, completely covering their faces. They then tied a rope around each of their necks in a noose. The two men supporting the youth turned him loose, and he crumpled to the floor with the rope around his neck. I saw the sheriff pick up a sharp looking broad-axe, and as he raised it, I closed my eyes. I heard the broad-axe strike, and I opened them. The four men were dangling in the air. A woman screamed near me and fell to the ground. Many of the people turned their heads from the scene and walked away.

After leaving the hanging, we drove on home, where we found the folks all overjoyed to see us. It was the longest I had ever been away from home, and my father killed a large turkey gobbler, and did all he could to make things pleasant for us. My mother was so proud to have her boys home with her again.

CHAPTER XVIII

I GO TO JAIL

THE day after we got home was Sunday, and in the afternoon I rode over to make Gertie an informal call. I hoped she would be glad to see me, and I wondered what she would think of my plans. As I rode along, I pictured to myself as I would appear to Gertie and her family. A year away at school, nice fitting clothes, and my improved accent should put me head and shoulders above any town beau that might aspire to her hand. However, I thought it best not to go into details about the lovely house that I was going to build for her; it would be best to wait a year for the wedding to take place. I intended to propose in the regular formal way.

When I arrived at Gertie's home, I found a carriage of young people there, who had come in to visit her that afternoon. They were mostly kinsfolk, and they talked loud, sang, danced, laughed and ran over the yard. Of course, I had no chance to be with Gertie alone. I could see that she wanted to talk with me, but as the company showed no signs of leaving at all soon, I did not stay long, and left saying that I would call again. I saw where I had made a mistake in calling informally, and decided to wait about two weeks and let her know when I was coming, so I could have the afternoon alone with her.

After staying around home a day or two, I realized that it was time to see about my summer's employment. I rode over to Greasy Valley and talked with Squire George about my old school.

The Squire wanted me to teach the school, but mentioned that at the last annual school election Tucker Jenkins had failed of re-election, and Harmon Harrell was elected in his place. He said that there was to be a meeting at the schoolhouse on the following Saturday afternoon for the purpose of deciding on a teacher, and he suggested that in the meantime I call on Harmon and talk with him about it. I went to Mr. Harrell's house, but he was not at home.

Harrell was known to be a very meddlesome kind of a fellow. He was often stirring up trouble in the church and, like dynamite, he always went against the resistance and never agreed with anybody on anything. However, as far as I knew, we were friends, and I had no fears as to his support.

In a day or two Mr. Harrell came to our house. It was about noon, and he stayed for dinner. We knew of no business which might have brought him, unless he had come to talk with me about the school. He asked me if I was going to teach that summer, and I told him that I wanted to and had been over to his house to see him about the school. He seemed to think it would be all right and told me that they were going to have a meeting Saturday afternoon for the purpose of deciding on a teacher. He asked me to be present and went on to say it would be better for me to be on the ground, as there might be other applicants.

I went over to Greasy Valley that Saturday, and on my arrival I recognized Sam Gray, a school teacher. I saw Harrell whistle to Gray and point to me, as I was getting down off my horse. This did not look good to me, but I felt sure that, if the choice were to be left to the people, I would be selected over any other applicant. I stayed around in the yard, shaking hands with acquaintances, when Squire George came to me and told me that there would be no school meeting held. To my surprise he informed me that Harrell had ridden the day before to Gray's house, fifteen miles away, and had gotten Gray and came with him to old man Roper, the third school director. These two had then contracted with Gray to teach the school. They did not consult him, Squire George, as two constituted a majority. I did not have any ill feelings toward Mr.

Roper. Gray was his nephew, and no doubt Harrell told him that Gray was the people's choice.

I was sitting in the schoolhouse, thinking about going home, when I recognized Harrell's voice on the outside, saying, "Why, I'd a-rid till my laigs fell off, 'fore I'd a-seed thatar young upstart git this hyar school."

He followed this with a loud chuckle. I could not hear what the men around him were saying, but they probably asked him what his objections to me were, for he said, "Why, he is jis' too stuck up and biggeted. Both o' themar boys is too big fer their britches. Why, that brother o' his'n driv by my house t'other day an' didn't so merch as tarn his head."

I listened to Harrell about as long as I cared to, and then got up and walked out of the house and around to where he was.

"I couldn't help hearing you, Harrell," I said. "I heard every word you said."

"Listen hyar, young feller," he said, "I warn't talkin' to you. You git off from hyar. I've seed little boys no bigger'n you git they ears boxed."

"All right, Harrell," I said. "I am going to leave, but first let me give you my regards. You knocked me out of the school all right. You won over me; but any man that would use the tactics you did to defeat me is a lowdown thieving coward."

I was wrong. Harrell was no coward when it came to fighting. He was a strong man and had the reputation of being a fighter. I saw by the expression on his face that I had probably made a mistake.

"You young polecat," he said. "This is jist the chanct I been a waitin' fer. I'll slap you in the mouth fer that."

He walked right on toward me, and I do not think he had the least idea that I would attempt to offer any resistance. The first law of nature is self preservation. I looked around me, and the only thing I saw within reach was a two-by-four piece of scantling about three feet long. I quickly seized this, and with a swing that I had learned in playing baseball, I struck with all the force that I could muster. He instinctively threw up his arm to ward off the blow. The scantling struck his left wrist and his jaw, loosening two of his jaw teeth. The blow knocked him backwards, and he seemed to be stunned; but in a moment or two he was making for his knife.

As he started at me with his knife, Sam Gray caught hold of his arm and Ed Jones grabbed my scantling. Harrell was bleeding at the mouth, and they led him into the house and got some water. I stood around outside with the scantling in my hand, expecting him to renew the attack. He did not come out, but in his stead came Dwight Simpson with a paper in his hand. Simpson was the township constable, and he had a warrant for my arrest. Harrell had sworn out a warrant before Squire George against me for assault with a deadly weapon.

I got Simpson to take me home to see about making bond. When we got there, my father was just getting on his horse, with his shotgun in his hand. Some men had been by and told him about the trouble, and he was going to my rescue. Simpson was a hired hand of Harrell's, and he was very exacting about the bond and required it to be sworn to. After some trouble, however, we got the bond fixed up, and the trial was set for the coming Tuesday.

Harrell was a man of some means. He had lands and employed a few men. He was counted well-to-do among the mountain people; besides, he was a man that few people had any desire to get mixed up with. I had friends in Greasy Valley, but they were reluctant to declare themselves. Harrell was a man who would betray a friend and never forget an enemy. My father pranced over the floor and his eyes danced, as I related the encounter to him. He did not take much interest in my educational ambitions, as he, like many others of his time and place, looked upon book-learning as only a means by which people tried to beat work. But since I had fought with a man as well-known as Harrell, and had, as he considered it, come out ahead, he was proud of me and thought me a boy worthy to be called a son.

Jim came home that night and his countenance darkened as I told him of the encounter with Harrell; but he perceptibly brightened up when he learned that I was under arrest and had to stand trial. "I will defend you," he said. "I will get you out of it."

On Tuesday my father, Jim and I went to Squire George's house to be at the trial. Jim went in with a pair of saddle pockets stuffed with law books thrown across his shoulder. But we soon learned that Mr. Harrell had not been idle. He had gone to town and employed a lawyer to prosecute me. He wanted me hanged if that could be.

Jim and the lawyer, Mr. Reed, agreed to try the case before a jury. After examining the witnesses, Reed opened the argument, picturing me as a ruffian who, without any provocation whatever, proceeded to beat up a poor hardworking man. He pointed to Harrell, who had his jaw bandaged and his arm in a sling, and called attention to the fact that Mr. Harrell would be laid up from his work for a long time, while I was unhurt. He wanted me punished.

Jim followed him, starting off with the air of one much learned in law. He quoted from Blackstone, and employed such terms as *corpus delicti, lex scripti* and others. As he warmed up, he indulged in great outbursts of oratory. First, he had the jury chasing polar bears in the frozen north, next he had them dodging the poisoned javelins of the wild tribes of Australia. Now he had them shivering on the highest pinnacles of the Alps, then suffocating in Death Valley of California. He talked so fast that he got his history awry and had Byron swimming the Rubicon and Cæsar crossing the Delaware. When he got through, he took his seat with great satisfaction, and like many others, believed that he had made a great speech.

Reed rose and spoke in a low tone of voice in words that the jury could understand, and said I ought to be thankful that Mr. Harrell was dealing with me as lightly as he was. He said that the prosecution could have made the charge assault with intent to commit murder, which carried with it a penitentiary sentence. The jury found me guilty and assessed a fine against me of fifty dollars and sentenced me to a day in jail.

We went within a short distance of the county seat that night, and on into town the next morning. The cost had to be paid in cash, but we could shave the fine considerably by buying scrip. When a county was in debt, it paid its obligations in scrip, which passed as money and was worth on the dollar according to the indebtedness of the county. I have seen counties so badly in debt that scrip was worth only ten cents on the dollar. In that case a man employed by the county at a hundred dollars a month, actually got in ready cash only ten dollars a month. There were always men about the court house from whom scrip could be had. It was used in paying taxes and fines. Scrip in our county at that time was selling at sixty cents on the dollar, and that reduced my fine.

While Jim was arranging my fine, I was doing my time in jail. Two men escorted me to the jail, and one of them held a gun in his hand while the other one opened the door just enough to let me pass through. The one holding the gun shoved me in, while the other one closed and fastened the door. The jail was set off from the court house, but was on the same grounds. It consisted of one room about twelve feet by twelve, and was built of heavy hewn logs, fitting so close together that daylight could not be seen between them. It had a door made of solid iron, which swung on powerful hinges and fastened with iron bars and two large locks. This door, in opening and closing, creaked on its hinges with a grating sound that I shall never forget. The jail was lighted and ventilated by two windows about a foot square, which were studded with iron bars cross-ways and up-and-down. The floor and the overhead were of the same material as the walls: thick, heavy hewn timbers, fitted close together.

When I first entered the jail, it appeared dark. As my eyes became accustomed to the darkness, I observed four men in the room. The first was a medium-sized man with red whiskers, shocky hair and small monkey-like eyes. He was wearing the remnant of a shirt and a ragged pair of pants, one leg of which was missing from the knee down. I learned later that he was a maniac waiting to be taken to the insane asylum at Little Rock. To the left stood another man. He was a giant about six feet two inches tall, and looked about thirty-five years old. He was unshaven, and his hair was long. He was a very dangerous and repulsive looking fellow. It was said that he had held a billet of wood over the head of an old man and robbed him of sixty dollars. He was waiting to be tried at the next term of the criminal court.

To the left of the giant another man stood. He was a youthful-looking fellow of about twenty-five. His hair was matted, and his beard had grown out over his face in patches. He was barefoot, and wore a shirt made out of home-woven cloth, which looked as if it had never been washed, and pants of the same material and much too short. I was told afterwards that this was a young mountain farmer who one day at the dinner table in a fit of anger had brained his wife with a skillet because she burnt the cornbread. He was waiting to be tried for murder.

The fourth of my cell-mates was a small middle-aged man with black hair and black whiskers and piercing eyes. He wore heavy cowhide boots which came up over the bottom of his pants legs. It was said that he was a "hoss thief," and that he had stolen a pair of mules up in Missouri and was being held there until the Missouri authorities came after him.

All except the maniac had their eyes focused on me with a grin. He lay on his bunk and walled his eyes and occasionally jabbered something unintelligible. I was told that he had been violent the night before, and that the giant and the wife-murderer had beaten him almost lifeless. I doubt whether the poor fellow ever lived to reach the asylum.

The giant came up to me, and placing his hand on my shoulder, said, "Wot's the row, purty boy?"

"I'm in jail," I said.

"Wal, I do say," he replied. "Hit looks lak ye air."

The three of them chuckled at this.

"Wot ye bin doin'? Stealin' somethin'?" he asked.

"I am innocent," I said.

"At's wot we all say," he replied. "Wal, hit mout be the stripes fer ye an' hit mout be a necktie. But you'll look purty in either one." Again they all chuckled loudly.

"Come," he said, "fork over wot little chink ye got."

I did not understand, and he proceeded to run his hand into my pockets and drew out my purse and counted out one dollar and thirty cents, all the money I had. As he did so, he said, "Ye see, we air all one fambly now, an' wots yourn is ourn, an' wots ourn is yourn."

The giant went to the window, whistled to the jailor, and said, "Three pounds terbarker." He gave the jailor a dollar and twenty cents and put the other dime in his pocket. When the tobacco came, he handed a plug each to the murderer and the "hoss thief," and they tore into it with their teeth like hungry wolves. After taking a chew himself, the giant shoved the plug out toward me, saying, "Have a chaw, young feller?" I refused, and he said, "Wal, jist whensomever ye git tarred stayin' here, jist walk out. Rickoleck, we air not a-holdin' ye." Then they all laughed like demons. They were through with me now, and began jabbering to each other, while they chewed and spat right out on the floor.

I thought this jail was the filthiest place in the world. In each of the corners were piles of discarded cuds of tobacco. The floor looked as if it had never been swept or washed. The bunks were made of old straw that had never been cleaned or changed. The quilts were old, ragged, dirty and lousy. Lice and bedbugs were walking on the walls. The maniac had soiled his bunk, and the whole place was nauseous and stunk. I do not remember that a legal execution ever took place in our county, and no wonder. It would have been impossible for a human being to live in that dungeon three months without contracting a fatal disease.

Some time before sundown they turned me out of jail so that we might get home that night.

Failing to get the school in Greasy Valley, I now had to see about getting employment somewhere else. I heard of a school up in Bear Wallow, which needed a teacher. I rode up into Bear Wallow to the home of Mr. Jim Gipson, a member of the school board. Mr. Gipson was in the field and I walked across to where he was plowing. When Mr. Gipson saw me coming, he stopped his horse and turned around with his hands resting on the plowhandles. He waited for me with a pleased look. I supposed that he took me for a book agent and was thinking of how he was going to tell me all about how much better off the country would be if such fellows as I would go to work.

I walked up to him, and offering my hand, I introduced myself and told him I was a teacher. When he heard the name, he quickly withdrew his hand. He turned pale, breathed quickly and seemed to be powerfully agitated.

"See here, feller," he managed to say. "I'm not lookin' fer no trouble. Rickoleck I've got a wife and three chilluns, an' I've gotta work, an' I'm not lookin' fer no trouble. Ye unerstan'?"

The man's strange behavior almost took me off my feet. I stood bewildered. He managed to get his breath a few times and ventured further: "Mr. Harrell has been over here, an' we all hearn about you. We don' want our school teached by you, an' I don' want no fight nuther."

Of course, this explained it. About all I could think of to say was, "Mr. Harrell is a mighty nice man. I hope that you will find a teacher to his liking. So I will say good day."

The fellow seemed more astonished than ever that there was no outburst of violence, and he stood with his mouth opened and gazed after me until I got out of sight.

Mr. Harrell was a prominent church man. He visited all the big meetings, went home with the people and asked the blessings at the table in long prayers. Therefore, he was well known throughout all the surrounding country. I learned that immediately after the trial, Harrell had gotten on his horse, and under the pretense of hunting a strayed mule, had ridden all over the country, visiting the school directors. His head was bandaged up and his arm was in a sling, and when he was asked what the trouble was, he explained at length that I came to him and asked to teach the school. When he refused me the school, I, without warning, had seized a fence rail and tried to kill him, and would have succeeded had not friends interfered. He described me as a ruffian and a maniac, and cautioned them to be on the lookout for me and to be prepared to defend themselves when I came their way.

I had to have employment, but it seemed as if Harrell was going to make good his threat to run me out of the country. I decided that the only thing I could do would be to go back to the lowlands and work for Mr. Harris. I wanted to wait until the following Monday to leave, for I wanted to go to see Gertie Sunday. I hired Will Eubanks to take a note over to her, in which I asked if I could call at two in the afternoon on Sunday. Will came back saying that Gertie said, "Tell him yes." She mentioned that there would be no need to answer the note in writing.

CHAPTER XIX

THE STILL

JIM came home Saturday night, and on Sunday I washed and polished the buggy, borrowed his new kid gloves and straw hat, and drove to Gertie's house. The road offered an open view as it led up to the house, and with top down, and the lines in one gloved hand and the whip in the other, I urged the horse into his best gait as I approached. I expected Gertie to be dressed in her best and to find all the family on the front porch looking for me. However, they must have mistaken the hour, for when I drove up to the gate there was nobody to be seen. I hitched my horse, stepped upon the porch and rapped gently on the facing of the door. Mrs. Russell came to the door, invited me in and waved me to a seat.

"Gert's asleep," she said. "I'll go wake her up."

I protested about disturbing her, but she said,

"Well, it's time fer her to git up, anyhow," and went into the adjoining room.

"Gert, that thang's in there," I heard her say. I heard the girl mumbling something, but did not catch what she said.

"Well, go out and git rid of him somehow," I heard Mrs. Russell reply.

So far as I was concerned, all thoughts of the wedding were then off. I would have left, but I did not know how to go without appearing rude.

In a little while Gertie came in wearing a Mother Hubbard dress, her hair uncombed, and merely smoothed back, yawning, trying to smile, and saying that the weather made one so awfully sleepy. She didn't feel like playing the organ, she had played herself down, and that was the reason she had had to lie down. Nor could she take a buggy ride; it always did make her head swim to ride in a buggy. She would like to have a drink of water, though, if I didn't mind drawing it. She got the dipper and we went out to the well. I took hold of the water bucket and started to draw the water.

"You know," she began, "I was just thinking—well," she hesitated, then went on, "What are you coming here for anyhow?"

I set the well bucket down and stared at her, hardly knowing what answer to make.

"Because I was just thinking that if matrimony is

your intention, you could save yourself a lot of valuable time by——"

I interrupted, saying that it was not my intention; at that time my only intention was to get in my buggy and drive home.

"Well, you needn't get so mad about it," she said, but I went on out through the gate and got into the buggy and drove off, while she stood with the dipper in her hand, staring at me.

When I got home, I called Jim out to the lot and related everything.

"Then you came very near getting married," he said, "and the only reason you didn't was that the girl and her family objected."

"Well, anyway," I said, "you can talk to me now about that useful career. I am ready for it, either here or anywhere else. I want to do something."

That night Willie Burton came in from Happy Hollow, where his uncle lived. He said that they wanted a teacher in Happy "Holler," and suggested that I should not leave until I saw about it. The next day Willie and I rode up into that section, which was probably twenty miles from our house. We spent the night with Willie's uncle. That evening Willie and his uncle went out about the lot and talked a long time. The next morning his uncle told us to stay there while he rode over to old man Garrison's, a member of the school board. He said that he would look into the matter of the school. Willie explained to me that the people of the hollow were very particular as to who taught their school.

I had already been told that various teachers there had been made to leave, but there seemed to be a reason for that. Usually the teacher was a stranger, and he would not be there long before he became too inquisitive as to the chief industries of the neighborhood. In every case the people were not slow in impressing upon his mind that it would be healthier elsewhere. However, they had no fears about me. I was a native, living within twenty miles of them, and was a brother-in-law of Willie Burton, who had relatives living in the hollow.

Willie's uncle came back and said that he and Mr. Garrison had talked the matter over, and they had decided that I was the man they wanted to teach the school. I contracted with them to teach three months for one hundred dollars. Mr. Garrison had plenty of room, and I arranged to board with him. It was agreed that the school should start the following Monday. Willie had explained to them about the Harrell incident and that seemed to be in my favor.

There were about thirty families living in the hollow, and something like fifty children of school age, from six to twenty-one. However, there were only twenty pupils there to greet me, when I opened the school. They were from eight to fifteen years old. The school advantages of these children had been limited to say the least, but they appeared to be a smart and intelligent lot of boys and girls.

I was surprised at the scarcity of text-books amongst them. Three or four of them had old and worn copies of McGuffy's First Reader. A few had the old Blue Back Speller. Two had Bibles, one a Methodist Discipline, and a little girl had a Hostetter's Almanac. One boy had an ancient copy of Shakespeare, which had been published in London, and many of the words in it were spelled as the mountain people pronounced them. He was unable to tell me where the book came from. Afterwards I heard of other such books among the mountain people, and I have since regretted that I did not procure one of them and keep it, as no doubt such books are rare.

I managed to get along with the books which we had, until I could get Jim over there. He prevailed upon them to adopt the series of school books he was representing, and arranged with Mr. Garrison to handle them. Every child bought new books, and some of those who were not going to school bought books to study at home. Those children were hungering for book knowledge, and they eagerly devoured the lessons that I assigned them, learning rapidly. I had some juvenile books at home which I brought over, and lent them around amongst the children. It was interesting to see how enthusiastic they were over them. They had never before seen pictures of animals dressed up like people, and they were delighted with them.

One day Billy Osburn brought me a history of the James boys, saying, "I'd ruther git my lessons in this hyar book. Hit's a better book than them 'ar new uns."

I looked at the book and told him that it looked like a mighty interesting book, but it was a book of history, and as he was not far enough advanced to take up the study of history, it would be better to keep on studying the new books for a while. I turned the pages and expressed a desire to read it.

"Take it home wi' ye an' read it through," he said.

I took the book home and read it through that night. It was of the yellow back variety, and was one amongst many of such books which were then swiftly circulating through the country, detailing the most daring train and bank robberies that the mind of the ink-slinger was capable of imagining. It was profusely illustrated. I remember one of the pictures in which Jesse James had been cornered by a posse, and with a revolver in each hand he was firing rapidly, shooting his way to liberty. Another picture showed Jesse as he was being hotly pursued, holding the bridle reins in one hand, and firing with the other on his followers, while his horse was going at full speed. Another picture that I remember was one of a well-dressed and handsome gentleman seated in a parlor, talking across a table with a beautiful lady. Everything in this picture indicated wealth and refinement. Underneath were the words, "Frank James Wins a Bride."

It seemed strange that books of that nature could

find their way in large numbers among isolated sections where books were almost unknown. But every undertaking by Jesse James was crowned with brilliant success. So certain was he that his well-laid plans would be carried out minutely that on the occasion of several big bank robberies, before leaving his victims, he would hand them a copy, giving a complete detail of the robbery, all ready for the press, which he had prepared and written in advance. The real facts concerning the adventures of Jesse James would make far more startling reading than the most exaggerated fiction. Hence a history of his life was eagerly sought by both young and old. However, such books as the one I had appealed strongly to romantic youth, and no doubt the reading of such literature was the primary cause of the downfall of many an adventurous young man. The mountain people looked upon Jesse James as a hero, and many of them held him up before their sons as an example of the ideal man. But there is nothing strange about that. It is one of the characteristics of human nature to worship at the shrine of anyone who excels in any line, let it be for good or for evil.

The next morning I handed the book back to Bill, and he asked, "How'd ye lak it?"

I told him that I found it intensely interesting.

He then said, "Paw say hit's the best book he ever seed, an' he say ef you lak that book, you air the only teacher wot's ever been here that had any sense."

I made friends with the children, and occasionally

went home with various ones to spend the night. I knew many of the mountain songs, and they thought it entertaining to hear me sing such songs as "Little Brown Jug," "Frog Went a Courtin'," "Nelly Grey," "Molly Darling" and others. It was not long before I regarded everybody in the valley as a real friend of mine. Mr. Garrison had a couple of grown-up boys who were very friendly with me, and one Friday night they asked me to go with them to the still the next morning. I had never seen a still and was curious to know how it looked and worked. With the two boys and two hired men I left the next morning long before day to visit the still. It was about five miles off, and we walked.

Happy Hollow was a funnel-shaped retreat in the mountains about seven miles long. The mouth or opening was about four miles across, and the valley for about five miles was very fertile land, drained by a creek. The last two miles consisted only of a narrow, winding gulch, traced by a spring branch. The gulch had no outlet beyond, but at the head was a large spring with a swift outflow. Before reaching the spring, the gulch widened out to a spread of about a couple of hundred yards. Here the stills were located.

We walked within two or three hundred yards of the entrance to the gulch, when one of the boys fired his gun. In about three minutes he fired again. He was answered in about two minutes by the guards at the gulch, who fired a single shot. We continued on to within about fifty yards of the guards, when one of them said, "Halt and give the pass word." One after another, we cried out, "King's Ex!" "Yore name?" demanded the guard. We called off our names. "Whar do you live?" was the next question. "Over the way," we each said. "Advance, single file," he commanded. We filed up to the entrance and found two men holding shotguns in their hands. They held pine torches up close to our faces, so that they might be sure of our identity, then let us pass through.

We got to the still about daylight. Some of the men were up working at the still, others were frying bacon and making coffee, while still others were asleep. There were two log shacks furnished with bunks on which the men who had to stay there at night slept. Also in these shacks were several barrels of meal and shelled corn.

The still was built alongside the flow of a spring. First, a stone furnace was built and on top of this was placed a cone-shaped copper vessel of about ten gallons capacity. At the top of this vessel was a copper tube or pipe, extending downward and entering a wooden trough, placed in the water and through which the cold water flowed. The pipe ran along the entire distance of the trough, which was ten feet; then in an elbow it doubled back ten feet, and in another elbow it again went forward ten feet, making thirty feet of pipe over which cold water flowed. The far end of the pipe extended over the trough, and bent downward and entered the mouth of a jug. This thirty feet of pipe was called the worm, and the copper container was called the cooker.

I stayed around there all day, and it was interesting to learn how they made their whiskey. First, they filled sacks with shelled corn and let them soak in water for a day or two. Then they spread the corn out on boards in the sun and let it remain until it sprouted. Next they ground or beat the corn into "chops." One way to do this was to chisel out an excavation in a solid stump and pour the corn into it and beat it with a pestle. Another way was to place the sprouted corn on a flat rock and crush it by twisting another rock around over it.

In making the mash, they put about five bushels of coarse ground meal into a heavy oak barrel and added to this a bushel of the beaten-up sprouted corn, letting it stand for several days. They then filled the cooker with the mash, and a good fire of solid wood, such as the oak or hickory, was kept burning under and around it.

The steam coming from the cooking mash escaped through the tube at the top and on into the pipes which were lying in the trough. Here the cold water running over the pipes condensed the steam into a liquid, which emptied into a jug. This liquid was a kind of alcohol and was called "sanglin's." When the cooking was over, the sanglin's was poured back into the cooker and was re-cooked and re-condensed. The liquid from this second cooking was the whiskey. They had no tester

and judged the proof by the bead. When the proof showed too low, the product was called "backin's," and was put back into the cooker with the other mash and re-condensed.

There were about half a dozen stills in the locality. One of them had only recently been erected, and it was the subject of much comment. It had a second cooker called a thumper. The steam from the first cooker emptied into the thumper, and was condensed for the second time, cooking all the while.

Several men were lounging around each still, but it was noticeable that none of them were drunk or even drinking. There were fellows there that I knew would drink whiskey and get drunk, but I did not see them drinking at the stills. However, they probably considered that they were at work, and a man cannot very well get drunk and work at the same time. The kind of work that they had to do seemed to be strenuous, and those on duty were kept busy. Some of them were too lazy to go to the spring and fetch a bucket of water around their homes, but it seemed as if they delighted in doing the hardest kind of work around the stills.

The stills had to be operated on Sundays as well as on week days. It is true that many of the men who worked at the stills belonged to the church, but unless they could get somebody to work in their place, they could not attend the service. This was later overcome by having church on both Saturday and Sunday, and the young men would attend the stills on Saturdays and allow the older ones to go to meeting. Then the older ones would look after the stills on Sundays, permitting the boys to go to meeting.

I was curious to know the difference between the product of those stills and that of a legalized distillery, and why there seemed to be such a demand for the output of the illicit still. It seemed to me that the purchaser would rather buy from a manufacturer who was within the law. In explaining this to me, they said that there was a government tax on the manufacture of whiskey. As well as I can remember, they said that this tax was ninety cents on the gallon, and it had to be paid by the manufacturer. Therefore, the legalized still must add this ninety cents revenue to the selling price of the whiskey, which, of course, was passed on to the wholesaler, then to the dealer, and finally to the consumer. The liquor dealer, in buying the moonshine whiskey, not only got it for less money than he did from the legalized distilleries, but he saved this ninety cents revenue in addition. Furthermore, he took one gallon of this pure corn whiskey, and with chemicals made four gallons of whiskey which had the corn flavor, and which he sold for corn whiskey at a low price, about two dollars a gallon.

The government had agents out looking for these moonshine or illicit stills, and whenever they found one running, they arrested the operators and took them before the Federal Court, where they were tried for manufacturing whiskey without a license and for not paying the revenue. These agents were known as "revenuers."

I inquired further as to the profits in moonshining whiskey, and asked whether, if the same activities were directed along legal channels, it wouldn't be equally profitable and a great deal less of a hazard. Mr. Garrison cited himself as an example and explained it in this way. He had about fifty acres of land in a state of cultivation. He planted twenty acres of it in wheat, oats, sorghum, tobacco and potatoes, and this left thirty acres which he planted in corn. The corn yield was from fifteen to forty bushels to the acre, and he never made less than five hundred bushels of corn a year. He used about three hundred bushels in feeding his horses, fattening his hogs, and for bread. That left a surplus of two hundred bushels.

There was no demand for corn in the valley, except a few bushels now and then. Therefore, in order to market his corn, Mr. Garrison must haul it forty or fifty miles distant to the river farms where they raised mostly cotton. The capacity of a two-horse wagon was about twenty bushels in the ear. If he succeeded in finding a buyer for his corn, the price was not more than fifty cents a bushel, which amounted to ten dollars a load for his corn. He could not really make the trip for that, so the expense of marketing his corn was more than he received for it.

Now, by converting this corn into whiskey, he netted a good profit. Ordinarily a bushel of corn would run off about a gallon and a quart of whiskey, which he could sell for something like two dollars and a half a gallon. Therefore, Mr. Garrison's surplus crop of corn, when distilled into whiskey, brought him a gross sum of six or seven hundred dollars, which was a lot of money for one family. The moonshiner's equipment was rude and primitive, and the process of operation slow. If he was able to run off ten gallons a day and sell it for twenty-five dollars, he considered that he was making big money.

There were some families living in Happy Hollow who were not directly interested in the stills. But the stills offered them a market for their corn; also they furnished them with day labor when they were not working on their crops. Hence the whiskey industry was considered by the natives of Happy Hollow to be an asset to the community.

The moonshiners of Happy Hollow were practically immune from punishment by law, for there was no law against the possession or the transportation of whiskey. They could haul barrels of whiskey across the country without fear of prosecution. They took great precautions against government agents getting into the valley. It would have been mighty hard for a revenue officer to get to the stills, and had he been able, under cover of night, to get to the entrance of the gulch, he would have been stopped by the guards. It would have been difficult for one to come down the mountainsides into the gulch, and had he done so, he would never have lived to get out.

I was going home one afternoon with the Hope children to spend the night. On nearing Mr. Hope's house, we came upon several men with guns in their hands, standing around a man who appeared to be a "furriner." The man was white with fear, and was begging for his life. As I got a view of him, his face looked familiar to me, but I could not place him then. I looked around, and observed a sewing-machine wagon and horse, and it came to my mind then who he was. It was Mr. Owens, a sewing-machine agent, whom I had met on his trips to Greasy Valley the summer previous. The man was so agitated that he did not recognize me.

I stepped up in front of him and said, "Hello, Mr. Owens, what are you doing in here?"

He was astounded at hearing his name called, but he was so scared that he did not at once recognize me. I went on, "I am the school teacher who was in Greasy Valley last summer."

He fell upon me, shaking my hand, and said, "For God's sake, save me! Please explain to them that I am only a sewing-machine agent."

I turned around to the men and said, "He is all right, boys. I knew him in Greasy Valley. He is a sewing-machine agent."

The crowd was composed mostly of young fellows, and they were not easy to be convinced. One of them said, "Yes, an' by God we've got enemies in Greasy Valley, too." They chewed tobacco, and spat and scowled, eyeing the man. It seemed that it had been some time since they had killed a revenuer, and they did not like to be disappointed. I could see that they were eager to fire into him. One large fellow stepped up to me and said, "Air you willin' to stan' fer him?"

I had to stop and study a little before I could answer him. "To stand for him" meant with them that I would be willing to forfeit my life for any harm that he might do in the future. While I knew him as a sewing-machine agent, it would be possible for a sewing-machine agent to turn revenue officer. I answered him, saying, "I would not stand for my own father or brother if he attempted to go on any further, but if this man turns around and goes back, I will stand for him."

Then the fellow said, "Any uv uz would do that."

Mr. Hope was in the crowd. He felt sorry for the man and wanted to let him go. He felt the same way I did, but he did not want to get himself into trouble over him. He begged the boys to let him go. The boys yielded, but very reluctantly. Mr. Hope offered to take the man to his house and keep him overnight under guard, and escort him out of the valley the next morning. But Mr. Owens did not want to stay in that valley a minute longer than he could help. He begged us to take him right out immediately. Mr. Hope lent me a horse, and he and I rode along by the side of the man, as he drove out of the valley. The other boys dogged along behind us on their ponies, and I feared violence every step of the way. However, when we got beyond the limits of the valley and turned to go back, the boys went back with us.

I had kept up correspondence with several of the boys with whom I was associated at the school the previous year. At the beginning of the school term that year one young man, a very good friend, had gone to Little Rock to enter the Little Rock University. He wrote me a lengthy letter describing the school and mentioning the dormitories where rooms and meals were furnished at a very low price, and urged me to join him.

My school drew to a close, and I was ready to leave. In settling with Mr. Garrison, he would not take anything for my board, as I had assisted his larger boys with home studies evenings. He gave me a warrant on the treasurer for one hundred dollars, and I rode toward home.

CHAPTER XX

FOLKLORE AND SUPERSTITION

WHEN I came within sight of home, I saw some children playing in the road ahead of me. As I drew nearer, I saw that they were Lelia's children: Lou, six years old, and Eddie, four.

"Howdy, Uncle Wayman," said Lou.

"How Unc Wayman?" asked Eddie.

I stopped my horse, and they came running toward me with great excitement.

"Aint Nora's got a little baby," said Lou.

"Ah," said I, "I will go see it."

"No, Aint Nora is sick. Don't go up thar; they don' want nobody in the house."

"Well, well," I said, "I would love to see that baby."

"Hits a little bittie baby," said Lou, "an' hits a boy."

"I guess you are glad of it," I said. "When it gets big, you and Eddie will have somebody to play with, when you come over here."

Eddie was showing great interest.

"Wursh Gran'ma Harris would brang uz one," said Lou.

"Oh," I asked, "did Grandma Harris bring it?"

"Yes," she said, "hit war wile in the woods an' Gran'ma Harris throwed a rock and broke its laig, an' she cotched it an' brought it an' give it to Aint Nora."

"Well," I said, "come on. We can go to the house and stay in the kitchen while you tell me all about it."

Thus were the mysteries of life explained to children. Babies were thought by children to be wild in the woods and able to run with the swiftness of a rabbit; but when brought into captivity, they were helpless and had to be cared for tenderly, until they were adapted to civilization.

Grandma Harris was an old lady living in the neighborhood; she was known as a "granny," which meant a midwife. She attended women in labor and directed the delivery of the child. Women did not have the services of a surgeon or a doctor in cases of childbirth. It was not considered the duty of a doctor to attend such cases, and they were all looked after by a granny in her simple way. Grandma Harris' remedy in difficult cases was gunpowder. The harder the case, the more gunpowder she administered. Nora's was a very obstinate case. She was a couple of days in labor, and the old lady gave her one dose of gunpowder after another. I heard Nora afterwards telling some friends that she took enough gunpowder to blow her clear out of the state.

I had decided to join my friend at Little Rock University, and I stayed around home a few days, preparing for the trip. One day as I was coming into the house, I noticed a horseshoe over the door. I looked at it and laughed. My mother was standing in the door, and a dark expression came over her face, as she remarked, "The poor girl had a hard enough time as it was." A horseshoe nailed over the door was supposed to keep out bad luck, and I then realized that my mother had put the horseshoe there just before Nora's case of childbirth.

I saw how my mother felt about it and said, "Why, of course, I hadn't thought of that. I am glad you put it there."

My mother's ideas and beliefs were fixed, and I respected them. I thought it would be wrong in me to try to change her long cherished views. However, my association with books and educated people had taught me better than to cling to the superstitious beliefs of my childhood. I had learned that "haints" and "sperrits" were for the very ignorant only.

Now after these many years I am confronted with strong argument from some of the most learned scientists in the world to the effect that incarnate spirits do dwell among us, and that in some cases they direct the destinies, not only of individuals but of nations. If incarnate spirits do abound on the earth, they do from natural causes; and as isolated peoples live closer to nature than do others, perhaps their opinions about these matters are of more value than are those of scientists who are learned in the arts. Hence, I do not now denounce my mother's beliefs. In my childhood days I thought her views correct and her practices proper, but after awhile I was certain that she was all wrong. Now all I can say is that I do not know. However, some of the beliefs and practices in signs and tokens seem just a little queer. Here are some of the rules by which we were governed.

If you find a dress pin with the point towards you, pick it up. It means good luck.

When you find a grain of corn in the road, cover it up with dirt and spit on it, and there will be unexpected company at home when you get there.

To drop the dish rag means that somebody is coming hungry. I was at Bill Ward's one day for dinner, and Mrs. Ward had set four plates on the table and happened to drop the dish rag. She got another plate on the table, saying there would be somebody else there for dinner. Sure enough, just as we sat down at the table, Ed Jones rode up and came in and ate.

If a bird gets into the house, it is a sign that a corpse will be taken out of the house.

If a rooster crows in front of the door, it is a sign that a stranger is coming.

If a hen crows, it means that some misfortune will befall some member of the family, and my mother made it a rule always to kill the hen.

When you move, never take the broom nor the cat. It makes no difference how new the broom is or how good the cat is; leave them, for to move either is bad luck.

Never turn back when you start anywhere, regardless of how important it might be. To do so is bad luck.

Never come into the house with an ax or a hoe on your shoulder; if you do, walk out backwards.

Never start a new piece of work on Friday; for if you do, you will never get it finished.

If you see the new moon through the brush, it is a sign that you will get angry. I remember that one night, when my father and I were coming home, I saw the new moon. I called my father's attention to the new moon, and he was a little slow in seeing it. When he did see it, it was through a tree top. When we got home and sat down to supper, my father noticed that there was no cream on the table for coffee. He asked about the cream, and my mother gave reasons for there not being any. He went on to say that he had six cows giving milk and he could not understand why they couldn't give enough to go in coffee. My mother's excuses for there not being any cream were good, and she said something back to him. He took a swallow of coffee,

and it was hot and burned his mouth. He got angry, and threw the cup against the wall and broke it. I felt sorry for what I had done. I was the cause of it all. I had shown my father the new moon through the brush and that caused him to lose his temper.

In the mountains we had but few books and no daily papers. In fact, but few of us could read. Therefore the only way we had of passing the time, as we sat around the fireside at night, was to talk to each other. The great questions of the day which agitated the world did not bother us, as we never heard anything of them. We never heard much of what was going on beyond the limits of our own mountains. Hence, the general subjects upon which we could talk were but few. However, we could always find something to talk about: the Bible and religion furnished topics for inexhaustible discussions, although we knew only two creeds—Methodists and Baptists. To us a Jew was a man who had a store in town and sold goods, first asking a high price and then coming down to what he thought you could pay. We knew that there were such beings as Campbellites and Presbyterians, but none of them dwelt amongst us. The word "Catholic" was fearful and awful. We would have lynched an infidel or a Morman, and as for Mohammedans and Buddhists, well, we had never heard of such monsters.

When we tired of discussing religion and the Bible, we could turn to homicides, brawls and fallings-out. These subjects were always discussed with great animation and anything new of that kind was talked about freely and at length.

Then there were the adventures of the hunter and trapper. There was always something new taking place among them. When we ran completely out of everything else to talk about, we could call on the ghost, who stood always ready to furnish us something in the way of a topic. Illiterate peoples, whether of the mountains or anywhere else, are very credulous and quick to attribute to supernatural causes anything which they cannot readily explain. There dwelt amongst us ghosts. No, not ghosts, for we didn't say "ghosts" nor "haunts." We said "haints." If we wanted to talk in a little more dignified manner, we said "sperrits."

With us haints were dead people who came back to the earth; we did not advance any theory as to why or how. They were simply dead people's spirits and they exhibited themselves in various forms and characters. Haints usually dwelt in and around very old and long-abandoned houses and fields. Sometimes, however, they dwelt right in the house with people. There was a place down on White River, about a day's ride from our home, known as the old Hogan Adams place, old Hogan having been a well-to-do planter and slaveholder. There ran a story to the effect that years past there came up the river a tow-boat loaded with merchandise, such as the natives were accustomed to buying. It was occupied by six or seven people and two big yellow dogs, and they tied up at old Hogan Adams' place and began selling goods.

Not long after this the occupants of the boat seem to have disappeared, and it was whispered around that old Hogan had made his slaves murder the people and bury them under the church house that stood near by, so that he might appropriate their possessions. Anyway, people claim that the boat crew were never heard from again, while the boat remained in the possession of old Hogan Adams. Out of this story grew reports that the old Hogan Adams place was "hainted," and men going down from the mountains to work on White River would come back with hair-raising tales as to the haints that they had seen about the place.

One night I had the pleasure of hearing several of these tales related. We heard that Lee Spark's baby was "bad sick" and my father went over to the Spark home, only to return with the news that the baby was dead. That night he and I went over to "set up with the corpse," which rested in the back of the one-room house, and for hours we sat around the open fireplace, lighting the house by throwing pine knots into the fire. Late in the night, when the conversation began to lag for want of a subject, Dan Amous, probably thinking the occasion most fitting, introduced the subject of haints.

"They say," Dan began, "the ole house on the Bobbs place is hainted."

"I hyeard about that too," said Jim Maberry. "They

say thangs has been seed around thar ever sence ole man Bolden war found dead."

"Yeah," went on Dan, "Henry Smith say he rid by thar t'other evenin' 'twixt sundown and dark, an, jist as he got even with the gate, he seed a infernt playin' aroun' in the yard. He thot mebbe somebody had moved in the house, and he stopped his hoss and hollered and the infernt paid no 'tention to him and jist kept a-playin'. He said hit war plum neked and jist a-skimmin' around on the ground."

"The wust I wuz ever skeered by a haint war about five year ago down on the ole Hogan Adams place," said Maberry. "Me an' Serry and the chilluns war on our way to the bottoms to pick cotton an' we stopped an' camped in a ole house down thar. We tuck some churs in the house, an' way in the night arter we had all gone to sleep, I heard a racket that waked me up. The far made a dim light an' I looked an' seed somebody in the house. I riz up an seed a dead womurn settin' in a chur by the far an' a-lookin' straight at me. I shuck Serry an' tole her to git up; an' the dead womurn jist slid outen the chur an' up the chimbly."

"I will always rickoleck the ole Hogan Adams place," Ebbin Davis said. "Me an' a crowd war down thar a-feeshin' one night, an' we wuz campin' on the bank uv the river. We had cotched a passel of feesh an' we spread the table cloth down on the grass, an' we war all settin' around eatin' feesh and drankin' coffee; an' all onbeknownst a log chain fell right close by, an' the links scattered around in the grass an' jist vanished. We wuz all skeered, but Leander Cummins, he tried to ack bold an' he say, 'All right, Mr. log chain, jist so you don't fall on the table cloth and break none of our deeshes.' About that time a big log chain fell right in the middle of the table cloth and the links all scattered all around. We jumped up an' hitched the critters to the wagin an' driv off. Ef ever I go down thar a-feeshin agin, hit will be in daylight."

Old lady McAllister knocked the ashes from her cob pipe, drew her shawl a little closer around her shoulders and said, "Hit don't haf to be arter dark to see a haint at the ole Hogan Adams place. I rid by thar one day on that sorrel nag o' mine, an' as I war a-passin' the ole meetin' house, two big yaller dawgs come a-runnin' out an' rared up in front of the horse. The nag let on lak he didn't see 'em—mebbe he didn't. They run off an' then come a-runnin' back and rared up jist lak they wuz a-goin to tar the hoss all to pieces, an' then all at onc't jist disappeared."

"I'll tell ye what a furriner tole me," said Jim Hambright. "He said he stopped at ole Hogan's to stay all night one night, and when he layed down, a big dawg rared up on his bed. He hollered an' tole 'em thar wuz a dawg in the room, an' Hogan cussed the nigger an' tole him to git the dawg outen the room. Course, the nigger knowed what it wuz an' ole Hogan knowed, but they didn't want the furriner to know. The nigger come in with a candle an' looked around but couldn't see no dawg. Said hit must a run out when he opened the door. The furriner said he laid down agin an' the dawg rared up on his bed jist lak hit did before. He hollered agin, an' when the nigger come in, he got up an' hep him look fer the dawg, but no dawg wuzn't to be seed. The furriner stood by the door an' when the nigger went out, he latched the door and propped it with a chur. He laid down an' the dawg rared upon his bed agin, an' he got up an' saddled his hoss an' rid off."

"I've jist been a-settin' here an' a-listenin' to youens," said Josh Guffy. "I war a-workin' down thar fer ole Hogan an' one night I war asleep, an' sump'n waked me up. Hit war a hot night an' the moon war a-shinin' in the house. I looked an' seed a coffin. The coffin war a-goin' out at the door and sump'n war a-settin' on it and a-grinnin'. The coffin went on off and the thang jist set on the coffin and grinned as long as I could see it."

Now these tales were narrated by people of experience and maturity. They were told with sincerity and truthfulness to an audience which never doubted. They were not related as tales or ghost stories, but as actual facts: facts that were experienced by the narrators or their friends. To have doubted them in the least would have been giving the lie to the ones who told them. I used to listen to such stories in our home when we had company. I would sit up late as those tales were told, and would become so frightened that when I went to bed I would run and jump into the bed, for fear there might be a haint hiding under it to grab me as I climbed in; and I would get way down in the bed and cover up completely.

Witches, well, they were our neighbors too. However, I was not as familiar with witches as I was with haints, as I did not hear as much about them. Witches were a favorite pest of the older men and women. We younger folks did not take much stock in them. I was spending the day one Sunday with my father and mother at Aunt Lou's. Aunt Lou apologized for the milk's tasting sour, and said the witches were getting in it. She said that she had nailed horseshoes over the kitchen door, but still they got in the milk. It was a dry fall and the herbage was getting low, and it probably did not occur to her that the cows were eating some kind of bitter weed.

I was over at old Uncle Johnny Bledso's house one day, and he was "laying off" from his plowing. The reason was, he said, that the witches had ridden his horse all the night before and it was tired out and he would have to let it rest. Therefore, he would not plow that day. He took me out to the lot and showed me how the witches had tied knots in the horse's mane. The horse did look tired, probably from a hard day's work the previous day, and the old man was convinced that witches were responsible.

There was a child in our neighborhood who suffered from epileptic fits, and it was believed by some that he had been bewitched. People even went so far as to identify the witch: an old woman who was crippled and lived mostly by herself. However, there was only talk and no violence was ever attempted.

There was a belief in older times that, as gold was representative of the sun, so did silver symbolize the moon and thus possess feminine powers. It was thought that witches were immune from bullets of lead, but that their magic could not prevail against bullets made of silver, as the silver bullets possessed not only physical powers but also spiritual influences. Strange to say this belief was preserved by each generation all through the centuries and was finally handed down and became a superstition of the Ozark mountains. I have always heard it said that one must shoot a witch with a silver bullet in order to have a fatal result.

There lived across the mountain from us an old man by the name of Bill Winkler. Old Bill and his family dwelt in a lonely hollow through which the public road passed. Some kind of disease appeared among Bill's cattle, and he lost three or four head. Bill concluded, according to his belief, that his cattle had been bewitched. Now the thing to do to keep his cows from dying, he felt, was to kill the witch. Old Bill got some silver, probably a half dollar piece, moulded a silver bullet and loaded his rifle with it. He then went into the woods and raked up a ring of leaves about fifty feet across. Just before midnight he set fire to the leaves and waited for the witch. He had heard that the way to catch a witch was to make a ring of fire at midnight and the witch would come into it.

In preparing his ring of fire, however, Old Bill had made it across the public road. It so happened that Dr. John Gannoway had been off on a late call, and on his way back he rode into the ring of fire. He thought nothing of it, however, and simply supposed that somebody had set the woods afire. When he rode into the ring, Old Bill seized his bridle reins, saying "Hi, yi, John! I got ye at last." The doctor was taken by surprise and did not understand. He thought the old man must have gone crazy, and tried to get him to explain.

Old Bill chuckled, and holding on to the bridle reins with one hand and with his rifle in the other, he said, "I got ye whar I kin kill ye. Ye cain't git away." And holding up the gun, he said, "She's loaded with a silver bullet, and hit will kill ye."

The doctor tried to quiet him and get from him what he meant.

"Wal," said Old Bill, "I built a ring o' far an' ye run in it, an' ye air the witch an' I'm a-goin' to kill ye."

The doctor quickly shoved his revolver in the old man's face and made him hand over his gun.

Old Bill then began crying and said, "Why John, you know you'll kill all my cows and we'll starve to death."

The doctor then pointed out to him that he had built his ring across the public road and people had to travel the road.

CHAPTER XXI

I LEAVE FOR COLLEGE

JIM came in and we had the pleasure of being together a few days at home with our parents. Jim had done well during the summer, and in addition to his school books, he had made a few sales of school desks which augmented his commissions. He said that he would have more than enough money to take him back to school that year. I told him that I had decided to go to Little Rock, and he offered to assist me when my limited funds gave out.

We had been at home only a day or two when a man who lived across at Bow Springs came to our house. Jim's reputation as a young lawyer had gone beyond the confines of our own county, and this man, hearing of him, had come seeking legal advice. He said that he had given a merchant a mortgage on his horse for a small amount of merchandise, and according to his figures, he had paid it. But the merchant's books showed differently, and he had sent the constable to take the horse. The man wanted Jim to go over and get his horse back. Jim questioned him carefully as to the mortgage, and then told him that he would go over and get his horse back for ten dollars; and in case he failed to get the horse, he would make no charge. The man readily agreed to this.

It was about thirty miles to Bow Springs, but Jim wanted to make the trip, for the lawsuit would give him experience and introduce him to new people. Also, he thought he might do a little book business while there. He wanted me to go with him, and as I was at home on a little vacation anyhow, I went along. I remember how on the way over Jim told me that the profession of law was different from what we had been led to believe. He said that we had always been under the impression that a lawyer was one who could ask a lot of questions, getting the opposition's witnesses confused in order to discredit their testimony. He went on to say that he had now learned that a lawyer was one versed in law. In the case he was about to defend, he knew that the mortgage was invalid. He said that the merchant had allowed the time limit of the mortgage to expire and had not renewed it. Of course, Jim said, the merchant knew that, but as he was not expecting any resistance, he did the usual thing in such cases—just sent an officer and got the property. Jim said that he would make no attempt to prove the injustice of the claim, but attack the validity of the mortgage.

We were all day getting to Bow Springs. We went to a place where we saw the sign "Hotel," and got accommodations for the night. Jim and his client were busy all the next day with the lawsuit, and I had nothing to do but to take in the town. The place where we were stopping boasted of being the "leading hotel" of the city, and was a two story, wooden building, with three rooms upstairs and four below. It was built of undressed lumber, and was not painted, nor in any way ceiled on the inside. We seemed to be the only guests, but the place was alive with children. There seemed to be something like a dozen children, from one to fifteen years old, running over the house and up and down the stairs, all half naked and half starved. The man of the place did not work, as he was the proprietor of the hotel. As I started out, I told the landlady, who was also the cook and housekeeper, that we would be back for dinner. We were the first strangers who had struck the town for some time, and she hinted at wanting to know our business. I told her that my brother was a lawyer and was in town on legal business. "Well," she said, "he looked like a preacher, lawyer, doctor, fiddler or fool, and I thought he must be somebody."

I first visited the springs. There were three of them. Two were walled in with boxes looking like bee gums.

One of these was equipped with a spout through which the water escaped with some force; and the other had three holes bored in the casing near the top, through which the water slowly trickled. The third spring was boxed in with boards and was about four feet square. A kind of yellowish white substance in spots was visible on the water, and a man, looking on as I was, said, "Hit looks lak somebody's harked an' spit all over the sprang." It was called a sulphur spring.

The town consisted of about a couple of dozen houses and three small stores. They were all built of undressed lumber and were neither painted nor ceiled. The place also boasted of a blacksmith shop and a church which was used both as church and school. Some of the houses were vacant, having been built by nearby country people, who had abandoned them and had moved back to their farms. A few others were rudely furnished and were being rented to people who had heard of the healing qualities of the waters and had moved in to spend a short time at the springs for their health.

I went to the principal store. It was a small boxed building and was stocked with such merchandise as the people were in the habit of calling for. On one side were the drygoods, which consisted of a few bolts of calico, yellow domestic, cotton checks, and a bolt each of grey jeans and hickory shirting. On the counter was a show case filled with notions, and under the counter was a large wooden box containing men's brogan shoes.

On the shelves were pasteboard boxes which had in them women's shoes, and there were other boxes containing black cotton hose for women's Sunday wear. Higher up on the shelves were some tall round boxes, some of which contained men's wool and felt hats, and others had women's headwear. The only ready made clothing I saw were a few men's duck pants. At the far end of the drygoods side of the store were the drugs and stationery, which consisted of a few bottles of turpentine, castor oil and liniment; some log wood and copperas for dyeing cloth, and some camphor gum; also a ream of foolscap paper, a few bottles of ink, a few school books and school slates.

On the grocery side I saw plenty of canned oysters, sardines and salmon; a half dozen caddies of different kinds of tobacco, and an abundance of snuff in bottles and in five and ten cent boxes; a cake of cheese and a box of loose soda crackers. There were hanging against the walls curry combs, back bands, horse collars, plow lines, trace chains, and hames. On one shelf were different kinds of plow points and iron bolts and nuts; on another were field hoes, chopping axes and grubbing hoes. None of these implements had handles in them; the people made these for themselves. On still another shelf were jars containing different sizes of shot, some boxes of gun caps and several bars of lead. There were no meat, meal, flour, or molasses in the store, as people raised plenty for their own consumption. Nor did I see any soap. But there was no demand for it, since people made their own soap at home and used it plentifully. In the rear end of the store were a couple of slack barrels, one of which contained coarse salt and the other coarse brown sugar. There was also a fifty gallon blue barrel containing coal oil. On a shelf were some small round boxes made in the shape of cheese boxes which had in them axle grease. On the top shelf were some dishes made of a yellow-looking earthern ware, some lamps and lamp chimneys, tinware, and cedar buckets.

The town of Bow Springs was one among many of such places that were built around mountain springs, the waters of which were supposed to possess great healing powers. And like nearly all of the others, it was destined to flare up, shine brilliantly for a while; then flicker and die out.

It appeared that about five years before a man had come there from Springfield, Mo., and was so impressed with the place that he thought he would build a town there. He bought the land on which the springs were located, and surveyed it into blocks and streets, and platted it into lots. He then had some pamphlets printed which he distributed far and near. In these pamphlets he gave the location and topography of the springs, mentioned every disease that man has ever been afflicted with, and asserted that the waters were a certain cure for each and all of them. He went among the people of the nearby country, holding meetings in the school and church houses, and talked to them about his plans for building a town right there amongst them. He told them that the surrounding country was easily able to support a town, and that as the country needed a town, he would build one with their coöperation. As for the springs, he envisioned a famous resort which would be built within the next decade, and beside which the world renowned Hot Springs would pale in comparison. He sold lots, a great number of them; but vacant lots alone do not build a town, and within a year or two, the man went broke and left. The town which I now had the pleasure of seeing was the remains of what once was a flourishing city and famous health resort—on paper.

Along in the afternoon I saw Jim and he said that he had won his suit and suggested that we stay over for the show. We had noticed by the posters that there was to be a show at that place the next day. We went back to the hotel and waited till morning. By daylight the people began coming in for the show. Many of them, men, women, and children, walked across the mountains for miles. At about ten o'clock the show appeared, coming overland, of course. There was an elephant, a camel, and a bear, all being led; there was a wagon of trained dogs and another of monkeys. This completed the menagerie, but other wagons, in which the show people rode and hauled their plunder, had painted on their canvas sides every kind of wild beast found in the jungles.

The tent was soon erected, and a man stood up in a wagon and addressed the crowd, telling us that we were fortunate in having the opportunity of seeing the greatest show in the world. They had exhibited, he said, in Paris, London, Berlin, and many other foreign cities, and had come directly from St. Louis for our benefit. The show was ready to begin, he said, and it was all free for only fifty cents a ticket. The people rushed around to the ticket wagon and swarmed into the tent like bees.

The first thing to greet us was the menagerie. The sight of the bear occasioned no wonder, but the camel and elephant were curiosities, if not monstrosities. That was the first time that a show had ever been in this part of the country. Many of the people had never seen an elephant, and some had never even heard of one; and the attractions and performances, simple as they were, were thrilling to these mountain people.

I was standing looking at the elephant eat hay, when a family came along, consisting of a young man and a young woman, an old woman and a small boy.

"Looky thar," the old woman said, addressing the young man. "Ezra, what is that big varmint over thar?"

"Hit's a elefernt," replied Ezra. "I seed ten of 'em at a show when I wuz up in the Nation."

"A elefernt?" asked the old lady.

"Yes," replied Ezra, "hit's the biggest varmint in the worl'."

"Wal," the old lady said, "if Godamighty made that, he orter make one more an' quit."

A couple of young men who were teamsters on the road, came by, acting the part of clowns. One was wearing a white blouse suit and the other a Mother Hubbard dress. With their faces painted white and their lips red and their dunce caps, they quickly caught the eyes of all. Their funny looks, sayings, and antics were the occasion for almost side-splitting laughter; I never saw people laugh so much. Aged men would laugh until they fell over. Again I heard the old lady speaking to Ezra.

"What's them ar, Ezra? Air they varmints er rale people?"

"Oh, them air rale people," Ezra answered. "Them air clowns. I've seed a lot uv 'em. They air funny people."

"Wal," said the old lady, "they shore do look funny. I never seed such close on a humarn."

We were now informed by the spokesman that we were about to witness one of the greatest and most daring feats ever performed by any human being. Madame Roset, he said, was going to walk across the grounds on a suspended wire with nothing to hold on to. The people could not believe that this was possible; but the girl was soon seen ascending the tent pole, and on a small standing space, she kicked off her slippers, and with a balance pole in her hand, stepped on to the wire. The people, breathless and with their mouths open, looked on with awe as the girl made her way over the tight rope. I was near four or five rough looking fellows, and one of them said, "By jabbers, is that thang a gal er a boy?"

"Hit's a boy," another one said.

"You never seed no gal with clo'es on lak themar."

"Haw, haw, haw," another one joined in, "looks lak he's got on a hippen."

With a few performances by the trained dogs and monkeys, and some simple trapeze and acrobatic acting, the show was brought to a close.

Late in the afternoon of the day before, while the show was coming over a mountain, the wagon with the monkey cage turned over, the door came open, and the monkeys escaped. They got them all back but one. After wandering over the mountains all night, this monkey came to the home of John Rash, an isolated mountaineer. At about daylight John heard something outside, and he got up and went to the door and looked out. The monkey was perched on the gate post.

"Cindy, Cindy, come yare quak," John called.

"Let me alone, John Rash," said his wife. "You hain't a-goin' to git me up afore day, so gwan let me alone."

"Cindy, the devil's out thar, shore's you're born," John said.

"Wal," replied Cindy, "hit's arter you. I tole ye the devil'd git ye fer kotchin' feesh on Sunday."

"I hain't a-foolin', Cindy," John said. "Let me try ole one eye on it."

Ole one eye was his double barrel shotgun with one hammer gone. Cindy saw that John was greatly agitated, and decided to go to the door and see for herself what it was all about. The monkey was glad to see somebody. He was hungry and he wanted to make friends; so he was jibbering and gesticulating. Cindy went to the door, and looking over John's shoulder, saw the monkey, and cried out, "Oh Gawd, hit is the devil. What'll we do?" She fell in a faint.

The monkey jumped down from the gate post and started up the steps. John, with trembling hands, and at a short range, fired, killing the little animal instantly. Then he and Cindy held a council to decide what steps to take next.

"Take the thang to Bow Sprangs," said Cindy, "an' ax Brother Powers ef it's shore 'nuff the devil. Ef it is, I know he'll be powerful glad you kilt it, caze he won't haff to preach so hard to the sinners."

These two people had never seen a monkey before; they had probably never seen a picture of one. No doubt they had heard of such an animal, but they had no idea of how it looked. I heard John when he came in with the monkey and was relating the incident.

"Gawd dim," he said, "I never seed no sich a-lookin' varmint, an' I thought hit war shore the devil, an' when it started to come in, I throwed ole one eye down on it an farred an' kilt it. Gawd dim, I war shore skyeard nearly to death."

We went back home, and I packed up and made ready to go on to Little Rock and enter the Little Rock University. Owing to the mode of travel and the road conditions, Little Rock was considered a long way from home. My folks hated to see me leave. My father advised me to take what money I had and invest it in some land near home. He seemed to think that I had sufficient education to carry me through, and he would like to see me, he said, buy land and own a home while I was still young. While I knew that my father considered further education of little importance, I could not help feeling that he was prompted by a desire to keep me near him.

My mother wanted me to take my father's advice, for like all good mothers she wanted to keep all of her children at home. Lelia, however, encouraged me to go on to school. I was young, she said, and had a great future before me. Nora said that that was the advantage of being a boy: We boys could get out and make a living for ourselves, while she, being a girl, was forced to stay at home and marry the first rag tag of a mountaineer that came along. Nor was that all, she said; she would have to stay there and rear children to grow up and do exactly as she had done. Aunt Lou thought it strange that a school teacher had to go to school:

she said she thought that a school teacher knew everything that was to be taught.

Sam was going to Little Rock with a load of produce, and I went with him. As I slowly put distance behind me on my way to Little Rock, I did not know it at the time, but I was bidding farewell to my old home in the mountains.

CHAPTER XXII

FORTY YEARS

I SPENT about four years at Little Rock and then taught school at various places over the state. One day I received a letter from a friend down in the southeastern part of the state advising me that they were organizing a high school in his town and needed a principal. He asked me to come down and see them, and I accepted his invitation, with the result that I contracted with the school board for a year.

The music teacher in this school was Miss Gill, the daughter of a cotton planter. We became interested in each other and it would take over thirty years to tell the rest of the story. However, after we married, we lived there for about three years, and then moved to

Natchez, Mississippi, where I had accepted a better paying position. After living a year at Natchez, we moved to Memphis, where I went in business.

In the meantime my parents had sold out their old home in the Ozarks and moved south of the Arkansas River to a place in the Ouachita Mountains near Hot Springs. Sam's health had given way and he had gone to the Panhandle country in Texas, Lelia and the children soon following. Nora and her husband had moved with my parents. Jim had taken the law course at Vanderbilt and was practicing at Hot Springs. He afterwards moved to Little Rock.

All members of my family having moved from our native hills, I never had any particular occasion to visit my old home. However, after so many years of city life, with no other purpose than to view again the scenes of my childhood, I decided of a sudden to go back to my boyhood home, and so my wife and I got into an automobile and drove up into the Ozark Mountains.

I was anxious to know what changes, if any, had taken place in the mountains since I had left them; and as we gained the uplands the ravages of the lumbermen were everywhere in evidence. The stands of tall, stately pines that had adorned the hillsides had been cut into and the choicest trees felled and the body cut and hauled off, while the tops were left to decay. It looks as if Vandals had invaded the woodlands and in their greed had stripped them of their beauty. I noticed a difference in the houses. In many places the sturdy old log cabins had given way to houses made of undressed lumber. Also, in place of the old panel rail fence, I saw quite a number made of lumber nailed to posts. These changes are being made for economic reasons. A few railroads, by following the courses of the rivers, have wound their way through the hills, thus creating a market for the product of the sawmill and at the same time giving a commercial value to the Ozark forests. Logs are of more value than sawed lumber; hence people are selling their timber and building with lumber. But the board houses are just as small and just as unaccommodating as those made of logs.

I located Wayland Dent, the playmate of my childhood, and we made our way to his home. Wayland, wrinkled and tanned by constant exposure to the wind and sun, and stooped under the weight of sixty years, showed plainly his age. The Dent family received us with a hospitality such as is found only in the mountains. They all quit work and came to the house and "dressed up," sparing nothing to make us feel welcome. That night several of the neighbors came in to see us, which is characteristic of the mountain folk. Two of them brought fiddles, and as they played many of the old tunes with which I was familiar in my youth, I listened with the great satisfaction of knowing that the old time fiddling is far from being a lost art.

We stayed on at the Dent home for several days and mingled with the people of this isolated settlement.

It was interesting to hear them talk on subjects with which I had been familiar years back, and it was pleasant to hear the dialect of my early days. In talking with them I noticed that they did not care to dwell on subjects which were outside their immediate experience. They were not interested in such inventions as the radio and the airship. Several children were playing about the place, and we offered to drive them back to a town where there was a picture show. Although they had never been to a movie, they expressed no desire to see one. Their enthusiasm was completely taken up with a coming event which they were looking forward to with genuine excitement: the annual barbecue.

We attended the barbecue, and at first I began to look for "improvements" over the barbecues of forty years ago, but I soon realized that there can be no improvement in the old-time barbecue, and its equal can be found nowhere except in the mountains. I walked around over the picnic grounds on that day and marveled at seeing such a happy lot of people. There in an empire of their own, far removed from the conventionalities, the disadvantages and the problems of "civilization," they are still living the peaceful, free and easy life that they lived fifty years ago and that they will continue to live for a hundred years to come. One need not go to Mexico or foreign parts to find survivals of an earlier and simpler conception of life. The self-sufficiency and rugged independence of American pioneer days exist today in the Ozarks, almost untouched by Machine Age economics and material improvements. To a stranger these people might at first sight appear poverty-stricken, but they are far from it. Their wants are few and easily filled; they are rich because they are satisfied.

The next day Wayland agreed to accompany me to my old home. As it was difficult to get there with a car, we rode horseback, and after going across hills and through "hollers," we came to the site of my boyhood home; and here after an absence of forty years I find myself amid the hills over which I once played and roamed, the hills of my youth, unchanged, unchanging.

APPENDIX

EXPLANATORY NOTES

These notes identify events, persons, places, songs, and obscure references from *Back Yonder: An Ozark Chronicle*. Because most of the community names to which Hogue refers appear to be fictionalized, only those communities that can be linked to an actual place will be referenced in these notes. Likewise, most of the people mentioned in *Back Yonder* appear to be pseudonymous or completely fictional; no attempt will be made to describe them, except in rare cases in which Hogue makes reference to an identifiable person.

p. 8, line 4 A "letter writer" was a guide book for writing letters. Popular in the eighteenth and nineteenth centuries, the letter writer included information on basic letter-writing etiquette, as well as guidance in grammar and spelling. Examples include *The Belles-Lettres Letter Writer* (Cincinnati, 1853) and *Chesterfield's Art of Letter-Writing Simplified* (New York, 1857.)

p. 10, line 15 Here Hogue echoes the notion—quite popular at the time in the literature on "mountain whites"—that the ways of living, and of making a living, in the Ozarks had not changed appreciably for generations. This theory that the people of Appalachia and the Ozarks were the "contemporary ancestors" of modern Americans first appeared in an 1899 *Atlantic Monthly* article by Berea College president William Goodell Frost. Though subsequently propagated by generations of local colorists, missionaries, and other chroniclers of life in the southern highlands, the contemporary ancestors thesis has been widely refuted by historians over the past quarter century or more.

p. 15, line 27 A nubia is a light head scarf made of wool.

p. 17, line 9 The cane that Hogue refers to is *Arundinaria gigantean*, popularly known as switch cane. Once commonly found in almost all river and creek bottoms in the region, this giant cane with evergreen leaves provided an important food source for livestock and wildlife.

p. 21, line 12 The "Bad Boy" was a character in a series of books by Wisconsin politician and humorist George W. Peck, beginning in the 1880s. See http://www.georgewpeck.com/books.html, accessed April 7, 2015.

p. 21, line 18 "The Adventures of Dr. Rattlehead" refers to an 1851 book, *The Life and Adventures of an Arkansaw Doctor*, written by Marcus Lafayette Byrn under the pseudonym David Rattlehead. The book focuses on a series of humorous stories of humans and wildlife in swampy eastern Arkansas. In his introduction to the reprinted edition, folklorist W. K. McNeil called *The Life and Adventures of an Arkansaw Doctor* the "first volume solely devoted to Arkansas humor." David Rattlehead, *The Life and Adventures of an Arkansaw Doctor*, ed. W. K. McNeil (Fayetteville: University of Arkansas Press, 1989), ix.

p. 25, line 8 Gravel Hill would appear to be a fictionalized name of Hogue's home community. There are rural communities of that name in Van Buren and White Counties, both of which adjoin Hogue's native Faulkner County; the latter Gravel Hill is only about ten miles from Hogue's boyhood home. There is also a Gravel Ridge in neighboring Pulaski County. However, there is no evidence that the Hogue family lived in any of these communities.

p. 31, line 15 Though Hogue likely chose *Back Yonder*'s geographical terms based on their aesthetic or rustic sound, one can today find a Bear Creek (or Branch), a Greasy Valley, and a Bull Mountain on a topographical map, all within a thirty-mile radius of the author's boyhood home in Faulkner County.

p. 41, line 29 Max Frauenthal (1836–1914) was a Bavarian Jewish immigrant who fought for the Confederacy in the Civil War and established a store in Conway Station (as Conway was originally known) on the St. Louis, Iron Mountain, and Southern Railroad in 1871. He later sold out to relatives (who renamed the business Frauenthal and Schwarz) and founded the town of Sugar Loaf (Heber Springs) in Van Buren (later Cleburne) County in 1882. Jeanie Frauenthal, "Max Frauenthal 1836–1914," *Encyclopedia of Arkansas History & Culture*, http://www.encyclopediaof arkansas.net/encyclopedia/entry-detail.aspx?entryID=3184, accessed April 8, 2015.

p. 55, line 12 The Everet Howard/Sal Saucer story is likely either a creation of Hogue's imagination or a fictionalized account of an actual event. If the latter, it is possible that his own father may have served at least in part as the inspiration for Everet Howard. In 1906, B. F. Hogue, sixty-three years old at the time, married seventeen-year-old Lucinda Graves in Garland County, Arkansas. (Lucinda Graves was listed as eighteen on the marriage license, but the birth date on her gravestone indicates that she was only seventeen at the time of the marriage.) It is presumed that Hogue had been widowed (Charles W.'s mother Miranda Hogue does not appear in the 1910 census), but I have not been able to confirm it. See B. F. Hogue/Lucinda Graves Marriage License, Arkansas Marriages, 1837–1944, https://familysearch.org/ark:/61903/1:1:FQPM-

LXQ, accessed April 8, 2015; and for Lucinda Graves Hogue Tankersley's gravestone, Pleasant Hill Cemetary, Find A Grave, http://www.findagrave.com/cgi-bin/fg.cgi?page=gr&GSln=tankersley&GSbyrel=all&Gdyrel=all&GSst=4&GScnty=118&GScntry=4&GSob=n&GRid=5636524&df=all&, accessed April 8, 2015.

p. 59, line 4 Before the coming of the railroad, livestock transported themselves to market. Drovers seasonally came through even the most remote neighborhoods, paying cash for cattle, hogs, horses, and even turkeys, which they drove to market in the nearest city or the nearest railroad stockyard. In the antebellum era, William E. Woodruff maintained a "steam-boat ferry" and "house of entertainment" on the north side of the Arkansas River, across from Little Rock; the operation catered especially to drovers and offered corn and fodder as well as corrals for livestock. *Batesville News*, August 16, 1838, 3.

p. 59, line 21 Gus Blass, along with fellow Jewish merchant Max Heiman, opened the Gus Blass Department Store near a Little Rock steamboat landing in 1871. The store expanded along Main Street to become for many years Arkansas's largest department store. See "Gus Blass Department Store," http://honors.uca.edu/wiki/index.php/Gus_Blass_Department_Store, accessed April 12, 2015.

p. 60, line 8 In 1880, Little Rock had a population of 13,138. The city experienced a boom in the following decade that almost doubled the population by 1890. James W. Bell, "Little Rock," *Arkansas Encyclopedia of History & Culture*, http://www.encyclopediaofarkansas.net/encyclopedia/entry-detail.aspx?entryID=970, accessed April 12, 2015.

p. 62, line 12 The Hogues, and any other travelers visiting Little Rock from the north during this era, would have crossed the Arkansas River by ferry. The first non-railroad bridge linking Little Rock and North Little Rock, known as the "Free Bridge," was constructed only in 1897. Bell, "Little Rock."

p. 66, line 5 Kerosene first became widely available in the 1860s and gradually spread into rural areas in the following decades, replacing candles and torches. The kerosene, or "coal oil," lamp remained a fixture in the rural Ozarks into the middle of the twentieth century, when rural electrification finally put even the most remote hollers and coves on the grid. In Donald Harington's fictional Stay More, Arkansas, a New England peddler introduces kerosene to the rural Ozarks as "Willard's Miracle All-Purpose Hand Cleaner and Lubricant," thus bringing an end to the "Second Spell of Darkness." Harington, *The Architecture of the Arkansas Ozarks: A Novel* (1975;

New York: Harvest/Harcourt Brace Jovanovich, 1987), 202–4.

p. 69, line 24 The American singing school tradition is about three hundred years old, dating to early eighteenth-century efforts to improve congregational singing in New England. In the nineteenth century, singing schools gradually became a southern and western phenomenon, and singing-school teachers relied on shape notes. Dismissed as "dunce notes" by many trained singers and musicians, shape-note hymnals replaced round notes with shapes representing tones on the musical scale. The earliest shape-note hymnals relied on only four shapes until the seven-note system was introduced in the mid 1800s. A protracted struggle between the two camps continued through the rest of the century; by the late 1800s the converts to the seven-note system significantly outnumbered adherents to the older four-note method, especially in Arkansas and the greater Southwest. On the struggle between four-note and seven-note adherents, see Gavin James Campbell, "'Old Can Be Used Instead of New': Shape-Note Singing and the Crisis of Modernity in the New South, 1880–1920," *Journal of American Folklore* 110 (1997): 172. See also James R. Goff Jr., *Close Harmony: A History of Southern Gospel* (Chapel Hill: University of North Carolina, 2002) and Douglas Harrison, *Then*

Sings My Soul: The Culture of Southern Gospel Music (Urbana: University of Illinois Press, 2012.)

p. 76, line 15 In the Ozarks the most ubiquitous mills, known as gristmills, were those that only ground corn into cornmeal using millstones powered by water or steam. Mills that had the capacity to grind wheat into fine flour were often referred to as roller mills, because of the steel rollers used in the grinding process. By the late 1800s, it was not unusual for larger milling operations to perform both kinds of milling and to offer different grades of flour. See M. E. Oliver, *Old Mills of the Ozarks: Sketches* (Point Lookout, MO: School of the Ozarks Press, 1972.)

p. 77, line 10 House yards in this era were generally kept free of grass and other plant growth. This practice served a number of functions—to protect the house from wild fires, to ward off snakes and other creatures that might lurk in grassy areas, and to reduce the population of ticks and chiggers. As Hogue indicates, women routinely swept their yards.

p. 77, line 16 The treats that Hogue describes as "peach pies in the shape of a half moon" were likely fried pies, a popular southern delicacy in which a fruit filling is wrapped in dough and fried in a skillet.

p. 81, line 1 The Ozark chinquapin (*Castanea ozarkensis*) was once a common hardwood in the region, valued for both its edible nuts and its wood. Logging in the late 1800s and early 1900s endangered the species, and the arrival of the chestnut blight (*Cryphonectria parasitica*) in the 1950s all but wiped out the Ozark chinquapin. See http://www.ozarkchinquapin.com/, accessed April 12, 2015.

p. 85, line 29 This song, most often identified as "Weevily Wheat," was a popular play-party song containing a number of alternative lyrics and floating verses, or verses that appear in multiple songs. The play party was a common nineteenth- and twentieth-century alternative to the dance or frolic, an alternative that especially appealed to Christians influenced by a Victorian-era demonization of fiddle music and the sinful dancing that accompanied it. The play party was geared toward teenagers and young adults, generally featured no instrumental accompaniment, and relied on group-performed songs to provide the rhythm for square-dance-style movements. Vance Randolph, ed., *Ozark Folksongs*, vol. 3 (Columbia: State Historical Society of Missouri, 1949), 297–301; see also Goldy M. Hamilton, "The Play Party in Northeast Missouri," *Journal of American Folklore* 27 (July-September 1914): 290–91.

p. 87, line 13 Another popular song used at play parties, "Hog Drovers" appears in numerous folksong collections. It is derived from an old Irish play-song known as "The Nine Daughters." Randolph, *Ozark Folksongs*, 367–68. Listen to this 1969 version sung by Ollie Gilbert in Stone County, Arkansas, and recorded by Max Hunter: https://maxhunter.missouristate.edu/songinformation.aspx?ID=1043, accessed April 12, 2015.

p. 88, line 13 Hogue likely refers to a play-party song better known as "Shoot the Buffalo." Randolph, *Ozark Folksongs*, 306–9. To hear a version recorded in 1963, visit http://web.lyon.edu/wolfcollection/songs/ferrellchase1271.html, accessed April 12, 2015.

p. 106, line 20 Hogue likely had a familiarity with, and fondness for, the genre of literature known as Southwestern Humor, popular in the thirty years leading up to the American Civil War. The dialogue here and on the following page is strongly reminiscent of the braggadocio displayed by such notable fictional and nonfictional frontier characters as Mike Fink and David Crockett as well as the "ring tailed roarers" found in the fighting stories of Southwestern Humorists such as Augustus Longstreet and C. F. M. Noland. For an Arkansas example, see Leonard Williams, ed., *Cavorting on the Devil's Fork: The Pete Whetstone Letters of C. F. M. Noland*, with new introduction by George E. Lankford (Fayetteville: University of Arkansas Press, 2006), 180–81. See also M. Thomas Inge and Ed Piacentino, eds., *Southern*

Frontier Humor: An Anthology (Columbia: University of Missouri Press, 2010) and Ed Piacentino, ed., *Southern Frontier Humor: New Approaches* (Jackson: University Press of Mississippi, 2013.)

p. 108, line 10 For more on Fourth of July picnics in the Ozarks, see Robert K. Gilmore, *Ozark Baptizings, Hangings, and Other Diversions: Theatrical Folkways of Rural Missouri, 1885–1910* (Norman: University of Oklahoma Press, 1984), 113–24.

p. 114, line 19 Hogue's description of a Fourth of July political debate bears a strong resemblance, in tone and style of humor, to C. F. M. Noland's "Pete Whetstone" letter of May 5, 1837. The similarity of the two works, as well as Hogue's use of the geographical designation "Devil's Fork," the backwoods home of the fictional Whetstone, suggests that Hogue may have had a familiarity with Noland's work. See Williams, *Cavorting on the Devil's Fork*, 66–68.

p. 123, line 25 Hogue's description of the expulsion of church members likely reflects his penchant for dramatizing and exaggerating any actual event that might have inspired this chapter. Though it was common for evangelical congregations of the era to expel members for a variety of offenses, surviving church records reflect that the process was never as quick and arbitrary as Hogue portrays it. Practically any congregation would have assigned a deacon, elder, or committee to interview any accused member and investigate the alleged sins committed. Expulsion from the church roll was generally a final option invoked only when the accused refused to repent and ask the congregation's forgiveness or when the offense was deemed especially heinous. Hogue's list of offenses—dancing, drunkenness, gambling, swearing, etc.—were in fact among those most likely to result in congregational punishment.

p. 125, line 13 As with his discussion of the expulsion of church members, it would appear that Hogue indulged in a bit of hyperbole when describing the mourners' bench. Among the churches that would have been most common in rural Arkansas during his childhood—Baptists, Methodists, Christians (pejoratively Campbellites), Presbyterians, and Holiness—there are no known examples of denominations or congregations that adopted eighteen as the "age of accountability." In most evangelical churches, it was common for young children (under the age of ten) to have conversion experiences. It was also quite common, as Hogue suggests, for supplicants to approach the mourners' bench or altar multiple times before undergoing a full-blown conversion experience.

p. 133, line 5 This sacred song was likely an early nineteenth-century camp meeting song sometimes known as "On the Other Shore." For a version recorded as "Some Have Fathers over Yonder" in north Georgia in 1980, see Art Rosenbaum, *Folk Visions and Voices: Traditional Music and Song in North Georgia* (1983; Athens: University of Georgia Press, 2013), 228.

p. 134, line 27 These lines come from an early nineteenth-century *Sacred Harp* song, 160b, "Turn, Sinner, Turn," attributed to William Miller (lyrics) and E. J. King (arrangement.) See *Original Sacred Harp: Containing a Superior Collection of Standard Melodies, of Odes, Anthems, and Church Music, and Hymns of High Repute* . . . (Atlanta, Ga., 1911.)

p. 135, line 13 "On Jordan's Stormy Banks I Stand" is an eighteenth-century hymn written by Englishman Samuel Stennett.

p. 143, line 29 Quitman Male and Female College was a combination academy and college that operated under the auspices of the Methodist Episcopal Church, South, from 1870 until 1898. It was located in the small town of Quitman some twenty miles north of Hogue's home community. James E. Hogue did in fact attend Quitman Male and Female College. Nicola Davis Bivens, "Quitman Male and Female

College," *Encyclopedia of Arkansas History & Culture*, http://www.encyclopediaofarkansas.net/encyclopedia/entry-detail.aspx?entryID=6320, accessed April 8, 2015; Fay Hempstead, *Historical Review of Arkansas: Its Commerce, Industry, and Modern Affairs*, Vol. II, 613.

p. 151, line 17 Sweet anise is more commonly known as fennel (*Foeniculum vulgare.*) Mullein is the more common name of the flowering plants in the genus *Verbascum.*

p. 152, line 21 For more on the death and burial rituals and beliefs of rural Ozarkers, see Abby Burnett, *Gone to the Grave: Burial Customs of the Arkansas Ozarks, 1850–1950* (Jackson: University Press of Mississippi, 2014.)

p. 154, line 6 There is a Greasy Valley in neighboring Van Buren County, near the small community of Morganton. It is located about thirty miles northwest of Hogue's boyhood home.

p. 155, line 3 Going to the river bottoms to pick cotton was a common seasonal, money-making activity for families and young men within easy travelling distance of the Arkansas River Valley, from at least the post–Civil War era until the widespread adoption of mechanical pickers in the 1960s. For information on seasonal cotton pickers in the Arkansas Valley in a later era, the 1920s, see Genevieve Grant Sadler, *Muzzled Oxen: Reaping Cotton and Sowing Hope in 1920s Arkansas* (Little Rock: Butler Center for Arkansas Studies, 2014.)

p. 160, line 4 Hogue's story of an Arkansas gold rush in the Hot Springs area appears to be based on an actual mining boom and rush that took place farther west in the Ouachita Mountains. Based in Polk County and centered on the new railroad town of Mena, the rush created a number of mining boom towns in the late 1890s, including Eberson City, Baby Ruth City, and Camp Wilder. Charles W. Hogue would have been near thirty years old and living in southeastern Arkansas at the height of the rush. See "The Great Polk County Gold and Mineral Rush," *Looking Glass* 18 (June/July 1992): 6–11.

p. 163, line 23 Given Hogue's romantic fascination with the Ozarks, it is surprising that he locates the origins of the Arkansas Traveler legend in far southeastern Arkansas and not in the mountains. Perhaps his years living in Drew County influenced the geographical location of the story. It is also likely that Hogue's familiarity with David Rattlehead's *The Life and Adventures of an Arkansaw Doctor* impacted his version of the story since Rattlehead's action takes place in the eastern Arkansas swamps. See William B. Worthen, "Arkansas Traveler," *Encyclopedia of Arkansas History & Culture*, http://www.encyclopediaofarkansas.net/encyclopedia/entry-detail.aspx?

search=1&entryID=505, accessed April 8, 2015 and Brooks Blevins, *Arkansas/Arkansaw: How Bear Hunters, Hillbillies, and Good Ol' Boys Defined a State* (Fayetteville: University of Arkansas Press, 2009.)

p. 171, line 4 No animal has played a more crucial role in the folklore and legend of the Ozarks than the panther, or "painter" as they were colloquially known up until a generation or two ago. The Ozark panther is actually a cougar or mountain lion. While extremely rare today in the Ozarks, cougars were common enough in the nineteenth century to result in numerous encounters with hunters, trappers, and others in the backcountry. Panther/cougar stories, similar to the ones Hogue recounts, are common in collections of Ozark folklore. See John Quincy Wolf, *Life in the Leatherwoods*, ed. Gene Hyde and Brooks Blevins (Fayetteville: University of Arkansas Press, 2000); *Turnbo's Tales of the Ozarks: Panther Stories*, edited by Desmond Walls Allen (Conway, AR: Arkansas Research, Inc., 1989); and the searchable database of Turnbo stories maintained by the Springfield-Greene County Library at http://thelibrary.org/lochist/turnbo/.

p. 189, line 16 Though Arkansas was officially known as the "Wonder State" when *Back Yonder* was published, the prevalence of black bears (*Ursus americanus luteolus*) and bear hunters in the pre–Civil War era had led many to refer to Arkansas as the "Bear State." Almost extirpated by the middle of the twentieth century, the black bear population (with the help of restocking) has rebounded in recent years to the point that a limited bear-hunting season was reinstituted in the 1980s. See Matthew M. Stith, "'Women Locked the Doors, Children Screamed, and Men Trembled in their Boots': Black Bears and People in Arkansas," *Arkansas Historical Quarterly* 66 (Spring 2007): 1–17 and C. Fred Williams, "The Bear State Image: Arkansas in the Nineteenth Century," *Arkansas Historical Quarterly* 39 (Summer 1980): 99–112.

p. 192, line 7 In the antebellum era the terms "Bowie knife" and "Arkansas toothpick" were often used interchangeably. Nevertheless, modern historians differentiate one from the other. The knife described by Hogue may in fact have been more accurately labeled a Bowie knife. See William B. Worthen, "Bowie Knife," *Encyclopedia of Arkansas History & Culture*, http://www.encyclopediaofarkansas.net/encyclopedia/entry-detail.aspx?search=1&entryID=2738, accessed April 14, 2015.

p. 194, line 14 The Brothers of Freedom was a farmers' organization established in northwestern Arkansas in 1882. The Brothers championed cooperative buying and marketing as well as political causes that were considered beneficial to the interests of small and middling farm families. Another farmers' organization, the Agricultural Wheel, was also founded in 1882, in the Delta of eastern Arkansas. The Wheel grew even more quickly than did the Brothers of Freedom, and in 1885 the two organizations merged in a meeting at Greenbrier, in Hogue's native Faulkner County. See Matthew Hild, "Brothers of Freedom," *Encyclopedia of Arkansas History & Culture*, http://www.encyclopediaofarkansas.net/encyclopedia/entry-detail.aspx?entryID=6990, accessed April 8, 2015 and Edward J. Chess, "Agricultural Wheel," *Encyclopedia of Arkansas History & Culture*, http://www.encyclopediaofarkansas.net/encyclopedia/entry-detail.aspx?entryID=2091, accessed April 8, 2015.

p. 196, line 24 Community literaries and debates, along with spelling bees and "ciphering matches," were among the most common forms of public entertainment in the late-nineteenth and early twentieth centuries. For an entertaining analysis of such events in the Ozarks, see Gilmore, *Ozark Baptizings, Hangings, and Other Diversions*.

p. 196, line 29 Hogue's relative, Arthur Madison Shaw, who grew up in the same vicinity of Faulkner County, recalled a similar debating society/farmer's organization, though he identified the farmers' lodge in the community as the "Farmer's Wheel," most likely a misidentification of the Agricultural Wheel.

Lynn R. McClinton, ed., "The Journal of Arthur Madison Shaw," *Faulkner Facts and Fiddlings* 12 (Spring 1970): 10.

p. 202, line 16 Colonel Fletcher refers to Little Rock businessman and banker John G. Fletcher, a candidate for the Democratic gubernatorial nomination in 1884 who was defeated by Simon P. Hughes.

p. 203, line 16 The names Hogue uses do not match those of any known Arkansas feud. It is possible that Hogue invented the feud story entirely. More likely he embellished an actual feud story, such as the Lively and McCool feud of nineteenth-century Perry County, Arkansas, to which Hogue's family moved in the 1880s. See Goodspeed, *Biographical and Historical Memoirs of Pulaski, Jefferson, Lonoke, Faulkner, Grant, Saline, Perry, Garland and Hot Spring Counties, Arkansas* (Chicago: Goodspeed Publishing Co., 1889), 666.

p. 206, line 3 Feuding and the twentieth-century survival of "Elizabethan" English were popular tropes in the public's imagination of Appalachia and the Ozarks. Modern scholars have largely debunked the sensational and romantic elements of these alleged mountaineer characteristics. See Altina L. Waller, *Feud: Hatfields, McCoys, and Social Change in Appalachia, 1860–1900* (Chapel Hill: University of North

Carolina Press, 1988) and Michael Montgomery, *Dictionary of Smoky Mountain English* (Knoxville: University of Tennessee Press, 2004.)

p. 229, line 14 Hogue's story of a legal execution in Clarksville is a fictionalized version of the hanging of bank robbers Fred Derham and George Underwood in 1903. Given that Hogue was already a father of four living in Memphis at the time of the execution, there is little reason to believe he actually witnessed the hanging. See Jennifer S. Koenig, "Johnson County," *Encyclopedia of Arkansas History & Culture*, http://www.encyclopediaofarkansas.net/encyclopedia/entry-detail.aspx?search=1&entryID=780, accessed April 8, 2015.

p. 253, line 18 Happy Hollow is another geographical entity that Hogue "re-purposed." Faulkner County's Happy Hollow (or Happy Valley) was only about five miles from Hogue's boyhood home. The author may or may not have taught a school in the community, but his previous and frequent flights of fiction suggest that there is little reason to believe the actual Happy Hollow sheltered a community-wide moonshining operation.

p. 272, line 24 The most comprehensive work on the subject of superstitions in the Ozarks is Vance Randolph's *Ozark Magic and Folklore* (New York: Dover Publications, 1964.)

p. 277, line 7 The illiteracy rate of Conway County (from which Faulkner would later be carved) was roughly 12 percent in 1870, slightly less than the US average of 14.6 percent and much lower than the Arkansas average of 27.5. *The Ninth Census, Vol. I: The Statistics of the Population of the United States* (Washington, D.C.: Government Printing Office, 1872), 396, 402.

p. 277, line 22 The term "Campbellites" was a term of derision used to identify adherents of the churches that emerged from the early nineteenth-century American restorationist movement, whose primary founder and spokesman was Alexander Campbell. They were generally referred to as Christians or the Disciples of Christ in the nineteenth century. An early twentieth-century schism produced a rural offshoot, the Churches of Christ, a group that is still quite numerous in the Ozarks today.

p. 286, line 13 Hogue based his description of Bow Springs on Pinnacle Springs, an actual healing water boomtown in northwestern Faulkner County. Founded in 1881 by a Christadelphian preacher from Springfield, Missouri, Pinnacle Springs grew steadily for a few years, attracting tourists and entrepreneurs catering to them. At the height of the town's prosperity, in 1885, three different hack lines transported visitors from the Conway depot and back, and Pinnacle Springs boasted two hotels, twelve bath houses, a skating rink, and a weekly newspaper. As the mineral-water craze slackened in the latter part of the 1880s, Pinnacle Springs citizens attempted to revive the town's fortunes by founding the county's first college, Arkansas Christian College. The college failed in 1890, and the once bustling boomtown disappeared from the landscape shortly afterward. See Jimmy Glover, "Pinnacle Springs," *Faulkner Facts and Fiddlings* 7 (Summer 1965): 21–27 and Faulkner County Historical Society, *Faulkner County: Its Land and People* (Conway, Ark.: River Road Press, 1986), 317.

p. 292, line 17 Hogue's relative, Arthur Madison Shaw, who also grew up in eastern Faulkner County, recounted attending a similar show, or circus, in 1878 at Lewisburg, on the Arkansas River a mile south of Morrilton. See McClinton, "Journal of Arthur Madison Shaw," 4.

p. 297, line 4 There was no institution known as Little Rock University in the late 1800s. If Hogue attended college in Little Rock, it is almost a certainty that he would have attended Little Rock Commercial College, a for-profit business training school that offered courses in penmanship, bookkeeping, commercial law, civil government, electrical sciences, and telegraphy, in addition to a smattering of traditional higher-education courses in languages and mathematics. See Goodspeed, *Biographical and Historical Memoirs of*

Pulaski, Jefferson, Lonoke, Faulkner, Grant, Saline, Perry, Garland and Hot Spring Counties, Arkansas (Chicago: Goodspeed Publishing Co., 1889), 506.

p. 300, line 5 Hogue's parents, B. F. and Miranda Hogue, actually made their move south of the Arkansas River about a decade earlier than he suggests in *Back Yonder*, settling in Casa Township of Perry County in the mid 1880s. At some point during the following decade, the family relocated to the Hollis community in the Ouachita Mountains of southwestern Perry County, where B. F. Hogue acquired a 138-acre homestead. This is where the census taker found the couple in 1900; no children remained at home, though B. F. and Miranda were raising a teenaged granddaughter. By 1910, B. F. Hogue, remarried to a woman more than forty-five years his junior, had moved farther southward into Garland County. He would remain in the Mountain Valley community north of Hot Springs apparently until his death in 1921. Manuscript Census, Tyler Township, Perry County, Ark., 1900; Manuscript Census, Bain Township, Garland County, Ark., 1920; and B. F. Hogue gravestone, Find A Grave, http://www.findagrave.com/cgi-bin/fg.cgi?page=gr&GSln=hogue&GSbyrel=all&GSdy=1921&GSdyrel=in&GSst=4&GScntry=4&GSob=n&GRid=3135808&df=all&, accessed April 8, 2015.

CORRECTIONS

p. 6, line 5 hangings] hanging
p. 41, last line Frauenthall's] Frauenthal's
p. 55, lines 26 and 27 Bobb] Bobbs
p. 56, line 23 Bobb's] Bobbs's
p. 59, lines 21, 22, and 25 Blas] Blass
p. 68, first line Boob] Bobbs
p. 101, line 13 Slew] Slough
p. 106, line 25 Granvil] Granville
p. 151, line 15 Gensing] Ginseng
p. 151, line 18 Anice] Anise
p. 151, line 19 mulein] mullein
p. 179, line 21 placed with my] placed my
p. 187, line 28 chaumping] chomping
p. 279, line 24: Amos] Amous
p. 300, line 6 Ouchita] Ouachita